I0788561

RULE ONE

A Dent McCreary Mystery

RULE ONE

A Dent McCreary Mystery

MICHAEL LUCKER

RULE ONE
A Dent McCreary Mystery

Copyright © 2025 Michael Lucker

ISBN: 9781959811855 (Hardcover)
ISBN: 978195911862 (eBook)
Library of Congress Control Number: 2025903054

Book Cover Design: Okamoto
Interior Design: Amit Dey
Editor: A.E. Williams
Author Photo Credit: Amisha Nair (@avncreatives)

1st Edition

Website: www.wordeee.com
Twitter.com/wordeeeupdates
Facebook: facebook.com/Wordeee/
email: contact@wordeee.com
Published by Wordeee in the United States, New York, New York

Printed in the USA

ADVANCE PRAISE

"Michael Lucker delivers a high-octane thriller with *RULE ONE*, seamlessly blending explosive action, relentless pacing, and profound emotional depth. In a world where nothing is ever truly black or white, Lucker paints a landscape of moral grey, where the path forward is carved by gut instinct—the universal drive to do what's right, even when the lines are blurred. He surrounds us with an unforgettable cast of characters, all flawed, relatable, and painfully vulnerable—making every twist and turn of this wild ride hit that much harder. This is an unexpected and gripping thriller that stays with you long after the final page."

—Christopher Dawson,
Producer, CNN

"Michael Lucker's *RULE ONE* is a fast-paced novel of gruff realism and noir fiction reminiscent of Elmore Leonard's *Get Shorty* and *Rum Punch*. Packed with witty dialogue, and memorable characters, Lucker's novel reads like a literary film script. This is an impressive debut."

—William Walsh,
Author of Lakewood and Haircuts for the Dead

"*RULE ONE* is a heart-pounding page-turner. Starting on page one Lucker puts the pedal to the metal and takes his readers on a wild and winding ride full of twists, turns, and surprises. Once I started reading I couldn't put the book down. I polished it off in two days. Michael Lucker's characters are interesting, flawed, compassionate, and maddening all at the same time. Dent McCreary is a classic crime thriller hero in the vein of Alex Cross. What a great first novel. Bravo! I can't wait for Rule Two!"

—Peter M. Green,
Executive Producer and Partner, Shoulderhill

"Michael Lucker has crafted a wickedly clever thriller that's equal parts grit and wit. His distinctive voice shines through every page of *RULE ONE,* delivering a perfect blend of dark humor and pulse-racing action."

—Trace Conger,
Author of the Mr. Finn and Connor Harding thriller series

"Michael Lucker's lively writing propels *RULE ONE* along like a crash-boom Hollywood car chase. The protagonist—a bottom-of-the-barrel, booze-addled FBI profiler—takes off on a cross-country chase in pursuit of a brutal serial killer who's leaving a gruesome trail of victims. It's a high-speed odyssey, stuffed with colorful characters, that will keep you flipping pages faster than you can grab your next breath . . . if you're able."

—H. W. "Buzz" Bernard,
Author of the multi-award winning WHEN HEROES FLEW series

"A pulse-pounding thriller filled with shocking twists and relentless suspense. *RULE ONE* will keep you on the edge of your seat until the final page."

—Dana Ridenour,
Author of the award-winning Lexie Montgomery FBI Undercover series

"RULE ONE is a rollicking high-tech whodunnit that is sure to please thriller fans and readers of hardboiled crime alike. This is a strong debut from author Michael Lucker. Well done!"

—Baron Birtcher,
Award–winning author of the best-seller, Knife River and Roadhouse Blues

"Brilliant Hollywood screenwriters know exactly what it takes to suck you into a story, and Lucker is a master. In his heart-pounding thriller, *RULE ONE*, you'll feel the danger as an FBI agent races to find a serial killer. He's picked out his next victim, and time is running out."

—Nathan Goodman,
Author of the Special Agent Jana Baker Spy Thriller series

"From the decorated screenwriter who wrote the book '*Crash! Boom! Bang! How to Write Action Movies*' comes a bold debut novel that reads and moves like a thrilling whodunit you'd see on the big screen. Lucker's dynamic characters, crafty prose, and twisty plot make *RULE ONE* an engaging page-turner."

—Dr. Aaron Levy,
Author of Blood Don't Lie

RULE ONE breaks the rules: A thriller where you find yourself pulling for both sides of this adrenaline-filled, funny, and daring mystery. Lucker's vivid, visual style plays like a movie in your mind.

—John Coveny,
Executive Producer & Writer, Longmire/The Closer

DEDICATION

For Butterball

CHAPTER 1

MANHATTAN BEACH

Santa Maria Rivera Rodriguez was the prettiest of her sisters. At least, that's what she was told. Of course, her sisters were told that too. The men of Manhattan Beach, California would tell a woman anything to get them into bed. But Maria had reason to believe it. She had the longest of legs, the softest skin, and the kind of eyes for which most men would die. Despite her genetic gifts, Maria somehow maintained a humility that could melt any ape's heart. *The Great White Buffalo.* That's what they called her, for she was the one girl in the South Bay no man could capture. Maria was holding out for someone special. And she knew he was out there somewhere.

Vomiting over the side of the Manhattan Beach Pier had become a ritual for JR Popper. After a half dozen shots of Jägermeister, or Goldschläger, or whatever the hell the bartender was pouring at the local watering hole, he would stumble his beefy ass down the main drag to the long pier, stick his finger down his throat, and yack what was left of his Kraft macaroni dinner into the waves of the Pacific. That way he had room for more.

By the time JR made it to Harry O's Tavern, there was a line around the block to get in. Scantily clad beach girls sporting baby oil tans and Walmart miniskirts sucked on Marlboro Lights trying their best to maintain their stick-thin figures. But it was the girl on the far side of the street that piqued JR's interest. A dark-skinned beauty in blue jeans and sweatshirt, toting a backpack of books on her way home from community college.

"It's from Columbus," Maria said with an intoxicating accent. "His ships? The *Niña, Pinta, Santa Maria?*"

That was how Maria got her name. She could have been talking Swahili for all JR cared. She was the hottest thing he had seen since his three minutes that morning on Pornhub. Between his pretty boy looks and college boy charm, JR had little problem talking Maria into a cup of joe at the corner coffee shop. That's the trick all real ladies' men knew. If they wanted a girl to trust them, they didn't take them to a bar for God's sake. They took them for coffee. There was no harm in that. Little did Maria know that while she was freshening up in the powder room, JR slipped two drops too many of Rohypnol into her cappuccino. An hour later, she was frolicking naked in the surf in the light of the moon thinking she had met Prince Charming.

JR never carried a condom. The indentation in his wallet would ruin any chance he had of getting laid the moment a girl saw him pay a bill. Not that he ever did. But given the fact Maria was three sheets to the wind, JR had little trouble convincing her he would pull out.

Six weeks later, Maria had a hell of a time tracking him down. It seems he didn't actually work as a film producer for Paramount but as a film processor at Walgreens. When she told him she was pregnant, he nearly choked on his Dentyne. After work, he begged her to have "The Big A." But no good daughter of an illegal, immigrant, Catholic shipbuilder would ever consider an abortion. So, JR split town. Took a prestigious management position in the south of Guam was what he told her. Months later, word leaked he was selling tractor parts for his uncle in Schenectady—but to JR, that lacked the same panache.

Given the quantity of steroids swirling through JR's body, Maria had twins. Now she had two kids on her hands and a family that disowned her for having babies out of wedlock. It was her turn to open the laundromat that morning, a job she hated but one that allowed her to have the girls with her, save money on childcare, and put a little extra away to one day return to college. She frowned when she saw the lock on the back door broken. It was six in the morning and still dark but for a sliver of pink on the horizon. She looked around the back alley parking lot and saw no one. *Surely nobody would harm a mother with two babies in her arms.*

The door creaked open on rusty hinges, allowing Maria to peek inside. Before she made it to the light switch . . . *WHAM!* The wind blew the door closed behind her, leaving her and the girls in the dark. One of them began to cry, so the other did too. That's the thing about twins. Everything happened in stereo. A loud *THUMP* sounded in the front of the laundromat. Maria's eyes widened. She prayed to God for her daughter to be quiet but knew no God would answer her. At least according to her mother. Maria laid the twins on a blanket in a laundry basket. The *THUMP* sounded again. Nervously, she grabbed the metal bar used to secure the back door to defend herself, slowly made her way to the light, and flicked the switch.

At the far end of the long room, a lone commercial dryer circled round and round. *THUMP. THUMP. Strange.* The store had been closed for hours. Someone would have had to put more than twenty dollars in the machine to keep it turning all night. She put the bar down and went to put an end to the racket. Nearing the dryer, she stalled seeing a heavy chain wrapped around it.

"*Cómo qué?*" she muttered.

THUMP. THUMP. Closer she stepped, seeing a padlock fastened to the chain. Suddenly her face paled, and she screamed at the top of her lungs. Through the dryer window, she saw, going round and round, a man. His body contorted in some sadistic pose like Cirque du Soleil, his eyes swollen like a beaten bullfrog, and his blood splashed against the circular window like the crimson suds of Satan.

CHAPTER 2

CUCARACHAVILLE

"Of all the gin joints in all the world, she had to walk into mine." The words dribbled from Bogart's lips on the last black and white TV this side of the Mississippi. Dent McCreary didn't care. About almost anything these days. All he knew was those words struck a chord. Actually, a whole symphony. After the worst breakup of his whole miserable life, he laid painfully alone in a dingy, hole-in-the-wall apartment in the heart of North Hollywood with Chiquita Banana yelling a blue streak of Spanish through the neighboring wall.

"Shut the hell up!" he bellowed.

The last thing he wanted to hear was a woman's voice. He still had his ex-girlfriend's pompous groan bouncing about his brain like a steel ball in a pinball machine. It's not that he wasn't used to it. He grew up in a house full of women who hated men.

"Men are evil." "Men suck." "Screw men," they would say.

When his old man had walked out on him, his chain-smoking mom, and anxiety-ridden sister, his mom had rented out a room in their ho-hum ranch house to make ends meet. What entered was a bevy of jeered and jilted females dumping their unpacked daddy baggage at the dinner table. The "bitchin' kitchen" is what he called it. The place where he was taught, by guilt of association, that he was bad. Since then, he tried to make amends for all the bad things other men had done to other women—throughout history. It was a lot for an eight-year-old, and it took its toll.

Bam-bam-bam! Dent banged his fist on the wall to quiet Chiquita down. *The bitch banged back.* He turned up the volume on his TV and aimed it at the wall to try and drown her out. The problem was now he didn't hear his phone. His cell buzzed on the kitchen counter, right next to an empty bottle of Jack and a half-empty bottle of Jose. Dent's two best friends of late and primary reason for his current condition. His wistful hair lay matted to his bedhead, his three-day beard cried for a razor, and his bloodshot eyes strained to open. A wrinkled grey tee and black sweats clung to his tall frame. The specimen of a man who in his twenties had a twelve-minute shot at a modeling career now in his early forties couldn't get his picture taken at a camera convention.

The woman volleyed back with her musical weapon, "La Bamba." She must have had surround sound, too, because the volume of her system put Dent's TV to shame. He pressed it against the wall for maximum effect. A fat roach scurried off from behind it.

"Para bailar la bamba," blared her music.

Dent's cell phone rang.

Ilsa pleaded on TV. "Kiss me as if it's the last time!"

"Son of a bitch," Dent grumbled.

Water filling his eyes, he turned for something, anything, to rectify his situation. He reached for his bedside table where an empty vial of aspirin, wadded-up Kleenex, and Glock 9mm sat. *That would do the trick.* Then he spied his Louisville Slugger leaning against the wall and thought better of it. He swung the bat like Roberto Clemente. It crashed through the cheap drywall. Dust sprayed. Pictures fell. The TV tipped. Ilsa stopped. La Bamba stopped. And Chiquita went screaming off down the hall in terror leaving Dent alone in his apartment realizing what he had done.

"Fuck," he said.

His cell phone rang politely one last time. And then it stopped too. Dent craned to the screen. It simply read "Missed Call." He sighed. Soon he would check his messages to learn he had to go to work. A man was found dead in a dryer in Manhattan Beach.

CHAPTER 3

CRIME SCENE

Yellow police tape labeled "DO NOT CROSS" roped off the Manhattan Beach laundromat, keeping beachy bystanders at bay. Still, nosy reporters with too much collagen tried to annoy their way past uniformed patrolmen trying to do their jobs.

"Oh, come on, Dave. Just a few shots," said a puffy-lipped photojournalist with Cloroxed hair.

"Can't do it, Misty," said the debonair officer in a neatly pressed black uniform. "It's a murder scene."

Her brow furrowed as much as it could, given her plastic surgery. "Who died?" she asked.

"No idea. But it's not pretty."

She smiled seductively. "I'll make it worth your while."

He rolled his eyes. "That's what you said last time."

She huffed a breath. "I did blow you."

"Once. And not for very long," he replied.

"That wasn't my fault."

Boom. A Buick LeSabre circa 1998 popped the curb pulling to a stop nearby. Out the door crawled Dent, half clean, half sober, and nursing a Styrofoam cup of black coffee. He donned his usual ratty sport coat, black jeans, black boots, and black tie he never pulled up.

"Dent. How's things?" said Lieutenant Mack Lenowitz, a wry social climber whose third time failing the bar exam steered his career off a cliff into the muddy ditch of law enforcement.

"Shitty, thanks," replied Dent.

"Least you're consistent."

"So are you, Mack. What ya got?"

"One poor bastard curled up in a dryer that turned all night."

Inside the laundromat, Dent peered in the dryer and got a glance at what was left of the tangled body lying in a shallow pool of pale flesh and red blood.

"Looks like a giant bowl of SpaghettiOs."

Lenowitz grimaced. "You got an interesting way of looking at things."

"That's why I get paid the big bucks." Dent craned. "Why am I here?"

Murders happened all the time in Los Angeles County the LAPD could handle just fine. Lenowitz nodded to the wall above the dryer. Written in blood in a circle was . . . "#1."

"Lovely," said Dent. The writing implied, of course, that there would be more murders, and serial killers were unquestionably the jurisdiction of the FBI. "Any witnesses?" Dent asked.

"One. That poor girl over there." He nodded to Maria standing in the corner with a baby in her arms. Her younger sister, Nina, held baby number two. She was just as beautiful as Maria but not quite as tall. Or naïve. Dent raised a brow.

"Jesus. They friggin' models?"

"Nope. One on the left works here. The other at the car wash up the street."

Dent shook his head. "I live in the wrong neighborhood."

"You and I both, brother."

"Get prints? Video?" asked Dent.

"Dusting now." He regarded an officer brushing the back door. "No cams though."

"How 'bout there?" said Dent, pointing across the street to the First California Bank. It was a bit more modern a building with stucco walls, tinted windows, and security cameras pointing in every direction. Mack nodded. "We'll get it."

Dent stepped over to Maria and Nina in the back of the laundromat.

"Ladies. Which one of you is Maria?"

"I am," she said, her face weary from the day's events.

"Cute kid," Dent said, eying her child.

"*Gracias.*"

"You the sister?"

"*Sí.* Who you?" spat Nina.

"Name's Dent McCreary. I'm with the FBI."

"You the asshole they keep us waiting for?"

"Uh, yeah," he said, unfazed.

"You FBI? You look like shit," Nina continued.

Maria scowled at her sister. "I'm sorry. *Mi hermana es* a little . . . rough on the sides."

"It's alright," said Dent. "I'm used to it."

Maria smiled.

"Mind if I ask you a few questions?" asked Dent.

"Don't tell this pig shit!" said Nina.

"*Claro que sí.* Whatever you like."

Maria handed her baby to her sister.

"*Poneda los bebés le parte de atrás, por favor?*"

Nina rolled her eyes and curled away with the babies, grumbling in Spanish.

Maria turned apologetically to Dent. "She has a bad day."

"Worse than yours?"

"Guess not," she acknowledged.

"I know you already answered questions for the police. But we do things a little different."

"I understand," she said.

He smiled to put her at ease. She took it the wrong way. That was the thing about Los Angeles. Flirting was in the water. If anyone smiled at anyone, they would think they wanted to sleep with them. So, no one smiled anymore.

"Can you tell me, when you got here, was the door locked?"

Maria shook her head. "No, no. It was broke."

Dent glanced toward the door.

"You were alone then?" Dent asked.

"*Sí*. Just the babies. I open. The manager close."

He went on to ask her a variety of routine questions about the manager, the employees, the customers, and herself, which she answered bashfully. Growing impatient, her babies began to cry.

"Maria!" called Nina.

"May I contact you later . . . if I have any questions?" asked Dent.

Maria nodded and scribbled her number on a piece of paper.

"Call anytime."

CHAPTER 4

THE OFFICE

"**A**re you high?" barked Special Agent in Charge, Richard Parker. The tall, lean gentleman with a clean crop of silver hair leered over his desk at Dent in the doorway of Parker's cookie-cutter corner office at Los Angeles's FBI headquarters. The office was adorned in boring, tan furniture, beige chairs, and one-too-many Olan Mills photographs of his average wife and pale kids. On an off-white wall behind him hung a large-framed photo of the president of the United States with a broad smile of bleached teeth.

"That a trick question?" Dent replied.

"You smashed a hole in your neighbor's wall?"

"Well, technically it was my wall."

Parker tossed down a manila folder with frustration.

"Dang it, Dent! What am I supposed to do with you?"

Dent raised an eyebrow. He was not surprised by his supervisor's Boy Scout expletives; it was that he still used them after twenty years on the job. "I can't keep covering for you. Day after day you violate department ethics, bureau code, and California state law. Can you give me one good reason not to ask you for your badge?"

"No," said Dent flatly. "I can give you seventeen."

Parker tilted his head. "Seventeen?"

"That's how many arrests I made this year."

It was eight more than anyone else in the office, and Parker knew it. The rest of his team was not incompetent. They were just a bunch of straight arrows from Ivy League schools who did things by the book. But "by the book" didn't cut it in LA. Given the statistics, Parker granted Dent a little latitude.

"You arrested fifteen. The other two you killed."

"Semantics," Dent said.

Dent's smart tongue was handed down to him by his father. A fraud and a forger, Bruce McCreary lived life on the edge. Until he was thrown in prison. It wasn't until Dent was in high school that he learned his father didn't actually leave his family—*he was taken.* Occasionally, Dent would visit him at Somerset Penitentiary but found every time he did, his father would whip him with words. Eventually, Dent stopped going altogether. He fought tooth and nail not to turn out like his old man. But he assumed he had him to thank for his ability to think like a criminal.

After low marks and high truancy in high school, Dent enlisted in the army. It was on a whim, hungover, on a Tuesday. He stumbled into the local recruitment office in the heart of Pittsburgh with three cigs left in a pack and two dollars in his wallet. He signed his signature four times, and the next thing he knew, he was on a plane to Fort Benning, Georgia for basic training. Quickly, he found his street fights as a youth on the south side of Pittsburgh aptly prepared him for hand-to-hand combat as an infantryman. There he met a senior intelligence officer who admired his gumption and taught him to track and attack. Three tours in Afghanistan left him with one purple heart, two gold stars, a medal of valor, twenty-two confirmed kills, and more scars than he could count. When he returned to the States, he could have stumbled into politics had it not been for the drinking. But watching the guts of friends and enemies blow out of their bodies required a little something to take the edge off. Fortunately for Dent, his commanding officer landed a high-ranking position at Quantico and recruited Dent to pay him back for saving his life in a late-night siege in Kabul. So began the career of one of the few non-college grads in the bureau's recent history.

Exasperated, SAC Parker leaned back in his bland chair.

"I can cover you with the DA. He owes me some favors. But I'm afraid I can't help you with this."

Parker handed Dent a piece of paper stamped "EVICTION" in bold red letters. Dent sighed.

"Your landlord's quick on the draw," said Parker.

"She's a lunatic," said Dent.

"You're the one who put a bat through the wall."

"Fair point."

"But we're going to have to change things up around here."

Dent didn't like the sound of that one bit.

"What do you mean?"

"It means no more flying solo."

Dent's stomach churned. "Wait. What? Why?"

"We have a new agent coming in. They're going to need training, and you need a babysitter."

"I don't do well with partners. You know that," said Dent.

"Clearly, you don't do well without them. This is the only way I can keep you off the books and on the job. You don't like it, put your badge on my desk and your resume on Monster."

Dent weighed his options. There appeared to be none.

CHAPTER 5

THE GIRLS

Orange County was everything awful it was rumored to be. Aristocratic. Conservative. And unconscionably white. If the residents had their way, automobiles under sixty grand would not be allowed in the county. Behind "the orange curtain," as they called it, residents had to drive a BMW, Lexus, or Mercedes. That was if you were riffraff. Something north of those brands if you were made of real money. But by all means, drive what you were worth so everyone would know. Belonging to a country club was a rite of passage. Being in the right AA group, a calling card. But it was the private schools that really separated the haves from the have-nots. Fifteen thousand a year for your eighth grader to learn basic algebra was standard fare. Daycare, on the other hand, was the holy grail of echelon. High-net-worth parents with low self-esteem would fight tooth and nail to get their four-year-olds into the highest-priced preschools in the country.

Fairmont Academy was the crème de la crème. Nestled on the hill of Newport Beach above the crashing waves of the Pacific, the pristine, white stucco compound for mini millionaires boasted a ninety percent success rate for turning tykes into tycoons.

Standing on the white-washed sidewalk beside the black-washed parking lot waiting for the daily kiddie stampede to exit was a gaggle of sun-tanned soccer moms in designer tennis outfits from the Olivia Langinger collection. *Who screwed who? Who divorced who? Who made who rich in the settlement?* Those were the topics of the day, and well, every day, frankly. So, it took quite a hiccup in the matrix to turn these ladies' heads.

Bam. Dent's old Buick rattled into the lot loaded to the gills with everything Dent owned. Which, granted, wasn't much. Still, through the dusty windows, the mommarazzi could see a rusty toaster, cracked microwave, stained luggage, wrinkled coats, and wadded-up comforter.

In the middle of the herd stood Melody Bancroft, the statuesque beauty who recently put Dent through the emotional Cuisinart that left him in his current state. She slinked angrily over to where he parked beside the dumpster.

"What are you doing here?" she groaned.

"I came to see Butter," he said.

"What makes you think you can?"

"Today's her recital."

"Today *was* her recital. It ended an hour ago."

"Ah, crap." Dent melted. The last thing he wanted to do was let Melody's little girl down. She had come to mean more to him than anyone ever had. From one to three years old, he was her surrogate daddy, teaching her to walk and talk and play poker. And she taught him to love. So, when Dent and Melody split, his spiral into depression had nothing to do with losing his girlfriend. It had to do with his losing her daughter.

"Big Daddy!" a small voice cried out with glee.

Dent turned and smiled for the first time in weeks.

"Butterball!" he exclaimed.

Amid a thundering herd of preschoolers fleeing the compound came Riley Bancroft. She raced across the asphalt as fast as her Converse would take her and leapt into Dent's open arms with a big smile. At five years old, she embodied everything that was good in the world. Her blonde bob haircut and little round cheeks were what led

Dent to nickname her "Butterball." Having no children of his own, he showered her with everything he could every day.

At Christmas, he went hog wild. Not one to plan ahead, he was ill-prepared for the last-minute onslaught of panicked parents fighting through the aisles at Toys "R" Us. Ramming shopping carts, yelling moms, screaming children, war-torn dads, and Dent, a deer in headlights. Ever determined, he crammed every toy he wished he'd had as a kid into the oversized cart. Super-soakers, foam darts, nerf guns, plastic swords, toy tanks. If it was the weapon of a soldier, knight, or ninja, it went in the basket.

"How old is your little boy?" asked the freckle-faced teen at the register.

"She's a girl," said Dent.

The teen's jaw dropped.

"She's four," he said.

"Oh," she said, quickly ringing up the maniac to get him out of the store. "I'm sure she'll love it."

Dent went all in because Melody never did. Despite her ninety-grand-a-year salary selling IT for Cisco Systems, she never bought Riley a thing. Didn't want her to grow up with false expectations in life, she said. Didn't want her to grow up with what Melody never had, Dent deduced.

Melody grew up in the sticks south of Atlanta on ten acres that served as a haven for her parents' work with the airlines. She was the youngest of five and there never seemed to be enough toys or food or love to go around, so when she got knocked up, she swore she would raise her daughter different. Away from Riley's father. Away from her parents. And away from anything nice.

"What's with the *Beverly Hillbillies*?" Melody said regarding Dent's packing job.

"I'm moving," he said deflecting.

She raised a brow. "Forget to pay your rent?"

"Can I stay with you for a night or two?"

"Are you serious?" said Melody without a thought.

"Is Big Daddy coming to live with us?" asked Riley.

Melody scowled and pulled her into her arms possessively.

"No, Big Daddy doesn't love us anymore," she said. Riley coined the name Big Daddy after returning from a visit to her biological father's house. She named him Tiny Daddy. It was the best a four year old could do to keep them straight. Dent was fine with it. Tiny Daddy, not so much.

"I do love you," Dent said. "I just can't live with you."

"Because Big Daddy doesn't love us," said Melody.

"What's the matter with you?" said Dent.

"You're the one taking psychotropics," she said.

"It's heart medication."

"Web MD said it makes you suicidal."

"Not everyone."

"I want to go with Big Daddy," Riley said reaching for him.

Dent reached for her, but Melody stepped in.

"Don't touch her," she said. "I'll slap an injunction on you so fast your head will spin."

Legal jargon spilled from Melody's lips with remarkable ease. She and her attorneys had been battling with Tiny Daddy over custody of Riley since the day she was born. With no paternity rights himself, Dent was left with no power over what he loved most. Which left him powerless. Which made him furious.

"I hope you get some help," said Dent.

"You're the one who's homeless."

"Fuck you," he said.

Knowing the drill, Riley slapped her hands over her ears.

"Watch your language," said Melody.

She opened the door to her burgundy BMW and plopped Riley in the car seat. She began to whimper.

"Riley, shush!" Melody turned to Dent. "See what you've done?"

"I love you, Butter," said Dent.

Melody climbed in the car and started the engine.

"Say goodbye, Riley. You'll probably never see Big Daddy again."

"Bye, Big Daddy," said Riley stifling her tears.

Dent sighed as Melody backed her car out an inch from him.

"I guess this means I can't stay with you."

"Don't ever contact us again," said Melody.

She hit the gas and peeled away, leaving Dent standing alone in the middle of the now-empty parking lot.

CHAPTER 6

THE MOTEL

Ding. Dent rang the tiny bell on the front desk of a shithole motel on the worst side of Culver City. A fat, old veteran sat slumped over his cane snoring in a corner. His faded T-shirt had a pointed cannon and read: *Go Ahead, Take My Gun.* The carpet was filthy. Water dripped somewhere. A TV played *The Price Is Right.* On a rusty stand, brochures with smiling families summoned one and all to the delights of Disneyland, Universal Studios, and The Magic Castle. *Ding-Ding.* Dent rang the bell again. Finally, a troll of a woman with heavy eyes and a light beard waddled from a back room in a low-cut dress better suited as a tablecloth.

"Can I help you?" she grunted.

"I need a room," he said.

"License and credit card."

He put them on the counter. She scooped them up.

"Do you have Wi-Fi?" Dent asked.

"Sometimes."

"How 'bout a soda machine?"

"End of the hall."

Dent pulled a book of matches from a glass jar. On the back was a sketch of a shapely stripper and an address for The Wild Goose.

"How many nights?" grunted the clerk.

"What?"

"How many nights?"

It hadn't dawned on Dent until that moment that he had no idea. As far as he knew, this was his home for the foreseeable future.

"Not sure."

"Three nights," she said.

"What?"

"Lost souls. Lost souls get three nights. That's usually how long they stay before they wander elsewhere. If not, you get another three nights."

"Fair enough," said Dent.

"Sign here." She held out the pen to him like "The Devil and Daniel Webster," taunting him to sign away his soul.

Screw it, he thought. *Where else I got to go?* He scratched his name across yellow parchment. She handed him two keys, which was optimistic of her, he thought. He had absolutely no one to invite. And if he had, he sure as hell wouldn't bring them there.

The room was worse. A paisley bedspread that Dent would not want to take a blacklight to. Peeling wallpaper. Faded paint. The words "Eat Me" carved into the headboard. Dent tossed his faded green army bag onto the bed. It was the one thing he never let go of from his time overseas. It got him to hell and back once. He figured it could get him back again.

Click. Dent flipped on the fluorescent lights above the sink in the bathroom. Caught a glimpse of himself in the mirror. Bags under his eyes. Scruff creeping up his cheeks. And his hair, once dark and full, was beginning to thin and grey.

"Christ."

He unpacked a large plastic baggie. Razor, dull. Toothpaste, mangled. Hairbrush, warped. And an airplane bottle of Jim Beam. How that got in there, he had no idea. But he was glad it did. He twisted off the top to take a drink but found it empty. His cell phone buzzed on the desk. It read: *DICK.* His loving nickname for his SAC supervisor. It was followed by a text:

"Meet your new partner, Charlie Norris, noon tomorrow."

CHAPTER 7

THE PARTNER

A shot of brown whiskey sat on an oak bar in a dark restaurant yearning for attention. Dent tossed it down his throat like a champ, clicked his teeth, and sucked in the customary breath.

"God bless happy hour," he said.

"It's lunchtime," said the bartender. He was a grey-haired lifer named Cally who worked every casino in Las Vegas during his sunless existence and escaped to the beach for his swan song. Venice Beach boasted plenty of seafood restaurants. How a Red Lobster made it past city ordinance was anyone's guess. But here it sat, three blocks from the ocean from which surely none of its fish originated. It was dark, empty, and the stench of ammonia still filled the air from its morning detox.

At the end of the bar sat a cute coed-looking girl with long, thin hair, horn-rimmed glasses, and a tan corduroy jacket. She sipped a pink drink and read a brown book. Dent squinted to see it, his eyesight beginning to fade.

"What ya reading?" he grumbled.

The girl turned, cheery and spry, her porcelain features lit by the red light coming through the lobster-colored window.

"Oh, it's Dostoevsky," she said.

"Dostoevsky?" he winced. "You a student?"

"No, I'm just reading. For fun."

"You read Dostoevsky for fun?"

"Sure," she said as though everyone did. *"Crime and Punishment.* It's incredible!"

"Sounds painful."

He wasn't sure what to make of her.

"You by yourself?"

"Not anymore," she said.

Dent grinned. "Can I buy ya a drink?"

"Oh, that's not necessary."

"C'mon, I'm miserable and lonely. It'll be good for my self-esteem," he said.

She smiled politely. "Well, okay, just one I guess."

"Great. What ya having?"

"A Shirley Temple."

"A *what?*"

"A Shirley Temple. It's a quarter cup Sprite, one and a half tablespoons grenadine . . ."

"I know what a Shirley Temple is," he huffed. "I just didn't know people drank 'em."

"We do!" she said cheerfully.

Dent felt like he tumbled into a fairytale.

"You're just a breath of fresh air, aren't you?"

"I've been accused of that," she said with a smile.

Dent beckoned the bartender. "Cally, can we get my friend here a Shirley Temple? And I'll take a Jack and Coke."

Cally nodded, knowing better than to interrupt whatever was brewing between the two.

"Jack and Coke?" she asked.

"Yeah, helps me get through the day. Jack to tolerate the bullshit and Coke to keep me . . . peppy."

"You don't seem very peppy," she said.

"Yeah, that's why I'm drinking 'em."

She waxed curious. "Do you come here a lot?"

"Just when I have to."

"Why 'have to?' "

"Eh, I'm supposed to meet someone I don't want to. Don't want them to know much about me, so I pick this numb-nut place so it won't reveal any of my secrets."

Her eyes lit up. "Ooh, you have secrets?"

"Doesn't everybody?"

"No. I don't."

The drinks come just in time.

"Well, you're young. You will."

Dent takes a hearty sip.

"Thank you," she said to the barkeep. She bit the cherry off the little plastic sword and swirled it in her pink drink. "Why do you feel you have to keep secrets?"

He considered her words, decided to confide.

"I'm an FBI agent. And a drunk. And an asshole. You can't go down the road of life with those stripes on your sleeve without having to sweep a few dust bunnies under the rug."

"That's a shame," she said. "That you see yourself that way."

"Yeah, well, I know where I've been."

"Jesus died for our sins, you know," she said. "You're free to be free again . . . from all that."

Dent raised an eyebrow. That explained her cheery fucking attitude. And the gold cross around her neck. She was a Bible-beater. He tossed back the rest of his drink with a flourish.

"Think you and I see the world a little different."

"That's okay," she said with a smile. "I like you all the same."

Dent grinned. He needed that. "Likewise. My name's Dent."

"I know," she said.

He blanched. "You do?"

"Yeah. I'm Charlie. I'm your new partner."

CHAPTER 8

THE CORONER

The security camera footage from the bank across the street from the laundromat yielded nothing for authorities to see because the killer came and went through the back. The fingerprints were clear as day but not in any database foreign or domestic. *Who could commit a crime this heinous without any priors?* Dent wondered. He and his new partner, bubbly, bright Charlie Norris, intended to find out.

Together, the mismatched duo drove down Pico Boulevard through a tunnel of palm trees to the county coroner's office. Charlie sat shotgun peering about Dent's dirty Buick like a nun in a whorehouse. The bulk of his belongings had been dumped in motel hell, but the grime and stench of days gone by still lingered. Charlie wiped a streak of brown dust from the dash.

"You could use a maid," she said, not one to mince words.

"You do that a few more times, I won't need one."

"I think you need a professional."

She was already getting under his skin, and it hadn't been ten minutes.

"That was pretty low of you, ya know. Yesterday. Not telling me who you were from the get-go."

"It wasn't low. I got to know the true you, didn't I?"

"I guess. A little," he admitted.

"And you got to know me."

"What did I get to know about you?"

"That I'm good at my job."

She had a point. It's not often Dent was duped. Well, at least professionally. Personally, he had a long list of failures. If he was being honest, he would admit he did wonder if the young woman at the end of the bar might have been single. But that was off the table now. Never in a million years would he cross the line of sleeping with a coworker. He was too thankful for this thankless job and wouldn't want anything to jeopardize it. Besides, they were clearly cut from different cloths.

"And the whole Jesus thing. That part of your act too?"

"None of it was an act. I just chose not to reveal everything. 'The Lord establishes the steps,' " she quoted from Proverbs 16:9.

Dent winced. No God had ever given him the time of day. And now he was saddled with a beauty queen disciple preaching the Word to him in his own damn cockpit.

"You got a boyfriend? Girlfriend?"

"A fiancé," she said proudly.

He peeked at her. "Little young for that, aren't ya?"

"I'm twenty-seven," she said.

"You look younger."

"Yeah, I get that. It's the height."

At five foot two and butterscotch blonde, Charlie was the last person you would expect to be a homicide investigator. And that was the idea. She could slip in and out of anywhere without anyone noticing. Growing up in Kansas on an unhealthy diet of Investigation Discovery, she long had her eye on the bureau. And they on her. After four years at Princeton majoring in criminal justice and three years at Yale Law, the bureau offered her a deal. She graduated top of her class at Quantico and trained in forensics in Cincinnati but wanted more. It seemed the tedium of actual FBI work and the glamour of *I (Almost) Got Away With It* were non-reminiscent. Now, she was Dent's apprentice. Or babysitter, depending on how you looked at it.

Dent steered the Buick into a half-empty parking lot of a bland building on the ugly side of town. The worn sign above the gloomy entrance read "Los Angeles County Medical Center."

"Ever seen a dead body?" he asked.

"Many," she said flatly.

Dent raised a brow. Young Charlie Norris was full of surprises.

Two stories beneath street level housed the coroner's office, a cold, metallic dungeon for carving up bodies and investigating their deaths. The view was grim. The smell putrid. It didn't seem to faze the coroner or his techs in back. But for Dent, it brought back a wave of death from his days in the Gulf. They say smell is the strongest of senses, triggering memories long lost in the furthest reaches of the amygdala. But to Dent, those sights and sounds were front and center. It was all he could do to keep his morning McMuffin down.

The coroner was a balding Black man in his sixties with a wrinkled face, grey coat, and quirky wit. He carved up frogs as a child which led to therapy, which led to medical school, which led to carving up people for a living. He went by Dr. Cone. He pulled back a bright white sheet covering the deceased to reveal a filthy, gooey mess.

"Never gets old, does it?" he said with a wink.

Dent grimaced. "Any prints?"

"Not that we could glean."

Charlie bent over to look closer. "DNA?"

The doctor prodded at the sinewy skin with a shiny scalpel. "No, no, it seems his tumble in the dryer was accompanied by a rather stringent agent."

"Bounce?" joked Dent.

No one laughed.

"Hydrofluoric acid."

In his twelve years with the bureau, Dent had seen horrible things. Not that his time overseas was a walk in the park. But the homicides the bureau were called in to investigate churned the stomachs of even the most stalwart veterans.

"Dental?"

"Bingo," said the doctor. "We found a few."

He rattled teeth around in a glass jar with a jingle.

"Run 'em through IAFIS?"

"We did." He called out, "Barley!"

One of the female techs turned in a white lab coat opened a button too low for her ample chest. Tattoos ran up her strong arms. A glint shined in her green eyes as they took in Dent.

"Yessir," she said, reporting for duty.

"Do we have data for Agent McCreary on the deceased?"

"Sent the specs to division. Haven't heard back."

"Got an ETA?" asked Dent.

"Yessir."

"Good work," said Dent.

Barley smiled and handed Dent a paper with the data.

"My number's at the top there. If you have any questions."

Dent wasn't sure how to respond. "Miss . . . ?"

"Barley. Just Barley," she said with a smile.

"Like Shakira," said Dent.

Charlie rolled her eyes and grabbed the paper. "We'll be sure to call you."

CHAPTER 9

BEVERLY HILLS

The ID on the teeth came through. The family of William Bartholomew Horvath III was notified their loved one was the unfortunate victim found in the dryer in Manhattan Beach. "The Cleaner" is what the press began to call the killer, running in a thousand directions with errant presumptions. Maybe the victim was dirty. Or diseased. Or just plain evil. And the killer thought he needed cleaning. Or at least drying. Social media was worse. Spinning yarns left and right that the victim was part of a cult. From another planet.

Dent had the inside scoop. He had seen the scene. Interviewed the witness. Smelled the body. And was now on his way to meet the newly widowed wife. In Beverly Hills, of all places, the most lavish city in America. *Maybe William Bartholomew Horvath III was laundering money.* That would explain things.

The Buick stood out like a sore thumb cruising through the manicured lawns and grandiose estates of North Palm Drive. Unaffected by it all sat Charlie. Not that she was used to it. She was focused on Dent.

"Is that your thing?" she asked.

"Is what my thing?" he replied.

"Flirting. The flirting."

"What are you talking about?"

"Miss MMA back there, me. Is that what you do?"

"I didn't flirt with her, you. She—she flirted with me."

"You don't have to flirt back, you know," she said.

"I didn't!" Dent replied.

"Well, you don't have to get defensive."

"I'm not getting . . . ."

"You don't even realize it."

"I'm friendly."

"Friendly. Ha."

"What?" said Dent.

She considered her words. "You don't realize the effect you have."

He considered her words. "What are you talkin' about?"

"You give them . . . hope," said Charlie.

"Hope? Of what?" asked Dent.

"Of being . . . rescued."

"Have you been hittin' the Shirley Temples?" he said.

"It doesn't matter if you ride in on a horse or a . . . what is this . . . a Buick?"

"Buick *LeSabre*, thank you."

"It's hope of a better life from . . . whatever life they're living."

Dent sighed, tired of her two-bit profiling. "I think you're projecting, Chuck."

"*Projecting*? I'm not projecting."

"I know projecting. And that sounds like projecting."

"I don't need rescuing. *Didn't* need rescuing," she said.

"Now that sounds like denial."

"Denial. Please."

"I *am* a profiler, you know. That *is* my thing."

"Sure. Old school," she said pointedly.

He chuckled. "And what, you, you're new school?"

"We do have the benefit of knowing what you know. And building upon it."

"Believe me, sister. You don't know what I know. And you don't want to."

She sat with that for a second. "I bet that works too, doesn't it? The wounded puppy thing?"

"Oh, for Christ's sake," said Dent rolling his eyes.

"Were you victimized as a child?" she asked.

"I'm being victimized *now*."

They rested. They breathed.

"Look, can you try not to profile me, please? My heart can't take it," said Dent.

Charlie turned to face him. "You were raised by women. Who taught you the passive-aggressive two-step? You couldn't say what was on your mind or you would be tossed in with whoever screwed them over. So, you learned to dance. Around it all. That's how you learn how women think. Manipulate. Control."

He was speechless. Which was kind of an oddity.

"Too bad they didn't teach you better," she said.

"You're talking about my mother, ya know? My sister!"

"Did you sleep with them? Were they attractive?" she asked.

"Jesus Christ! What's the matter with you?" Dent said.

"Just chitchat," she said with a smile.

"Chit . . . cha . . . You're evil!" he exclaimed. "A wolf in this little lamb body of yours."

"Would you rather have it the other way around?

"I'd rather not have it at *all*."

The Buick pulled to the ornate gates of a grandiose mansion. Green-ivy-wrapped iron fence rods. Dent rolled down his dusty window. A male voice came from a shiny speaker in a stone wall.

"May I help you?"

"Agent McCreary to see . . .'"

"Horvath," said Charlie eying her notes on her phone.

"Mrs. Horvath," said Dent. He craned to Charlie. "Or would it be Miss now?"

She shot him a look.

"Too soon?"

After a moment, there was a buzz. A click. And the gates yawned open. Thus was the way of bureau work. Cadavers and coroners in the morning. Mansions and movie stars in the afternoon. You never knew what you were going to get.

The house had curb appeal. Towering white pillars. Walls of tinted glass. And a wide berth of stone steps inviting the few and famous to twelve-foot doors. Shiny Mercedes, Land Rovers, and police cars dotted the circular driveway.

A soft-spoken housekeeper of Hispanic descent met Dent and Charlie at the doors and showed them inside. A marble staircase spiraled from a shiny foyer past a ten-foot Andy Warhol painting to a second-story landing. Waiters carried trays of crackers and cocktails past tired cops and weary mourners. Plump leather couches surrounded oak tables in the living room. Books from Aristotle to Shakespeare lined shelves in a library.

"Well, if the wife's the heir, we have motive," said Dent.

"Let's not jump to any conclusions," said Charlie.

"That's what we get paid to do."

A voice called to them from across the living room.

"Detective McCreary?"

Elenie Horvath was the matron of the manor. Not that she fit the part. Faded jeans, black tee, and old boots. Her long, black hair hung across her brown eyes. Her bronze skin radiated an unusually healthy glow. An easy smile made it to her supple lips despite the fact her husband was just found in a glob.

Charlie stepped forward. "It's *agents*, actually. I'm Agent Norris. This is Special Agent McCreary."

"What makes you special?" Elenie asked Dent.

Charlie glared at him.

"It's a long story," he said nonchalantly.

Elenie smiled. "They told me you might be coming."

"We're sorry for your loss," said Charlie.

"Thank you. It's all been so sudden."

Dent and Charlie read her like a book. It's Murder 101. When a body is found, suspect the spouse. The lover. The mistress. The mister. Whoever had the most to gain by losing the dead.

"If you don't mind, I'd like to have a look around," said Charlie, knowing Dent could get more out of her alone.

Elenie nodded. "Of course."

Charlie eyed Dent and wandered off to explore the estate.

"I know you've already been questioned by the police, but you mind if I ask you a few questions of my own?" Dent asked.

"Not at all," said Elenie. "Would you like to sit down?"

"No, but a little air might be nice." He knew getting her away from others was the best way to get her to open up. She showed him onto the broad back patio that overlooked a beautiful stone pool. A handsome pool boy in tight whites swept for sunken leaves.

"May I ask what your husband did for a living?"

"Other than live off his father, you mean?"

Dent raised a brow.

"Don't get me wrong. William is . . . was a smart man. Accomplished in his own way. But he had a head start."

"And you?"

"I am, was, a makeup artist. In the biz. That's how we met. William was a producer. On *Doctors and Nurses* on CBS. Well, a pretend producer, I call it."

"What do you mean?"

"A consulting producer. He just tells people what they're doing right and wrong. Kind of like our marriage."

"Any idea why anyone would want to kill him?"

Elenie blew her bangs from her eyes.

"He was pushy, impulsive, petulant. Who knows?"

Dent looked around the lavish grounds.

"What happens with all this?"

"Hell if I know," said Elenie. "There's a will. But I've never seen it. He has two exes, three grown kids, was screwing his assistant, and Lord knows who else. Could be a free-for-all."

Dent was unaccustomed to such candor. It was kind of refreshing.

"So, I have to ask. Where were you night before last?"

She smiled. "With him," she said regarding the pool boy.

Dent caught him looking their way and raised a brow. "Any proof?"

She nodded with a smile. "Sure. We have video."

In the study, Charlie perused framed photos of the deceased with TV stars—flamboyant, beautiful, and rich. There were screenplays on a credenza. Diet Coke cans in the trash. Diplomas on the wall. But something in the corner drew her eye. On the panel beside the fireplace was a framed stethoscope. "Best of luck with your new adventure!" was emblazoned beneath.

"What are you doing in here?" a man's voice said.

She turned like a kid caught with her hand in a cookie jar and found LAPD Lieutenant Lenowitz standing behind her.

"Just looking," she said flashing her credentials.

"Charlie Norris, FBI," he read.

"Who are you?" she asked turning the tables.

"Lieutenant Lenowitz, LAPD. You must be Dent's new girl."

She didn't appreciate the insinuation.

"We work together if that's what you mean."

She continued perusing the room.

"About time they got some new blood," he said trying to compliment her.

"How long have *you* been on the force?" she asked.

"Fourteen years," he said sheepishly.

"Huh," she uttered.

"We can handle this just fine without you, you know."

She eyed him flatly. "Like you handled the O'Reilly murder in El Segundo? Or the Townsend Twins in Westwood? Or the MacIntyres in Marina Del Rey?"

Lenowitz's eyes widened. "How did you know about . . .?"

"Save your breath," said Dent wandering into the room.

Charlie and Lenowitz turned.

"She's three times smarter than me, and I'm twice as smart as you."

"Seriously. How did she . . .?

"She's got a whole Doogie Howser thing going on."

"Doesn't everyone investigate the people who are investigating who they're investigating?" said Charlie.

"No," said Dent and Lenowitz together.

"Huh. Old school," she said and sauntered away.

Lenowitz looked after her. "What is she, twelve?"

"Too young for you," said Dent.

"I'm married."

"Like that ever stopped you."

Dent turned to leave.

"Hey. Let me know what you find out on this, will you? My boss is up my ass."

"Don't I always?"

"Not once."

"Well, why break a streak?"

"Seriously. The 'number one' has got people freaked. Everyone wondering if there will be a number two."

Dent stopped at the doorway and peered back.

"The question is not *if*, Mack. It's *when*."

CHAPTER 10

BEND

A river ran through it. That was the only explanation for this town. In the middle of the desert of Central Oregon lay the magical oasis of Bend. Cute as a button, the eight square blocks of cafes, galleries, and breweries along the gentle rapids of the Deschutes River gave birth to a rustic refuge for wealthy retirees escaping Silicon Valley and the hordes of stoned snowboarders serving them. Nearby Mount Bachelor boasted a couple easy runs on a few feet of snow a couple months a year. The mountain was too far to see from the city, but close enough that real estate agents could claim it a "ski town." Older couples enjoyed enormous chalets with pebbled drives and koi ponds. Younger folks packed ramshackle houses two to a room and parked dented Subarus across dirt yards. No matter what side of the river they were on, people needed to eat, drink, and get their hair done. But it was healthcare that really took root here. After all, retirees and skiers both broke bones, sprained ankles, and tore ligaments on a semi-regular basis. Orthopedics came in droves. The hospital system exploded. Private and public healthcare options grew by leaps and bounds. Bend became a major dumping ground for San Fran ex-pats with asthma to Zika and everything in between. With it came the progressives. The Pacific Northwesterners who thought outside the box.

Inga Haelstrom was one of them. Originally from Germany, the eldest daughter of industrialists from Frankfurt was raised on bratwurst, sauerkraut, and strudel. Suffice it to say, her intestines were a bit overworked. Vegetables were not generally sought after in her neck of the woods either, so what followed was daily indigestion. Left unchecked, it led to esophagitis, gastroenteritis, and irritable bowel syndrome. Long bouts with the toilet were commonplace in the Haelstrom household. And with five children, two parents, a grandmother, and one and a half baths, this proved a problem. Pissing outside in the woods behind the shed was easy for the boys, but the girls had a rougher go. Still, they did. It was that or piss their pants. Inga was sure when she got older, she wanted a big house, a small family, and a cure for her intestinal woes. She studied night and day to get perfect grades. A degree in biometrics from a university in Dusseldorf gave her the springboard to America to attend medical school. The University of Washington offered her a partial scholarship and discounted housing.

One night in the laundry room, she met Damen Johannsen, a dapper medical student from the right side of Spokane. After trading barbs and folding clothes, the two threw back one too many beers and screwed like rabbits in the back of Damen's Volkswagen. You would think a couple of medical students would be thoughtful about using contraception at the height of the AIDS epidemic. But you would be wrong. Young love, cold beer, and raging hormones trumped all. Inga dropped out of school after three years to have her first child. Then popped out two more before they divorced. Once the child support ran out, Inga was left to her own devices to pay the bills. Holistic healthcare was hot and heavy in the Seattle area at the time, and she quickly found that a six-month night course for $1,500 would equip her with a certificate in "Holistic Integrative Medicine." Using the finest ingredients from the most questionable manufacturers, she could hang out a shingle as an "H.I.M. Practitioner" to heal others with tummy troubles. The school website boasted a first-year graduate could yield $80,000 a year. In a town like Bend, it could yield more. So, a month after graduation, Inga loaded up her kids and moved to the mountain town to set up her own practice in the trendy Northwest.

It was near dark outside Inga's little health café when she locked up. Being the first to arrive and the last to leave was something ingrained in her German upbringing. Bags in hand, she shuffled past the cacti shrubs and patio seating to the empty parking lot. Her Volvo sat in the light of the crescent moon rising on the horizon. At five foot eleven, Inga could take care of herself, but when she was approached by someone from behind, she was surprised.

"Oofta! You startled me," she said in her German accent. Then suddenly her eyes gaped at a taser pointed her way. And then she felt it. A stinging sensation exploded through her pale-skinned body like a thousand bolts of lightning. Her body convulsed, her eyes rolled back in her head, and she hit the pavement face down, breaking her nose with a crack.

Sunrise in Bend was as pretty as it got. Slivers of pink slinked through wispy clouds with a painter's precision. Dew glistened, streams gurgled, and sparrows sang. Along the river ran a three-mile trail for hikers, bikers, and joggers.

Marsha Bagby was a knockout for these parts. At twenty-four and a CrossFit diehard, her Nike-clad frame simply glided along the trail. Long dark hair tied neatly in a ponytail, she was sure today was the day she would break her 24:37 time for running the entire route. There was no one in her way at this hour, and Justin Bieber was rocking her AirPods. Her breaths pumped in and out with piston-like rhythm, blowing little puffs of cool air like a choo choo. Until she turned the corner at Drake Park. Suddenly, her eyes widened, her gait slowed, and her jaw dropped. Something awful caught her attention, and she forgot about beating her time. Hanging from the bottom of the Newport Avenue Bridge was a woman's body, naked as a jaybird, arms akimbo, tied to a steel support beam. Her white feet dangled toward the rushing river below and the number one was painted on her stomach in blood. But the most striking thing of all was . . . the long medieval sword shoved up her ass through her torso and out the top of her head. Its sharp, shiny tip glistening in the rising Oregon sun.

CHAPTER 11

THE FIANCÉ

Colby Lewis was his name. A fresh-faced young lad from a good home in a nice neighborhood with two loving parents the Lord Almighty had seen fit to keep together. He went to the best public school in his small town, rose to valedictorian his senior year, and graduated with straight A's. He could have gone to any college he wanted, but sure enough, ol' Colby wanted to follow in his father, grandfather, and great-grandfather's footsteps, pursuing an honorable career in the military. Three days after graduating, Colby signed up. He set his alarm for 7:00 a.m. sharp, showered, shit, shaved, and made himself a balanced breakfast with all four food groups. With the stroke of a pen, he signed his life away for the next five years with every intention of making the Marines his lifelong career. The shining star of basic training, Colby quickly rose to officer. He swore himself to God and country and would surely die for either. Perhaps that's what Charlie saw in him. She, too, was raised with the oft-forgotten notions of honor, integrity, and respect. These values they held in common, along with a strange affinity for *The Andy Griffith Show* reruns and butternut squash soup. People had married for less. So, when Colby dropped to his knees on that glorious spring day at Charlie's favorite soda shop, she squealed with delight. Now they were engaged, set to marry at the church where Charlie was baptized, and living as close as they could to one another without cohabitating. Carlsbad was the cutest town they could find between her Los Angeles FBI field office and his San Diego military base, Camp Pendleton. The drive for each was grueling, but that's what one did for love, they told each other. She lived in a quaint condo with a roommate in nursing school and he lived with a pile of grunts in a not-so-shipshape soldier pad two blocks away.

Colby reclined on a fluffy pile of lace pillows in Charlie's bedroom watching her pack. He was in grey military sweats emblazoned with "US Marines." She was on the verge of a blue pantsuit preparing for her very first work trip.

"Are you taking your sweater?" Colby asked.

"Yes, I have the blue one," she smiled.

"Do you need another? It might be cold there."

"It's Oregon, sweetheart. Not Belarus."

"I just don't want you to be cold."

"I'll be fine," she said.

He squeezed her teddy bear in his strong hands.

"I wish you didn't have to go."

"It'll only be a day or two."

She knew his ego was being tested since she was shipping out before him, but she had faith he would overcome.

"Still, it makes me wonder," he said.

"About what?" she said plopping her shoes in the suitcase.

"You know . . . us." He patted the bed with a grin.

She turned three sheets of red. "Colby Lewis!"

"We *are* engaged, you know," he said.

She waved her meager ring. "Why yes, I do! But that doesn't mean we have to . . . you know, mess up my bed." She snickered.

Colby finally sat up. "Come on, sweet pea. I'm the only one in the house who hasn't done it. In the whole platoon!"

She shut her suitcase and rested her hands on his shoulders. "That doesn't mean you have to."

He looked down, dejected. She lifted his chiseled chin.

"We're months from being married, honey. We've waited this long. Do you really want to soil ourselves now?"

"I guess not," he muttered.

"I didn't think so. Besides, it will make that first night all the more special."

He smiled and rose, shoulders back like he was taught. Hating to admit that he admired her conviction.

"Walk me to the car?" Charlie asked.

He nodded, plopped his camouflage cap on his crew-cut noggin, and grabbed her suitcase. She rewarded him with a peck of a kiss and grabbed her .45-caliber Smith & Wesson from the top drawer of her white dresser. She holstered it promptly and snapped the leather clasp closed with a click.

"I love you," he said with pride.

"Not as much as I love you."

LAX was its usual construction-ridden clusterfuck. Taxis, Ubers, Lyfts, and limos jockeyed for position around a general obstacle course of orange cones, barricades, and detour signs. On the far side of the airport, a different story. The private entrance off Imperial Avenue was where the city's elite rolled their Range Rovers through a gate past a barbed-wire fence to board their private planes. So, too, would federal authorities.

Charlie was excited. She had never flown on behalf of the bureau. It was like a medal of honor to be invited on the jet. It meant she mattered. It also meant the case she and Dent were working on was important. She parked her Chevy Cavalier in a numbered spot, gathered her things, and hustled across the tarmac to where Dent stood at the staircase of a Gulfstream G550.

"You're late," said Dent over the roar of the engine.

"I'm sorry," she admitted.

Dent couldn't find it in himself to condemn her. Sooner or later, he knew he would be late. Or drunk. Or both.

"Well . . . try not to be late again."

She smiled thanks and climbed the steps. Dent followed, and the pilot pulled the door closed behind them.

CHAPTER 12

THE SWORD

Homicide was not commonplace in Bend. The last one was a year and a half before Inga's demise. A simple domestic disturbance that led some put-upon housewife to take a frying pan to her abusive husband. They said, the whack to the parietal lobe didn't even do it. It was his neck snapping on the kitchen counter on the way down. Nevertheless, the jury took pity on the woman, and she got three to five with good behavior—as long as she stayed out of the prison kitchen.

Word spread fast about the lady on the bridge with the sword up her ass. A rookie coroner's assistant named Ben had Inga laid in a body bag in the back of the coroner's wagon. Firefighters had the area cordoned off with yellow tape. The Department of Natural Resources patrolled the river in boats keeping kayaking rubberneckers from tampering with evidence.

Regional FBI agents combed the grounds in blue jackets. Dent and Charlie stood side by side at the back of the wagon staring at the "#1" carved in Inga's bloated tummy.

"Now, my math may be a little rusty but . . . doesn't two come after one?" asked Dent.

"Maybe he lost count," said Charlie.

"On two? Who loses count on two?"

"Maybe he's . . . impaired."

"Oh, he's impaired alright." Dent craned over the bridge. "How'd he get her up here?"

"How'd he get a sword up her ass?" said Ben.

Dent and Charlie craned.

"Pardon my French," he said apologetically to Charlie.

"That's okay. I speak a little French myself," she replied.

Dent couldn't take the cuteness, drew a cig, and fired it up.

"Alright, let's get her to the coroner and see what we can find out."

Ben zipped up the bag.

Dent and Charlie stepped to the railing of the bridge and looked out over the town.

"Doesn't make sense," she said. "A TV producer in Beverly Hills? A holistic nutritionist in Oregon? Both numbered one."

"That's the problem with profile training. They train us to look for patterns. But the people we're trained to profile are so batshit crazy, most of the time, there aren't any patterns."

His cell phone buzzed. The screen read "PSYCHO."

Charlie blanched. "Friend of yours?"

"My ex-girlfriend," he said matter-of-factly. "Excuse me."

He stepped away to take the call. On the other end of the line was Butterball.

"Big Daddy!" she said, full of cheer.

"Butter! How you doin'?"

"She's sad," said Melody cutting in on the speaker.

Dent's shoulders slumped. He was used to the bait and switch.

Melody drove through Newport Beach, top down on the BMW, Riley pinned in her car seat in a dirty soccer uniform.

"What's wrong?" he asked.

"Riley thought you were coming to her game today."

Dent tried to remember if he forgot. Melody was an expert at gaslighting. Most people with borderline personality disorder were. They grew so accustomed to lying to justify their means, they forgot which lies they told, and wove a tapestry so complex no one else could tell either.

"You never invited me," said Dent.

"Yes, I did," said Melody. "It was today at noon."

The worst part was Melody was gaslighting Riley too. *Big Daddy was supposed to be here. Big Daddy doesn't love you.* And Riley was left with a five year old's mind to sort it out.

"I'm sorry I wasn't there today, Butter."

Riley looked out the back of the car, wind whipping through her little blonde locks, her mind a thousand miles away.

"She doesn't want to talk to you," said Melody.

Dent shook his head with anger.

"Can you take me off the speakerphone?"

He knew she wouldn't.

"We have to go," said Melody. Even though they didn't.

"I love you, Butter," said Dent.

"Say goodbye, Riley. We may never talk to Big Daddy again."

"Melody, goddamn it, I swear. . ."

Click. She hung up.

Dent was used to having his buttons pushed, but Melody took it to a whole different level. One night when he was dropping her off, he had damn near had a heart attack. It wasn't a Fred Sanford, grab-your-chest kind of thing. It was like being struck by a small bolt of lightning. He broke out in a cold sweat, short breaths, and felt an ache in his arm. Right in front of Melody in front of her condo. One of her tirades brought it on and was what led Dent to meet a doctor, a cardiologist, a psychiatrist, and a kooky old therapist named Doctor Blume.

"When you met Melody and Riley, they were in a proverbial raft . . . with a hole in it . . . in the middle of the ocean," he said. "Once you got in, you started bailing water to keep everyone afloat. But you can't do it any longer. And if you don't get out, you'll go down with them."

It was hard to hear, but Dent had known it was true. He had to save himself, knowing he was leaving Riley behind to drown in her mother's dysfunction.

Bam-bam-bam! Dent banged a fist against the soda machine in the hall of the Hampton Inn on the outskirts of Bend, trying to get his soda out, his money back, or both.

"Maybe you should talk sweet to it," said Charlie.

He looked up, finding her standing in a matching terry-cloth robe and slippers.

"That ever work?" he asked.

"Does for me," she said with a smile.

He looked around. "You just walking by?"

"I heard banging," she said.

"You investigate banging?"

"Sworn to protect." She pulled her gun from her robe pocket.

Dent grinned. He liked her. Maybe because he saw himself in her. Or her in Riley.

"What did you want?" she asked.

"What?"

"Your soda. What do you want?"

"Oh. A Coke."

"Not diet?" she joked.

"Easy, Chuck."

She pressed the button, and a can ejected into the bin.

"How'd you do that?" he asked pulling it out.

"You have to press the button after you put in your card, not before," she said matter-of-factly.

"How'd you know that?"

She shrugged. "New school."

He frowned, popped the top, and took a sip.

"What'd you think about today?" he asked.

She realized she was being debriefed. Right then right there.

"I think we're dealing with a clinical sociopath with no moral conscience, adept at human interaction, and intentional in objective. But unlike others, he has no regard for his own life, exhibiting characteristics common to patients suffering from histrionic behavior disorder."

"What makes you say that?" he asked.

"A laundromat in the middle of a commercial district? A bridge in the middle of town? He doesn't care if he gets caught. Or if he dies. And that's what scares me."

Truth be known, it scared Dent too.

CHAPTER 13

THE TIMES

It took balls to drive a car in New York City. Riding a bike was simply asinine. Still, everyday bike messengers, delivery boys, and flower girls took their lives in their own hands to get across town. The cabbies were horrible, relentless in their pursuit of the almighty dollar. But at least they knew where they were going. Ubers were the worst, helmed by a bunch of broke, lost suburbanites from Rockland County who braved the Tappan Zee Bridge each week to try and make enough dough off the city socialites to cover their rent.

Hauling ass over elbows up Eighth Avenue at the crack of dawn on a white Roebling nine-speed was a wiry young Black dude with shoulder-length dreadlocks named Lyle Packard. But everybody called him Pac-man. *HONNNNK!* A beat-up MTA transit bus sporting a Clairol ad with an emaciated model nearly sideswiped him.

"Watch out, motherfucker!" bellowed Pac-man.

He hit the brakes, popped the sidewalk, and dodged a hotdog cart before regaining control and navigating the last of his commute to the glass tower of *The New York Times* world headquarters.

In the two-story, broad marble lobby, Pac-man hustled through the morning slew of journalists, couriers, and executives vying for entry through the NORAD-like security system. SWAT, cops, and suited officers manned a barricade of metal detectors and video cameras three layers deep.

"What's the haps, Pac-man?" said one large Black security officer in a black suit, black tie, and with a black sidearm. Pac-man threw his backpack on the moving belt and dropped his shades, keys, and iPhone in a little red bucket.

"Ya know, ya know, JP, same shit, diff day."

Pac-man swaggered through the detector in his shiny bike pants, worn Air Jordans, and faded Boston University sweatshirt, flashed his tethered lanyard, and gathered his things.

"Counting on you to keep us straight," said the big man. Pac-man knew JP was referring to the newspaper as a whole but simply spoke for himself.

"Just a cog in the wheel, my man."

The tenth floor was way too busy for this time of day. A giant digital clock on the far wall clicked "7:01 A.M. NEW YORK." Beside it were other clocks for London, Bangkok, Sydney, and more. Pac-man slid past the morning scribes of the crime division and plopped into his cubicle with customary panache. He dropped his backpack on the desk and pulled out his Mac Air covered in stickers touting hip-hoppers of yesteryear. His fabric walls were covered with Post-it notes scribbled with story details, photos of LeBron, Malcolm X, Rhianna, Otis Redding, and a poster that read "BLM, BITCH."

From the other side of the cube rose a nebbish Long Islander named Oliver who always had the sniffles.

"Hey, Pac, how goes, brother?"

Without looking up, Pac-man responded.

"Easy on the 'brother,' Oliver. Black folk gonna think you tryin' too hard."

"Sorry," said Oliver, angry at himself.

"It's all good. Least you tryin'."

That gave Oliver some solace.

"You hear about that laundry killer in LA?" he asked.

"Hell yeah, whacked, right?"

"He struck again."

Pac-man looked up. "Whaaaaaat?"

"Right? Bend, Oregon of all places."

"Where the hell's that?"

"Middle of the state, just east of the Cascades. They claim to have three hundred sunny days a year."

"How far is it from LA?" Pac-man said, Googling it.

Up on his screen popped a faraway photo of the Christlike image of Inga strewn to the bridge.

"What the Jesus?" he said eyes wide.

"I know. So much for the laundryman moniker."

"How do they know it's the same guy?"

"Painted a big number one on her stomach."

Oliver pointed at the screen, and Pac-man zoomed in.

"Sonuvabitch. Beaker put anybody on it yet?"

"Nope. That's why I'm telling you. You're serial guy."

"That was once. Two years ago. And I was lucky."

"Well, maybe you'll get lucky again," said Oliver.

"PAC-MAN!" barked a voice from the corner office.

Pac-man popped up, looking over the top of his cube.

At the end of the hall stood the editor of the crime department, Edgar Beaman. But folks called him Beaker because he looked like the Muppet with cropped red hair and bug eyes.

"Sir!" said Pac-man standing to attention.

"Get over here. I got a job for you."

Beaker was a tough guy from Queens with three ex-girlfriends and two ex-wives and up to his ass in alimony, palimony, and child support. He loved his job more than any of the women, or the kids, and it showed. He was always at the office, on his phone, on his laptop, or at a breakfast, lunch, or dinner meeting. That didn't leave a lot of time for bedtime stories or shenanigans. As a result, they all bitched and moaned and left. *So be it*, Beaker thought. He always had the paper. His employees were like family, people he hired, trusted, and fought alongside. Like him, they were raised and reared on Murrow,

Cronkite, Bernstein, Thompson, and Rather, and were passionate about uncovering and exploiting the truth.

"Screw 'em" is what Beaker said when they cried *fake news*. "YOU WILL KNOW THE TRUTH, AND THE TRUTH SHALL SET YOU FREE" hung framed on a shiny plaque above his messy oak desk.

"John 8:32," Beaker would say. "Nobody screws with John."

Next thing Pac-man knew, he was boarding a plane for Portland, Oregon. From there, he would hop a nineteen-seat turbojet to Bend. *God knows why they called it a Turbojet*, Pac-man thought. Damn thing felt like a flying go-cart, rocking and rolling on buffets of air like an old jalopy on a mountain road. He clenched the armrests like they were going to fly away and sweated his coffee out through every pore of his body. A cute flight attendant noticed.

"Never flown in a small plane?" she asked.

He just shook his head. He couldn't speak.

"You'll be okay. But there's a sickness bag in the pocket in front of you if you need it." Pac-man peered down to the bag before him. He hadn't thought of vomiting until she mentioned it, but now that she had, it seemed like a good idea.

He landed in Bend a little before 10:00 p.m. Pacific Standard Time, not at all surprised to find he was the only Black man in the terminal. And outside the terminal. And on the rental car bus. He rented a Camaro, drove eight miles to town, and checked into a ho-hum hotel overlooking the river. He dropped his bag on the dresser and landed face down in the bed exhausted. He was asleep in seconds and needed every ounce of it for what was to come.

CHAPTER 14

THE CLINIC

Bend's finest taped off the H.I.M. clinic where Inga was abducted. Her SUV sat in the same spot. Forensics dusted the vehicle for prints and combed the ground for clues. They found a smidgeon of blood where her face hit the pavement. Reporters had gathered in customary fashion, vying for entry past the police to no avail. And a little grey terrier barked like the world was out to get her little grey-haired owner looky-looing across the street.

A regional FBI agent named Monica Swann pulled up in a standard black fed-issued sedan. Her short, black hair hung to her faded blue FBI jacket. From the passenger side stepped Dent, nursing a cup of black coffee like a magical elixir. From the back seat stepped Charlie, chipper as the crisp Oregon air.

"Thanks for picking us up," said Charlie.

"No problem," said Monica. "Figured it'd give us a chance to chat."

Over breakfast, the three talked about the case. What they knew from Manhattan Beach. What they didn't know. What they knew about Bend. What they hoped to learn today. They would divide and conquer to make the most of their time. Monica was the local, so she took the community. Charlie was the clue hound, so she took Inga's SUV. And Dent took the clinic staff.

Ding. A little bell rang on the door as he pushed inside. The clinic walls were decorated in cheesy Zen-ful musings printed on airbrushed beaches with phrases like . . . *Let the flow come from within.* A few cops roamed around trying to look like they knew what they were looking for. Two female staffers sat nervously at the front desk, wide-eyed and shell-shocked. One was young and cute who checked the patients in and out. The other was withered and haggard from doing the books, charts, and orders of vitamins, supplements, salves, ointments, and tinctures that filled the shelves behind them. Talking the two up was a young Black dude with dreadlocks in a faded T-shirt that read "ANTIFA AF."

Dent showed his badge to the attending officer by the door.

"What's with Snoop Dog?" he asked, peering at Pac-man.

"I don't know. He was here when I got here."

Dent shook his head. Flatfoots were useless. He sidled past the cop to the desk where Pac-man and the women talked freely.

"Ladies, how are ya?" He showed them his ID.

"Agent . . . McCreary," Pac-man said leaning to read the print. "How are you, sir?"

"You all work here?" said Dent diplomatically.

"We do," said the bubbly one, regarding her and her elder.

"I'm with *The Times,*" said Pac-man pretending to reach for his lanyard that he knew was not hanging around his neck.

"Oh, forgot to put this on," he said pulling it from his pocket. Dent leaned in to read the small print.

"Lyle . . . Packard."

"Everybody calls me Pac-man."

"Long way from home, aren't ya?"

"All the news that's fit to print," said Pac-man, touting the century-old motto of *The New York Times.*

"You're not supposed to be in here, you know that."

"Nature called," he said pointing to the bathroom.

"Back to nature, newsman," said Dent eying the exit.

The ladies stood stunned, more from Pac-man being from New York than *The Times.*

"Aye-aye, Cap," said Pac-man, saluting Dent on his way out. "Catch ya on the flip."

"Not if I can help it," said Dent.

"Just you wait, Agent M., you gonna love me!"

Dent couldn't help but grin.

After asking the desk brigade the usual questions, Dent stepped outside to get some air, which, for Dent, meant smoking a cigarette. He peered at Inga's SUV, wondering how and why she was taken. What link was there between her and William Horvath III? These questions kept all investigators tossing and turning at night. But for Dent, they were sustenance. He needed them to survive. To keep his brain alive. If not, he would be like Bobby Fischer without a chess board, crazier than the day was long.

"Dent," called Charlie. She stood with the little grey dog, now in the frail arms of the little grey-haired woman—more to keep the dog quiet than safe.

"This is Mrs. Merrill," said Charlie. "This is Special Agent McCreary."

"How ya do," he managed.

"Mrs. Merrill is retired, lives up the street, and walks Fifi here four times a day."

Dent knew what that meant.

"I saw him," said Mrs. Merrill. "He was driving a white van. I knew there was something off about that. A white van in this neighborhood, that time of evening. Something off, I said."

Charlie updated Dent on what Mrs. Merrill told her.

"Male, Caucasian, six foot three, shaved head, black clothing."

Convinced Charlie had gotten what they needed on the suspect, Dent moved on.

"Tell us about the van. What made it stand out? Was it dirty? Broken headlight? Any dents?"

"No, no, no, none of that. Just your average, everyday rental van."

That stopped Dent and Charlie in their tracks.

"How do you know it was a rental?"

"Well, it had a Hertz sticker on the bumper," she said as though it meant nothing. "Don't think they just stick those on any old van."

Twenty minutes later, they were in Monica's sedan doing seventy miles per hour in a thirty-five miles per hour zone with a police escort in front and behind them, flying west on Newport Avenue toward Northwest Warehouse Incorporated. Dent was on the phone with the local police captain orchestrating back-up. Charlie was on the phone with Sanjay Amble, their able IT counterpart at their home office in LA. He handled all things computer-related from his three-screen workstation in the bureau bullpen on the fifth floor.

"You're two miles out," said Sanjay watching their blue beacon soar across a large, high-tech GPS screen toward a red X marking their destination. Some rental car companies now required their vehicles to be mounted with tracking devices that could be accessed with the flip of a switch. This allowed them to track deviant road trips of mischievous renters and, more frequently, retrieve high-end autos when stolen.

Sanjay was a slender descendant of Indian American parents who immigrated to the US in the '70s on work visas with the British Embassy. Counterintelligence was their specialty, and shop talk around their nightly kebab rubbed off on their third child. A scholarship to MIT led Sanjay to a master's degree in computer engineering which led to an FBI recruiter knocking on his McCormick Hall door his junior year. Trained by the best brains in the country, Sanjay could hack his way into and out of any mainframe on the globe. It was just a matter of time. When he wasn't staring at screens in the office, he was staring at screens at home, playing Fortnight until all hours of the morning. Beating every game in record time caught the eye of global manufacturer Epic Games. They flew him to their Cary, North Carolina headquarters and offered him a job helping design the next wave of video games. Despite the colorful collection of Lotuses and

Lamborghinis in their parking lot, Sanjay declined. He was happy with his day job. He liked real stakes, catching real bad guys.

"Turn right, turn right, turn right!" Sanjay exclaimed. He saw Dent and Charlie getting close. The red X was locked on a storage unit on the back row of the last warehouse leaving Bend. Frazzled management opened the metal gates for the caravan of police, SWAT, and agency cars to file in. Lights were swirling, but no sirens blared. They didn't want whoever it was that killed Inga to know they were coming. Still, the small-town cops couldn't help but let their tires screech when they stopped. This was the most action they had in years.

Boots hit the ground as Dent, Charlie, Monica, and a hoard of Bend police swarmed the facility quickly and quietly. Dent motioned for a few cops to move around back. He and Charlie moved to the metal front door. SWAT officers joined the fray in flak jackets, combat helmets, and face shields. Positioning themselves on either side of the door with a battering ram and assault rifles, they awaited Dent's cue. *BAM!* They cracked the door and tossed two flash bombs inside, exploding in a loud cloud of smoke. SWAT went first, as was customary, the red lasers of their rifles swirling through the grey. Dent and Charlie followed. Waving away the haze, they discovered the small, abandoned warehouse was filled with a maze of rusted machine parts . . . and a white Hertz van. Sweeping the room, the cops called "Clear! Clear! Clear!" At the van, a different story. Dent and Charlie approached slowly, weapons drawn, and found no one in the front seat, flung open the rear doors and found nothing but plastic wrap streaked with blood. Dent dumped a breath. Charlie holstered her weapon. *TING!* A metal sound reverberated in the back of the warehouse. Everyone swung their weapons. A myriad of red lasers landed together on only a frightened rat scurrying through a hole in the cement wall.

An hour later, doors and windows were open, lights were on, and the place was swarming with investigators.

"Dent," said Monica. He and Charlie stepped over to a large metal worktable mounted with wrist, ankle, and torso clamps covered in traces of dried blood.

"Looks like this is where he did it," she said. Their eyes fell upon the end of the table where a heavy, motorized vice stood agape and ready for action.

The next day, they would learn from the local coroner that, judging by the enzymatic secretion during blood loss, Inga Haelstrom was alive and well when the two-hundred-millimeter Oakeshott XII sword was inserted into her anus, through her intestines, stomach, lung, esophagus, throat, brain and out the crown of her head, courtesy of an industrial machine pump. Simply put, the killer wanted her to feel the pain. Or at least feel as much of it as she could before she passed out from shock and blood loss. So, too, would the Los Angeles autopsy prove was the fate of the TV producer in Manhattan Beach. William Horvath III died *in* the dryer. Not before. Whoever was killing these people wanted them to suffer.

CHAPTER 15

THE HOOKER

The idea of returning to the motel in Culver City made Dent sick to his stomach. But he had nowhere else to go. Tossed from his apartment, abandoned by his ex, tracking the nation's latest serial killer, it simply had to do for the time being. As the sun set, he pulled his Buick into the cracked parking lot outside his rundown room and turned off the engine. He wiped his weary face and eyed his motel room door. To his surprise, it was slightly ajar. He raised a brow and lifted his Glock from the passenger seat where it lay beneath the *New York Times* front-page headline: "THE #1 KILLER STRIKES AGAIN." The byline read "Lyle Packard."

Dent moved quietly toward the motel door. Pushing it open, he found the bedside light on. Per protocol, he checked behind the door, cautiously swept the room, the closet, the beds, and that's when he heard it. A *click* in the bathroom. He tensed, swallowed, cocked his weapon, and stepped to the door. Though he had been in similar situations a hundred times, he never got used to it. Perhaps that's what kept him alive. The knob on the door turned before him, the door opened slowly, and out curled a beautiful woman in a tight-fitting white sundress and a wild mane of curly blonde hair. Dent's pistol landed beside her head.

"AH! It's me, it's me!" she bellowed in a Russian accent. Her English was broken, but the way the words dripped from her lips made up for it. The sound of her voice could slay a thousand men, and for all Dent knew, it had. But he didn't care. Evgeniia Volkoff was her name. But Dent just called her Evie.

"What the hell are you doing here?" he asked.

"You invite me!" she exclaimed.

He squinted trying to remember.

"You forget," she said.

He lowered his pistol and head in shame. "Sorry."

She took his head in her hands and kissed it softly.

"How did you get in?" he asked.

"Frances."

"Frances?"

"The maid."

Dent shrugged. *So much for security.*

She smiled and it lit up the room. "You have bad day?"

"Bad month, more like it."

"Well, let's see what we can do for that."

Gingerly, she took his gun from his hand and laid it on the bed. It was seldom, if ever, Dent let anyone take his weapon from him. But Evie was someone he could trust. Perhaps the only person. Partly because they had been through so much together, and partly because he knew she had been through so much before they met.

The last daughter of a supposed import/export titan of produce from Verkhoyansk, Russia, she knew her father was something else entirely. Never was there so much as an orange around their six-bedroom hillside estate surrounded by barbed wire and armed guards. Reared on meat and potatoes and lies, she knew she had to make it out of her town before she graduated secondary school or she would never make it out at all. At sixteen, a pretty friend of hers from school gave her the number of a man in Yakutsk who knew a man in Kostroma who knew a man in Moscow who could sell them through an international marriage service to lonely American businessmen for $40,000. Ten percent of which would be given to the girls. It wasn't much, but it was enough for them to escape the cold winters of northern Sakha and start a new life. The firm promised American buyers the marriage would last forever, but the US courts allowed the betrothed to file for legal separation after eighteen months. It usually took another twelve to make it through the courts. By the time Evie was nineteen, she had fled her family forever, sailed a freighter to New York City, and married an overweight heir to a garbage disposal service in Flint, Michigan. The day she got her green card; she filed for divorce. Twelve months later, she was hitchhiking her way across the great plains to Hollywood. She didn't plan on becoming a prostitute. It just sort of fell in her lap. Mister Michigan had a prenup protecting him from sexy suitors milking him out of house and home. But Evie knew there was more to life and love than money. She hit the road with the same clothes in the same sack she landed with in America and $1,200 in her purse. *Dasvidaniya, motherfucker,* she thought as the bus roared away from the Greyhound station.

Landing in LA was never what a wannabe actress would have thought. The irony was that one was led to believe it would be all sunshine and roses in the first place. The truth: the City of Angels was a soulless vacuum of a million attractive, intelligent, talented people fighting one another for ten thousand jobs. What was left were depressed bartenders, waitresses, and hookers in a trail of tears in empty alleys and bathroom stalls, embarrassed they never lived up to their family's expectations. New to Los Angeles, Evie met a handsome man in a well-to-do lounge in a high-end hotel on the Sunset Strip. Initially, she shunned his advances. But then he offered her $5,000 to spend the night with him. He came in sixty seconds and paid her happily, more out of shame than anything else. He never called her again. But his friends did. And she upped the price with each call. Now she was making $8,000 a night, two nights a week. Before she knew it, she had an eleventh-floor condo with twenty-four-hour security at the Westford, a shiny black BMW X7, and a half-decent guy who loved her for who she really was . . . Dent.

Never would the two have met had it not been for the sting operation. The California Bureau of Investigation had been tracking high-end call girls for fourteen months in and around the hotel where Evie met her first John. She wasn't involved with the eighteen women operating through a "boutique modeling agency," but she was in the bar the night FBI agents flooded into the marble lobby and took them all down. It was just the disconnect Dent needed to get her off the hook.

Arguing over what to play on the radio en route to the jail, the two found common ground for the Stones and the Kinks. He asked her out. She said yes. So instead of taking her to the federal building, he took her home. Evie had never met a man who didn't want to rip her clothes off the first night they met. So that led to a second, third, and fourth night of talking, laughing, and listening to music. He kissed her goodnight, but they never disrobed. She felt safe with him, and he felt appreciated. Gradually, their slow-motion romance evolved into part-time lovemaking. He didn't want any whips or whip cream like the others, just someone to share his time and body. When Dent woke the next morning, Evie was always gone. Nothing but a dollar left on the bedside table so there would be no confusion about who was using whom.

CHAPTER 16

THE PUBLIC

Now that two bodies had been found, both labeled number one and left gruesome and bloody, the public was up in arms. It was more than just Los Angeles and Bend. The whole country craved word of the killings and fear ran rampant. News anchors and talk show hosts espoused ill-gotten and ill-formed theories. Spectator video of Inga's strewn carcass flashed across social media. What was left of her home, family, and past was ripped apart by reporters and investigators like ravenous wolves.

The Los Angeles Federal Building was a zoo. News vans lined the curb, reporters jockeyed for interviews, and police tried desperately to direct traffic. On the fifth floor, the elevator opened, and Dent wandered out with a hot cup of Dunkin' in hand. He wasn't opposed to Starbucks, but he always found their LA stores too filled with broke and desperate screenwriters. The vibe just didn't make for a positive start to the day.

"What the hell's going on?" he muttered to no one in particular. Charlie passed with a handful of file folders.

"You're late," she said with a smirk.

"Sorry not sorry," he said flatly.

Mornings were not Dent's bailiwick. Ever since the army, sit-ups had been a staple of his morning. More often than not, they were followed by throw-ups since drinking was a staple of his evening. Balance was what he called it. Regardless, the two exercises kept his aging abdominal muscles in some semblance of shape.

He traversed the busy floor of walking, talking feds to his messy cubicle in the back. Photos of dead guys were strewn here and there, fast-food wrappers contained leftover scraps and scribbled Post-it notes hung every whichaway. Across from it, Charlie had set up her own desk. Neat and tidy and ready for *House Beautiful*. An adorable photo of her and Colby sat beside a matching purple stapler, tape dispenser, and pen holder. A pink tulip stood in a vase tied with a bow. Dent just stared.

"I straightened up," said Charlie taking her seat with authority. "I didn't want to disturb your things though."

"Good," he said. "I'm very particular."

He plucked a week-old magazine from his soiled chair and dropped it in the overflowing wastebasket.

"Dent, Charlie, don't get comfy, briefing in five," barked SAC Parker as he passed to the large glass conference room.

"There's a briefing?" grunted Dent.

"Don't you check your emails?" said Charlie.

"I try not to. Doctor says they're bad for my health."

Dozens of other suits filed into the conference room.

"Looks like friggin' prom night," muttered Dent.

The fact was, thanks to the press, more attention was being paid to the case which meant more personnel, more supervision, and, for Dent, more headaches.

"Everybody wants credit," said a familiar voice behind them. Dent and Charlie craned, finding Pac-man sauntering up with a caffe latte, red backpack, and faded Malcolm X T-shirt.

"Who let you in?" said Dent.

"That nice lady up front," Pac-man said pointing to a weighty receptionist named Gladys.

"You lie to her too?"

"I'm press, dog. We don't lie. We *embellish*."

Dent eyed Pac-man's T-shirt.

"*The Times* approve your wardrobe?"

"Got to blend in, brother. This the way of the world."

"God help us," said Dent.

"I'm trying," said Pac-man with a smile.

Charlie had less patience for him.

"Shall I show him out?"

"Whoa, whoa, Closer. I got something for ya."

Dent raised a brow.

"Make it quick. We got a meeting."

Pac-man drew a piece of paper from his coat pocket.

"The Bend woman. Haelstrom."

"What about her?"

"She was on the take," said Pac-man.

"What?" asked Charlie.

"It's all right here," he said handing her the paper. "Every transaction in the last eighteen months. Overcharging insurance carriers for services not even rendered."

"How'd you get this?" asked Charlie.

"I'm friendly," he said not divulging his sources. But Dent figured Pac-man charmed Inga's desk girls out of it.

"Told ya you'd love me," he said with a wink.

Dent grinned. "It's a start."

Pac-man beamed. "This mean I can stay?"

"No," said Dent curtly.

Charlie motioned toward the elevator. Pac-man shook his head.

"Aw man, I thought we were getting somewhere, you and me."

"Not today we're not," said Dent.

Moving for the door, Pac-man called above the fray. "You owe me, Holmes!"

The mood in the conference room was intense. Fluorescent lights bore down on a large mahogany table surrounded by twenty-six leather back chairs. The back wall had floor-to-ceiling windows overlooking the smoggy skyline of the gritty city. The end wall featured digital screens with data, graphs, charts, maps, and photos. The chairs and walls were filled with agents of every color and creed. This was ground zero for the case and a standing-room-only event.

SAC Parker presided over the meeting, calling on subject matter experts as he went. Dent's eyes roamed the room, seeing a host of familiar faces and one unfriendly one. An ornery bastard with a crew cut gritting his chipped teeth in the corner.

"Special Agent Reynolds will helm things from Washington, and liaise with Dent as needed in the field," said Parker.

"Don't make me come out there, Dent. Bad enough I had to come to LA," he said.

None of the LA contingent took kindly to his remarks, but Reynolds didn't care. That's what made him a good agent. At least in the minds of the brass. A bad one in the minds of his peers.

"We'll miss you when you go, Rey-Rey," replied Dent.

It was a nickname Reynolds coined for himself at the academy thinking it was cool only to learn later only douchebags coined their own nicknames. Half the room laughed. Dent was well-liked in the bureau, even if he had issues. But if the shit ever hit the fan, everyone knew they could count on him.

He and Rey-Rey were partners years earlier, but that quickly soured when their egos collided. Rey-Rey was a climber, a wannabe politician with his eyes on the prize. Dent was just trying to do a job. Rey-Rey was put on a desk and Dent was put in LA. It was a demotion for both, but one equally insulting so neither could balk. The brass realized the two rivals knew how each other thought and assumed they would be able to overcome their differences for the good of the case.

Parker laid out the facts for the group. His assistant clicked through corresponding images on the screens. The Number One Killer was the number one priority for the bureau. Because it was a priority for politicians. Because it was a priority of constituents. *Would their women, children, dogs, and cats be safe?* So came the calls.

So came the orders. Whoever had killed the man in the dryer and the woman on the bridge was obviously a crackpot. What kind of crackpot, what made them that way, what made them risk their life to kill in such public ways was what the group was tasked to unearth. Whoever it was, they were strong, smart, creative, ruthless, prepared, and . . . destined to kill again.

CHAPTER 17

UTAH

Baseball was America's favorite pastime. But in Salt Lake City, it had become religion. Which was saying something considering this dusty tundra was the den of the Latter-day Saints. The LDS, as they were known, were a tight-knit clan of God-fearing, baby-rearing hypocrites. *Celibacy until marriage!* But by all means, then marry as many women as you like. *No caffeine or alcohol!* But they were all jacked up on one antidepressant or another. Everyone swore off swearing. But jacked off to Instagram like it was going out of business.

A hop, skip, and jump from downtown lay picturesque Sugar House Park. Built on the ground of the former prison penitentiary, it was now covered in green grass, tall spruce, and a fair share of the white right frolicking footloose in the shadow of the Wasatch Mountain Range. At the Little League baseball fields, emotional parents cheered on their determined tykes like it was the World Series.

"Come on, Scotty! You can do it!" shouted Coach Dan Townsend. A handsome, well-coifed fella in a beige button-down, tan khakis, and grey Vans. A little dapper for the park, but he just came from the office to coach his son's eight-year-old T-ball team. *Crack!* Little Scotty got a rare hit and took off like a shot.

"Go! Go! Go!" yelled Dan, his fingers clutching the fence in the dugout.

Scotty's little legs churned as fast as they could, kicking up dust rounding first and second before sliding into third, just beating the throw.

"Safe!" said the portly umpire.

Parents cheered from the bleachers. And Handsome Dan grinned ear to ear with pride. It simply got no better than this. Sunset and seventy-five. Snow cones and SweeTarts. If Norman Rockwell were alive, he would have painted the shit out of it.

Watching from a distance, it appeared but a collage of sight and sound. Except for the *breathing*. Someone was watching. A menacing presence in the shadow of an oak tree. From here, there seemed a longing for the life Handsome Dan, his slugger son, adorable daughter, and beautiful wife were enjoying as they walked arm in arm, post-game, to their shiny white Range Rover. But the *breathing* was what stood out. Deep. Heavy. Raspy. Like a wild animal.

It was hot in Salt Lake, but the city welcomed it. Everyone needed to thaw out after the long cold winter. The happy-go-lucky fit in their picnics, their barbecues, their biking. Pools opened for a short spell and lemonade stands were aplenty. Fortunately, Handsome Dan's Range Rover had air conditioning. So did his two-million-dollar, three-story home embedded in the side of Neff's Canyon. Art deco with a pinch of southwest, the Townsend House came loaded with a movie theater, swimming pool, arched doorways, vaulted ceilings, and master bedroom hearth.

The Range Rover eased into one of the three pristine parking spaces in the expansive garage. Beside it was a shiny silver Mercedes-AMG GT Coupe. Just a little something to get the Missus to and from the store. Beside it were twin Ultra STX Jet Skis on a custom trailer, ready to soar at a moment's notice. The family was met with licks and wags from their stout four-year-old golden retriever, Gunter, who shepherded them happily inside. The Missus punched the six-digit code on the home security panel and dropped her Louis Vuitton bag on the kitchen counter. None too surprising, the innards of the home were also fitted finely. Stainless steel appliances, quartz countertops, marble floors, Italian paintings, and plush leather furniture.

Once the children were fed, showered, and tucked in for the night, Handsome Dan and the Missus got down to business. She was on top, as usual, grinding her Keto-sculptured ass into his tan hips like there was no tomorrow. Little did she know, no truer words could be spoken.

Downstairs in the kitchen, a black-gloved hand reached through the flap of the dog door. It gently twisted the lock on the knob and slid quietly back out. The doorknob turned. The door opened. The tall, dark intruder stepped inside. His raspy breath muzzled by a black mask; his large body obscured by dark shadows. As expected, Gunter greeted him with licks and wags until he was stabbed with a syringe full of midazolam, knocking him out cold. The intruder made his way past happy photos on the frig to the garage. Moonlight glinted off the aluminum oxygen tank protruding from the man's backpack. He made his way to the air conditioning unit in the corner and hooked a hose from the tank to the unit's intake line. Knobs were turned and gas was emitted. Inside the house, a slight scent could be detected if one were awake. But after eight glorious minutes of sexual ecstasy, Dan and the Missus were down for the count. And the gas would keep them that way.

Moving through the hall in a military-grade gasmask, the intruder walked past young Scotty's room, his little sister, and the bathroom before coming to the double-doored master bedroom. Pushing open the doors, his raspy breath picked up pace with excitement. He found the white comforter bent back, exposing the Missus's naked leg. Strangely, he curled the blanket up to cover it properly. Whomever this was had nothing against her, or the kids, or the dog for that matter. Handsome Dan, on the other hand, had another thing coming. The comforter was lifted from his side of the bed, exposing his lean body in nothing but his Calvins. Leather straps clamped to a steel chain were pulled from the backpack and attached to Dan's ankles. He was then promptly dragged from his bed, down the hall, down the stairs, across the Italian tile of the kitchen, past the slumbering dog, and out the back door of the house.

An hour later, a mounted track of bright, circular lights snapped on, blinding the flittering eyes of Handsome Dan who lay naked, arms and legs and head and torso bound with leather straps to a steel slab. His eyes flickered with terror at what had become of him. He would have screamed if he could have, but a red ball had been wedged in his mouth by a leather harness, keeping him from uttering a word. Never had he felt so vulnerable, so victimized, so terrified. And that was the idea. Looming here and there around the table silhouette in the light was the killer, clinging and clanging metal instruments in preparation for something horrible.

"You're awake," the killer said in a dark, raspy voice. Dan blanched at the sound of it, struggling to see his face but unable. Handsome Dan tried to mumble something, but his words were unintelligible. The last thing he knew, he was asleep, safe and sound beside his lovely wife beneath his fluffy comforter. Now he was here, in the den of hell, being presided over by what seemed to be the devil himself. It suddenly occurred to him he had no idea what had become of his family. His eyes shot wide.

"Don't worry," the killer said. "They won't be harmed. . .if you behave yourself."

A hanging plastic IV bag was rolled up beside him. Dan grunted and groaned, and tears streamed down his cheeks. *What had he done to deserve this?* The killer drew a long needle from the bag's supply tube and jammed it into the vein of Dan's muscular forearm. He groaned in pain. But the fun was just beginning. The killer wheeled one—two—three more IV stands around each side of the table and stabbed three more needles into Dan's remaining limbs. *What the hell was he doing?* The killer released the valve on each of the supply lines and a clear solution slowly began trickling into Dan's body. He could see the bags were labeled with simple saline solutions. But something else puzzled him. Each line was connected to another tube, funneling from the shadows. Something else was being added to the solution. Handsome Dan thrashed this way and that, muscles straining with all their might to break free from his predicament. But it was no use.

"I bet you're wondering what's next," said the killer.

He calmly walked to the corner of the room and flipped on a dim red light, casting a horrific hue on a sight fit for Dante. Thousands of teeming white maggots packed in a large glass tank squirmed anxiously for an exit through the tubes. Shock set into Handsome Dan's eyes, and he started hyperventilating. An industrial vacuum had been attached to the tank and IV lines.

"Karma," said the killer.

He flipped the vacuum switch, and it roared to life, sucking the maggots out of the tank in a flurry and sending them spiraling through the IV lines into every extremity of Handsome Dan.

" . . . is a bitch."

The insects squirmed beneath his skin. And the red room reverberated with his muffled scream.

CHAPTER 18

THE MOUNTAIN

Alta Ski Area was the closest slope to downtown Salt Lake. On a light-traffic day, you could do meetings in the morning on State Street, escape up the canyon for lunch, ski two diamond runs, and make it back in the afternoon to respond to emails. So was the way of many a Utahn. In the warmer months, the lifts catered to hikers and bikers who would enjoy a scenic escort to the top to roam above the tree line or simply revel in the ride down the hundred-degree incline to the bottom. Occasionally, a hiker or two would tire at the top and catch the lift down, so it was no surprise to eighteen-year-old lift operator Molly Bingham when she saw someone coming down in the distance.

As the lift chair neared, Molly noticed something odd. The hiker wasn't wearing traditional hiking garb. No boots courtesy of Merrell, no fleece from North Face, not even a Patagonia cap. They seemed to be in nothing more than a jumpsuit. A strange, tannish suit with ivory hues. Molly squinted to get a better look as she approached the lift controls. That's when she realized the suit was *moving*. And the hiker was not. In fact, the suit was no suit at all. It was actually thousands of maggots vigorously consuming every inch of what was left of the naked body of once-handsome Dan. Beside him, the chair painted in blood with a circled "#1."

The FBI jet landed at Salt Lake City International Airport in the afternoon. This time, the lowering Jetway was met by three local FBI sedans. Dent and Charlie came down the stairs followed by a couple of other agents in boring suits and a wiry Black dude in a white T-shirt with a black fist that read "Black Power." Clearly, it was the first time Pac-man had been on a private plane, or in the great state of Utah.

"You sure they allow brothers here?" he uttered to Dent.

"They're religious. Brotherly love and shit," Dent replied.

"Not sure I'm their kind of brother."

Pac-man stepped a Jordan onto the tarmac.

"One small step for man . . . ."

Two tightly wound, white-as-snow local agents met them as they deplaned. One called out over the whine of the idling engines. "Special Agent McCreary?"

"Dent's fine."

The lack of protocol surprised them.

"I'm Agent Barnes, this is Agent Conarro."

Everyone else introduced themselves.

"Sorry we're late. Had some trouble over Area 51," joked Dent.

No one laughed.

"They don't do sarcasm," whispered Charlie.

"What?" he didn't whisper back.

"Mormons. They don't get it. They think you're serious."

"Jesus," said Dent.

"Yeah, I wouldn't say that either."

He shot her a look.

"You shittin' me?"

"They don't cuss either."

"I need a drink," said Dent. Charlie frowned, not having the heart to tell him alcohol was hard to find here too.

"He with you?" asked Agent Barnes, regarding Pac-man grabbing his bag from the plane's berth.

"He's with *The Times*," said Dent.

"Press?" he said surprised.

"Yep."

"You let him ride with you?"

Press accompanying an investigation was highly suspect, but Dent felt that with a good reporter in tow, they could control the story, and good ones often obtained answers they could not.

"He was coming this way," said Dent.

"Will he be joining us in the SUVs?"

"Just one of 'em," said Dent.

Charlie shook her head, figured they'd be lucky if they got out of town without Dent killing someone here himself.

CHAPTER 19

THE SAINTS

The battalion of black FBI SUVs roared into the parking lot outside the mammoth lodge at the foot of Alta Mountain, which was bustling with police, press, ambulances, and fire engines.

"Looks like the gang's all here," uttered Dent, climbing from the SUV.

Charlie and the others emerged from their doors, their faces solemn, none too excited about what was next. Despite their extensive training in emotional detachment, seeing a dead body was difficult, especially a mutilated one. Yet, it was an important part of the investigative process. On the steps to the ski platform, they passed a couple of overwhelmed firefighters bent over with nausea. Charlie steeled herself. Pac-man took it in nervously.

"I never seen no dead body before," he managed.

"Well, don't worry, you won't see this one either."

"Aw c'mon. I'm a crime reporter, right? Got to see the crime to report it."

"No. You don't," she said, pointing to a bench.

She still wasn't sure she could trust Pac-man even though Dent somehow did.

Frustrated, Pac-man plopped on a bench like a scolded child. "Alright, alright."

At the chair lift, coroners pulled back a black tarp for Dent and company to see what was left of Handsome Dan, which wasn't much. Maggots were not known to eat live flesh, but the killer had funneled the hoard inside the good doctor's body . . . and they had to get out somehow. Most of the bugs had since moved on, leaving little of the doctor's skin intact except, ironically, a bit of a Tweety Bird tattoo above his right ankle. Agents Barnes and Conarro gagged the moment they saw him and stumbled off to vomit. Dent and Charlie just looked away. They knew it would take a few rounds of EMDR to deprogram the images from their two-second glances.

Eye Movement Desensitization Reprogramming was the latest form of trauma treatment. Using moving lights and electric impulses, it allowed patients to replace negative memories with positive ones. But to Dent, it was like luring an anaconda through traffic to try and tame it.

"Aw, fuck!" they heard someone bellow.

Despite Charlie's instruction, Pac-man had snuck up behind them to take a gander and regretted it the moment he did. He spun away in some convulsive MC Hammer–type twirl and wiped his hands over his face repeatedly as though he could somehow wipe the image from his memory.

A few minutes later, Charlie joined Dent on the broad stone patio behind the redwood lodge, overlooking the magnificent Alta Mountain. All was quiet. Peaceful. And green.

"People live here," he said matter of fact.

"Sure," said Charlie.

"Why don't we?"

"What do you mean?"

"It's like a damn fairy tale. All this nature, beauty, trees. We live in . . . traffic and filth and garbage. What's wrong with us?"

"We're saints," she said.

That stopped him. There certainly was a higher calling for their work. There had to be. After all, they didn't *have* to be FBI agents. They could work in sales, farming, manufacturing. *Hell with that.* People who chose a life in law enforcement did so for one of three reasons: One, they were wronged or knew someone who was wronged and wanted to—*no, needed to*—set it straight, vicariously; two, they were sons or daughters of men or women in law enforcement who grew up hearing valiant tales of adventure around the dinner table—and nothing else could hold a candle to the rush; or three, it was just ingrained in their DNA, programmed into their soul from their triumphs and travails of a past life. Maybe in some mystical, multi-planned way, those things were all connected.

"I suppose," he said.

He peered at the chairlift, his mind whirling.

"Maggots. A sword. A dryer. Not a lot of this in the books, is there?"

"None I read," said Charlie. "He clearly wanted the bodies found though."

Dent agreed.

"Exhibitionist? Narcissist? Obstructionist?"

"Resourceful," was all she could muster, eying the mountain, "how he got him up there without anyone noticing."

Dent found himself agreeing again. Charlie Norris may have been light and fluffy with a cherry on top, but damn if she wasn't smart as a whip.

Dent noticed Pac-man pacing circles at the bottom of the steps, talking to himself.

"Poor kid. Didn't know what he was getting himself into."

"He's in shock," said Charlie. "Want me to get him?"

"Be my guest," replied Dent.

As Charlie rose, they were approached by Agent Barnes.

"Agent McCreary. We got a possible ID on the victim."

Handsome Dan's pretty wife rose from her nitrous oxide-induced slumber that morning to find her husband missing, a few spots of blood on the kitchen floor, and nothing else amiss. Police officers summoned to the scene found the canister hooked to the AC unit in the garage and the dog a little groggy. Among the identifying characteristics she listed of her husband was a Tweety Bird tattoo he got in college as tribute to her.

"You want to talk to the wife?" asked Barnes.

"Not particularly," replied Dent.

"How far is she?" asked Charlie.

"Forty-five minutes. In Sugarhouse. His office is closer if you want to go there."

Dent shrugged. "What'd he do?"

The agent flipped through his notes on his phone.

"A doctor of some sort."

That stopped Dent and Charlie in their tracks.

"What kind of doctor?" Charlie asked.

"An infusion specialist, it says."

Charlie started dialing Sanjay. In her short time with the LA office, she learned he could use any information they obtained in the field to gather more information everywhere.

"What is that?" asked Dent.

"What is what?"

"An infusion specialist."

"Uh, they hook you up to IVs, I think. Pump you full of Vitamin C. Painkillers. Steroids. Antibiotics. What have you."

"There's a doctor for that?"

"Guess so."

"How far we from there?"

"Same. Forty-five."

"Good. Let's go there."

Truth be told, Dent's reason for wanting to go to the office first was so he would not have to be the one to tell Handsome Dan's wife what had become of her husband. That was the hardest part of the job for him. Not seeing the bodies. Smelling the bodies. Shooting the bodies. It was seeing the look in the eyes of their loved ones when he told them their husband, or wife, or child had been killed. In fact, he had established a pat, seated, side-by-side technique for sharing such awful news. It was the one way he could demonstrate he cared while not having to look them in the eye. That way it seemed more like a tall tale passed down through generations than an actual event. Some people clutched his leg, put a head on his shoulder, or even fell into his arms in tears. But that was on them. Dent would never, could never, initiate such contact. That would be frowned upon by HR and open him up for more aggravation than he could handle.

The parade of SUVs cruised through Salt Lake City like an army of ants marshaling their way to a picnic. Dent and Charlie rode in the backseat of car three like royalty.

"How'd Mr. Hollywood get in the mix?" asked Dent staring out the window as the city blurred past. "Two doctors and a *TV producer?*"

"Maybe he wasn't always a producer," she voiced.

"A *pretend* producer, his wife said."

"His pretend wife," Charlie rebutted.

"Everybody's got a pretense of some sort."

"Do you?" she asked.

"Me? No. I got a thousand."

She smiled. A man with no pretense about his pretenses.

"In his office," she recalled, "there was a stethoscope framed in a box on the wall. I thought was from a show. Maybe it was from *before* the show."

"He was a *real* doctor," agreed Dent.

The notion raised their pulses. This was the kind of thing investigators lived for. The connections. It was like reading—no, being—in an Agatha Christie novel . . . all the time.

"Let's see what Mr. Horvath III did before *Doctors and Nurses.*"

CHAPTER 20

SUGAR DADDY

Handsome Dan's infusion clinic looked like a ski chalet from *Elite Traveler* magazine. Long wood beams from ancient pine trees crisscrossed vaulted ceilings for no apparent reason. Tall, angular windows opened to breathtaking views of the Wasatch Mountains. Agent Barnes greeted the office manager at the desk, and FBI investigators fanned out across every corner, digging through files, drawers, shelves, and computers. With probable cause of a gruesome murder, no warrant was required. The staff stood to the side, frightened out of their minds, waiting to be selected for questioning at what felt like Nuremburg.

"Next!" called out Agent Conarro, exaggerating his masculinity. An older desk clerk nodded to a younger desk clerk, and she shuffled away into the private office.

Another agent at a file drawer looked to Dent. "Would you want accounts payable, sir?"

"I want it all," he said. "Patients, partners, employees, vendors, janitors. Anybody who ever stepped foot in this place. I want to know who they are, where they are, and why they were here."

Charlie hung up her phone and stepped to Dent.

"Sanjay rocks."

"Yes, he does. Crappy card player, but good at recon."

"Before embarking on his illustrious television career, Doctor William Horvath III belonged to South Bay Internal Medicine, a general practice in Manhattan Beach."

"Bingo," said Dent.

"He's pulling everything from there. Monica's pulling the medical files in Bend. We should be able to start cross-referencing everything tonight."

"Good work," said Dent. That was a lot from him, and she knew it. She nodded thanks.

"Where's Pac-man?" asked Dent looking around.

"He went to the hotel. Said he had a deadline."

"Probably curled up in the bathtub."

"Can you blame him?"

"Not really. I don't want to be here either."

Not exactly what she wanted to hear from her partner/mentor.

"You don't like this," she said realizing.

"Nope," he said without a thought.

"Did you ever?"

"When I was young, I guess."

"What happened?"

"A thousand days like today."

She could only imagine. She was sharp but young. Most of what she had seen was in photos, videos, and simulations. Between those and the real thing was a wide chasm.

"I just want to save one," she said matter of fact.

"One? One what?"

"One person. If I can save one person, I'll feel like I've fulfilled my . . . purpose."

"You say that like we have one."

"Of course, we do," she said as though it were obvious. "We all have a reason for being. We just have to find out what it is. That's the mystery of life."

"Your Bible says that?"

"Oh God, no."

He nodded somewhat relieved.

"My Bible teacher."

Across the room, Agent Conarro peered out of the office door to Dent. Inside he could see the pretty young desk clerk crying like a baby.

"What'd you do to her?" he asked.

The young woman was not interrogated to tears. She was sleeping with her boss. *Handsome Dan.* She was only twenty-two, a part-time grad student in physical therapy at the University of Utah, and grief-stricken to learn her sugar daddy was dead. Maybe because she loved him. Maybe because she couldn't cover her rent by herself. Either way, Dent didn't pay her much mind. There were plenty of red flags that flapped in the wind in an investigation. And this he felt was one of them.

CHAPTER 21

THE CAFÉ

Pac-man sat in the corner of the half-empty hotel coffee shop typing feverishly on his laptop. He was writing the story of his life about death by maggots. The coroner had come back with gory details, and the young reporter was doing his best to get it all down while it was still fresh in his mind. He hadn't eaten all day but had five cups of coffee. The empties were lined up before him like trophies. Everyone knew coffee was the writer's fuel, but for Pac-man, it was lifeblood. No matter the time of day or night, if he was writing, he was drinking joe. It beat drinking whiskey, he told himself and anyone else who questioned his caffeine intake. He was a fast writer to begin with, but coffee made him faster. Seldom would he have to back up, rethink, retype, respell. Once he had the structure of his story in his head and research done, he could write like the wind. And today he would need to. Beaker was always wanting tomorrow's story yesterday, but this story was breaking like wildfire. *The New York Times* had long been considered the seminal news source in the country, and Pac-man's firsthand tale from ground zero of the Bend desert had been picked up by the AP and, thus, every other news organization in the civilized world. Serial killers were hot property—in novels and comics and television and movies, but when it was real and coming soon to a town near you, it was the talk of every water cooler from coast to coast. Once the world found out the killer struck a third time, in Utah of all places, the wheels would plumb come off. *California, Oregon, Utah? Where would the madman strike next?* Pac-man mumbled as he wrote, forming the words on his lips as they sprang from his fingertips. Sometimes he would even snicker. It wasn't a big deal in the privacy of his own apartment, but it did strike folks a bit odd when he was out and about in the corner of a crowded pub. Or a hotel coffee shop.

"Who the fuck you talkin' to?" a gruff voice asked.

Pac-man looked up. The gruff guy was talking to him. And was one of a trio of good ol' boys in hunting gear who were obviously passing through town themselves. If Pac-man got put up in finer lodging, he wouldn't have had to deal with such ruffians, but the Hilton Garden Inn was about as fancy as *The Times* would go.

"Oh. Sorry. Was I mumbling?" he asked, staring into three doughy, white faces suited up in camouflage. A quick glance around the café revealed everyone else there was lily white, too, and now, thanks to the gruff guy, looking his way.

"You sound like a damn crazy person," said the gruff guy.

"Crazy like Monday morning or crazy like sexy cool?" Pac-man heard himself say before he could stop. That's the thing about being a journalist, and a New Yorker—filters were optional. And being both didn't bode well for him.

"You with them BLM?" the gruff guy asked.

Pac-man peered down to see he was still wearing his Black Power T-shirt. And realized he was about to get his ass kicked. In Philly or Boston or New York, he would have been surrounded by brothers who had his back. Out here, there were no brothers. And no Mormons were sticking their necks out for anyone. It was literally against their religion.

"It was a gift," he lied. "From your mother."

It didn't used to be like this, Pac-man recalled. Until racist politicians gave racist assholes the green light to taunt those whose race, or sex, or religion, was not to their liking. *They'll get theirs*, Pac-man thought, *when they get to the pearly gates*. But for now, Pac-man would have to fend for himself.

Wham! The gruff guy clocked him across his jaw. Black coffee splattered against the white wall. A frightened female manager phoned for help. And the other two hunters rose for business. One spun Pac-man's laptop crashing into a wall. And for a writer, that's like being castrated. Pac-man rose with renewed vigor, a glint in his eye, a spring in his step until . . . *wham!* The gruff guy put him down again. This time, blood spurted from Pac-man's lip. He peered up with fear in his eyes, realizing he was doomed.

"There a problem here?" asked a voice from behind.

The gruff guy turned, angry at being interrupted, and found Dent standing in the café doorway, the manager scared stiff, and the clientele quickly vacating.

"Who the hell are you?" asked the gruff guy.

"Just a concerned citizen," said Dent.

The gruff guy grinned smugly.

"They're three of us. Only one of you. What you gonna do?"

Dent pulled back his coat revealing his Glock.

"Actually, there are nineteen of me."

The gruff guy knew exactly what he meant. The Glock held seventeen rounds in the mag and one in the pipe. He changed his tune and held up his palms.

"Whoa, whoa, we don't want no trouble," he said.

"Then I suggest you exit lickety-split."

The three hunters promptly grabbed their belongings and departed.

Dent lumbered over and helped a bloody Pac-man to his feet.

"You okay?"

"Never better," Pac-man groaned.

Dent eyed his shirt, shook his head.

"You asked for it, amigo."

Pac-man huffed a breath. He knew it was true.

"How'd you know I was here?"

"Shit, I'm just trying to get a cup of coffee."

Dent nodded to the manager putting a Styrofoam cup on the bar for him.

"Uh, that's free," she said.

Pac-man shook his head. That afternoon, he got six sutures beneath his lower lip, a stiff drink at the hotel bar, and an airline ticket home. On the plane, he wore a cheery new T-shirt he bought at the airport gift shop that read "Utah—75% Mormon, 100% Sexy."

CHAPTER 22

THE PLANE

The bureau flight home was like a football team after a loss. Laconic and depressing. The cabin held sixteen leather seats, faux wood tables, fiber carpet, and a single bathroom. Everything designed in dreary gray. It was like a 1960s German train car flying five hundred miles per hour at thirty thousand feet. A few suits slumped here and there. One slender female flight attendant in a pantsuit tended to their snacks, sodas, and safety.

Halfway back, a weary but pensive Charlie sat riveted to her laptop, combing through pages of research. Dent sat in the back row half asleep, half-snoring into his balled-up coat against the window, until they hit an air pocket, stirring him from his slumber. He cleared his throat, wiped his eyes, and tried to make out what Charlie was doing. He couldn't. But he could see she wasn't enjoying it.

"Research?" he asked.

"Yes. It's infuriating."

"Wi-Fi issues?"

"No."

"Red tape?"

"No."

She wasn't very forthcoming.

"Can I help?"

"I doubt it," she said plainly.

He wasn't insulted, but he was intrigued.

"Try me," he said.

She sighed and spun her screen for him to see. It was filled with China patterns of dishes from Crate & Barrel.

"These stupid wedding registries are intolerable!"

Dent raised a brow.

"Well, gosh darn."

"There are too many choices . . . colors, patterns, textures, brands, models, trims, depths, widths, heights. How is anyone supposed to choose anything?"

"Would you rather there be fewer?"

"Actually, yes!"

Interesting, he thought. Here was a dynamic young mind, top percentile of her Ivy League class, overwhelmed by one of life's simple complexities.

"Our wedding is three months away and people are calling and emailing and texting and messaging and posting, asking what we want and where to get it, and I don't know what to tell them!"

"Checks," he said flatly and leaned his head back again.

She peered at him blankly. "What?"

"Just have 'em cut ya checks. That way you can get whatever the hell ya want."

She scoffed.

"What?" he asked.

"You can't just get checks," she insisted.

"Why not?"

"It's not . . . *romantic*."

"Oh. Well. Romance. Sure."

To Dent, the notion of romance was but a myth. Like Santa Claus. Or the tooth fairy.

"Weddings are a time to be enraptured . . . by splendor and ceremony!" Charlie said with a flourish. It was obvious she had dreamed of her wedding day since she could walk. She had it all planned out in her pretty little head. From the daisies hung on the outdoor cabana to the rose petals scattered on the ivory aisle. Lamb would be served with cranberry, champagne, and a hint of mint. Her doting father would give her away to the handsomest of men awaiting atop a red bandstand in a black tuxedo. The bridesmaids would be Mary, Melissa, Sally, and Tammy. The groomsmen, the swellest of gents this side of Wichita.

"Well, at least you got that to look forward to . . . ya know . . . if you can crack the dish puzzle," said Dent, rattling the ice in his glass.

"Have you ever been married?"

The question caught him off guard and an ice cube in his throat.

"Me? No. Got close a couple times. But ducked and swerved."

She sighed sadly. "Do you have *anyone?*"

He knew he couldn't tell her the truth. Not about Evie the hooker. Any Cinderella with such designs on Prince Charming would frown at that sort of thing.

"Used to." It was common for partners to learn about one another's personal lives. Inevitable, actually. Working so closely for so many hours in such tight quarters. There was no way to keep it all at bay. Even though Dent tried.

"What happened?"

He realized his diversion tactic was a poor one, opening up a whole new can of worms.

"Uh . . . she wasn't mine."

Charlie stared, confused.

"My butterball," said Dent.

"Your *butterball?*"

"My ex's little girl."

He flipped to a photo on his phone of him and Butterball together, arm in arm, on a blanket. She was four years old, adorable as always, and he was smiling.

"She's beautiful! And you're smiling!"

"I smile."

"I've never seen you."

"I save it . . . for special occasions."

It was comforting for her to see Dent had a soft side.

"I hope to make you smile one day," she said.

"Don't hold your breath."

He peered out the plane window, lost in thought. Miles of desert wasteland passed beneath them. Why anyone would live out there in the middle of nowhere was beyond him. He only knew he was excited to get past it. Then he remembered he didn't have much to return to.

"Dent," said the pilot leaning out of the cockpit.

"Yeah?"

"We're getting asked to reroute." The pilot was matter-of-fact. That's the way they were all made, or what piloting made of them. Either way, there was never any bullshit between them and Dent.

"What?" Dent said sourly.

"Coming from the top."

"LA?"

"DC."

"Fuckin' Rey-Rey," Dent muttered. "Reroute to where?"

CHAPTER 23

TUCSON

If Hell had a zip code, it would be 85719. Tucsonans claimed it was "just a dry heat," but that was only to allay their own misgivings about living there. Or to keep their real-estate prices from plummeting. Either way, a hundred days a year at a hundred degrees were enough to keep them sequestered all summer indoors. To compound matters, rattlesnakes, coyotes, and scorpions seemed to creep and crawl through every inch of the desert landscape.

Tucson also boasted the highest crime rate per capita in the nation. More than New York or Detroit, which was not entirely surprising since so many people from those cities migrated to Tucson to escape them. You would think they brought the crime with them. But they didn't. Right-wingers blamed it on the Mexicans crossing the border sixty miles south. Left-wingers blamed it on everybody else. Either way, the town had become a surreal, Mars-like landscape of adobe mansions with high-end Kolbe windows whose John Ford views were blocked by more steel bars than San Quentin.

Careening across the desert, leaving a rooster tail of dust, were five government-issued black Chevy Suburbans. It seemed that with each murder came more SUVs as public interest piqued and federal budget allowed. Never would they exceed the speed limit, and seldom would they don blue lights. The FBI was intent on remaining below the radar.

Not that there was anything discreet about five matching SUVs driving along in a row.

On the east side of town, they roared past the famous military airplane graveyard that extended for miles. Behind barbed-wire fence, but visible to all, was every decommissioned airplane and helicopter of the United States Air Force, Navy, Marines, Army, and Coast Guard in the last sixty years. It was at once humbling and infuriating to see that much of America's tax dollars put out to pasture.

The caravan twisted up a long, manicured drive in the foothills of the Rincon Mountains past lush grass, tall cacti, and ornate fountains to the world-renowned Canyon Ranch Wellness Resort. It was the end-all, be-all of wellness retreats for mind, body, and soul. If hotels were ranked on a five-star scale, Canyon Ranch was a seven. Accordingly, weekly room rates began at $8,000. Large in size, they were filled with every accoutrement from the finest designers in the northern hemisphere. Southwestern in architecture, the tall walls that surrounded the resort's 150 opulent acres were made of adobe clay. So were the arched doorways and curved corners of the bio-conscious two-story buildings. The magnificent cobblestone entrance was an expansive roundabout festooned with a towering fountain, rich botanicals, and the most attractive staff in America. Handsome, fit, tan male valets in tight black shirts, black shorts, and black ASICS, as though color bore no consequence in the Arizona sun. One smiley young lad opened the door for Dent. Everything he said was captured on a thin black headset as though car retrieval was of national security.

"Welcome to Canyon Ranch."

Dent looked around like he landed in *Fantasy Island*. He was there because a dead body had been found. But it didn't seem like anyone knew. Because, well, they didn't. There were no cops, no press, no coroners. There was nothing but peace and quiet.

"Agent McCreary?" called a sultry voice coming down the stairs. Dent turned to find Miss Ramona, a thirty-six-year-old, bright, talented, gorgeous PR executive in an ivory pantsuit that accentuated her dark skin and long, black hair. She held out a welcoming hand with matching ivory nail polish.

"Nice to meet you. I'm Miss Ramona. Head of public relations for Canyon Ranch. Welcome."

"How ya doin'?" said Dent.

Charlie curled around the SUV to join them.

"This is Agent Norris."

"Pleasure," Miss Ramona said with a smile. "Right this way please."

She escorted them up stone steps and out of the public eye. Dent craned, seeing the rest of the agents corralled to the visitor lot by the security staff who weren't the least bit intimidated. They, in fact, were composed largely of former Secret Service agents who semi-retired to this arid refuge, played in an adult softball league together, and respected the way of the West: *Whatever happened in the resort was kept in the resort.* And left to Dent and Charlie to unravel.

CHAPTER 24

THE RANCH

Walking through "The Ranch," as everyone called it, was breathtaking. The vaulted, sculptured ceilings, hand-carved wooden sculptures, broad stone fireplaces, and Balmoral furniture was beyond anything Dent and Charlie had ever seen. Miss Ramona gave them the two-buck tour like they were prospective guests. She spoke of the streams and gardens, golf courses and tennis courts, and the three-to-one staff-to-client ratio who passed them with gracious smiles and nods.

"Why's everybody so happy?" asked Dent.

"They're paid to be," said Miss Ramona.

"They don't know about the murder," concluded Charlie.

Miss Ramona shot her a curt smile. "We're discreet."

Dent raised a brow.

"I'm sure you understand," said Miss Ramona.

He did not. It had been weeks since the murder.

Pushing through the front doors of the health spa revealed an oasis within an oasis. Dry saunas, wet saunas, whirlpools, and Watsu pools, organic cafés, and smoothie bars. People felt healthier here just breathing the air. The entire staff wore black outfits that matched the valets.

A few guests lounged about in fluffy white robes on cushy white chairs. That way, there was a clear delineation between the guests and employees. Dent and Charlie could've sworn they passed a movie star or two. Or rock star. Or social media star. They couldn't tell anymore. They all seemed to blend together. But they knew some of them were someone.

The trio made it to an anonymous door with a digital card scanner. Miss Ramona swiped her black card through the stainless-steel scanner. It buzzed, allowing them into a long corridor that led to another door at the end of the hall. "Sorry about the mess," she said.

She slid her card through the second door scanner that opened to a white-tiled room housing a dozen dry saunas currently off-limits to guests. The hall was clean as a whistle. The end sauna was crisscrossed with yellow tape labeled "Under Maintenance." The walls around it were freshly painted. The tile freshly laid. Whatever happened there had recently been covered up. Dent ran a hand over the wall. Beneath the white paint was a faint stain of "#1."

"The police allowed us to freshen up the outside," she said. "But not the inside. They wanted us to save it. For you all, I suppose." She smiled smugly.

There was nothing "The Ranch" despised more than outsiders dictating inside protocol. She removed the tape and stepped back for Dent and Charlie to enter the sauna alone. It was now evident the only reason she was showing them the site was to get approval to refurbish it. Dent drew open the door, dust billowed out, and his jaw dropped. The sauna was like a different planet. Everything was blackened to a charcoal crisp. The planks of the floor and walls and ceiling and benches were all deep-fried, the metal heater destroyed.

"Where was the body?" asked Dent.

"Here. Near the door."

"We told the police and the local agents what happened."

"Right. Can you tell us?" asked Charlie.

Miss Ramona tried to hide her anger, but it seeped through.

"The fire started in the heater, slow and steady, late at night. Dr. Chen liked to come after most guests had gone home. He was a stickler for germs."

Dent and Charlie had already been briefed on the basics of the events by local authorities, but now was their chance to fill in any gaps. Dent combed the room for clues as Charlie fired questions at Miss Ramona. They knew that was a better tack since the PR pro showed no rapport with Dent.

"How did the fire start?" asked Charlie.

Miss Ramona blanched. "We were cleared of any wrongdoing by the fire department."

"We're not investigating the fire," said Charlie. "We're investigating the murder."

Miss Ramona swallowed. "There was a device . . . inside the heater that blocked the regulator. The system is supposed to max out at two hundred degrees."

"What did it go to?"

Miss Ramona hesitated. Dent peered at her.

"Two-fifty," she admitted.

"His towel," assumed Charlie.

Miss Ramona nodded. "It caught fire first."

Dr. Chen was next. The planks kindling. Charlie eyed the thick door.

"What prevented him from exiting?"

"He was trapped," Dent said kicking a metal rod in thick ash that covered the floor.

"Why didn't anyone notice?" asked Charlie.

"We close at 10:00 p.m. It started well after. The sprinkler and security system were disabled. The police believe he was drugged. Not until the cleaning crew smelled the smoke did anyone call for help."

"How'd you keep it quiet?" asked Dent.

"We're Canyon Ranch," she said flatly.

"Of course," Dent said to her chagrin.

Dent assumed every politician within a hundred miles had memberships to the club and reigns on every authority.

"Explains why he's grown more daring in his exhibitions," said Charlie.

Dent nodded. Their killer didn't appreciate his artistry being swept under the rug.

"Do you think this is connected to the Number One Killer?"

"Yes. But this was his first," said Charlie.

"Really?" she said as though it could buoy sales. Then caught herself. "What took you so long to connect it?"

Dent glared at her. "You."

CHAPTER 25

SHAYNA

Computer screens blurred with passing names and dates and codes in the FBI bullpen. Sanjay manned it like Mr. Sulu helming the bridge of the Starship Enterprise. His brows furrowed when he worked. His forehead perspired. His pulse quickened. His eyes darted back and forth like he was battling a Russian genius for the World Chess Championship. But this was more important, he told himself. At stake with competition was money. At stake here were lives. Speed of consequence. Mistakes deadly.

"You're sweating," said a young female voice.

Sanjay peered up. *Huh?*

"You're sweating," said a cute librarian-type with a short, dark bob looking his way from her cube by the window. Sanjay looked stunned. Maybe that someone interrupted him. Or that she was female. And cute. And young. Her five-four height, lively green eyes, and pink nail polish made her seem younger.

He pointed at himself. *Me?*

"Yeah, you."

"Who are . . . ?"

"Shayna. Shayna Gold. I'm new. In IT."

Sanjay wiped his face, snuck a sniff of his armpit.

"Oh, don't worry, I think it's hot."

Sanjay cocked his head. *What?*

"Yeah, the way you get into it. I feel safer just knowing you're on the case.

"What . . . ?"

"Whatever case."

He smiled, impressed by her instinct.

"You . . ."

"Finish your thoughts. Yeah, I do that."

"How . . ."

"It's freaky, I know. Sucked in high school. Kinda cool in college. But around here it's, like, totally appreciated."

"Uh-huh."

"I went to a psychic when I was sixteen. He said I had the gift, too, you know? And I didn't even need him."

"So, you're . . ."

"Twenty-five now. Twenty-six next month. I just look young."

"Uh-huh."

"Mind if I roll over?"

"Roll . . ."

Before he could compute, she wheeled her office chair over to his desk.

"Are you working on the Number One Killer?"

"Yeah," he heard himself say, figuring he couldn't keep it a secret if he wanted.

"I really want to be in investigation. I just took the IT job to get through the door."

"Okay . . ."

"What have you found?"

"Um . . ."

He peered down at her yellow credentials to make sure this woman even belonged in the building. But somehow got lost in her diamond pendant swinging from a chain in her ample cleavage.

"Shayna. Gold."

He shook from his trance.

"Right."

She sensed his reticence.

"Oh. It's confidential, is that it? Top secret?"

"Well . . . ."

"I know I'm just a yellow badge, but I'd love to watch and learn from you if I could, I mean, if you don't mind."

Her words seemed to all tumble out of her mouth at once. It was so adorable Sanjay didn't care what the hell color her badge was.

"Well, I suppose . . ."

"Great. I can help too! I mean, if you want. I have a master's in mainframe systems engineering from Rutgers and can run data analysis like nobody's beeswax."

Sanjay was used to being the smartest one in the room. But this girl was doing laps around him. And it made him positively giddy.

"Okay . . ."

"Hit me."

Sanjay turned to his screens.

"Well, we have three murders. Four now with Tucson.

"Tucson?"

"It happened five weeks ago, but nobody connected it until yesterday. Just hasn't hit the press yet. All with the same MO. Doctors, of some sort, killed in unique and untraditional methods and . . ."

"Labeled number one," she said.

"Right."

He pulled up gruesome photos of the dead bodies and their unorthodox surroundings.

"In LA . . . a dryer. Bend . . . a sword. Salt Lake . . . maggots. And Tucson . . . a sauna."

"A killer sauna?"

"Yeah."

"Cool!"

He blanched.

"What's the connection?" she asked.

"That's . . . what we're trying to figure out. I'm running cross-references now . . . with legal, financial, medical records, looking for any kinds of connections between them."

On the screens, different patterns formed, colors matched at a blistering pace.

"You're using DeMoivre's Theorem."

Sanjay blinked. No one knew that.

"Yes."

"I love that theorem!"

He loved her.

"You know . . . ."

"Doesn't everyone?"

He almost wet his pants.

"Accurint helped," he said.

"NEXUS didn't," she said.

"CODIS was too fat," he added.

"PYTHON too thin," she finished.

The usual fray of federal activity bristled around them with agents walking and talking here and there, but Sanjay and Shayna were all alone in their own little pleasure dome of nerdy bliss trying to solve the crime of the century. And happier than could be.

CHAPTER 26

THE STAND

"**Y**ou want hot sauce?"

"What?" asked Dent.

"You want hot sauce?" Charlie repeated.

"Mild," he said patting his chest.

She ordered from a roly-poly Mexican woman peeking down from a window at a roadside taco truck. Dent sat at a worn-out picnic table in a gravel parking lot surrounded by a few other beat-up tables with a couple salesmen and a daddy-daughter duo. Dent looked longingly at them. She was about Riley's age with cheese smeared on her cheeks. Her daddy wiped it off caringly. Dent smiled sadly. It was the man he wanted to be but could not.

Nachos buried in cheese and jalapeños landed on the table, breaking Dent's trance.

"This place is the real deal," said Charlie. She handed him his iced tea, sat down with her lemonade. "There's a whole family back there cooking away."

Dent plucked a couple pills from a couple vials.

"Vitamins?" Charlie asked politely.

He shook his head no. "For the ticker. And blood pressure."

"Anything I should know?" she wondered.

"Just if I go down face first in the cement, you should probably call someone."

"There a chance of that?" she worried.

"Not as long as I take my vitamins."

He popped them in his mouth and chased them with his tea.

His cell phone rang on the table. His heart skipped a beat. It always did at the thought of his ex calling. But his screen read "SANJAY." Relieved, he hit the speaker so Charlie could hear.

"Sanjay."

"We got a name!" exclaimed Sanjay over the phone.

"What?"

"We got a name!"

Charlie's eyes lit up. Cars whizzed past.

"Martin Livingston," said Sanjay.

Back at HQ, Sanjay and Shayna hovered over a speakerphone in the bullpen looking at the center computer screen with the name *Martin Livingston* highlighted in blue.

Charlie jotted down the name.

"Got a description?" asked Dent.

"Male, Caucasian, six-four, two forty, fair skin, shaved head. We're pulling photos now." On their screens were pictures of the suspect in his youth: thinner, happier, hairier.

"Tell him about the files!" chimed Shayna.

"Oh yeah."

Charlie raised a brow at the newcomer's voice.

"Who's that?" asked Dent.

"That's Shayna. She's new."

"Okaaaay."

Sanjay's enthusiasm grew. "The files. We used a variation on the DeMoivre's theorem, with a splinter feed of . . . ."

"Sanjay."

"Right. Sorry. He was a patient."

"A patient of who?" asked Charlie.

"All of them!"

Dent and Charlie peered at each other.

"What?" spat Dent.

"His was the one name that came up in everyone's files."

"What's he got?" asked Charlie.

"That's the thing. Nobody knows. Or knew."

"What do you mean?"

"His files are old."

"Old? How old?"

"Eight, ten, twelve years."

"What? Where the hell's he been?"

"Sick," surmised Charlie.

"I'll say," said Shayna under her breath.

"Okay. Send us Mr. Livingston's files. And run him through FHIR in Washington to get the rest of his medical records."

"We'll need a warrant."

"Talk to Parker. Let's find out what other doctors he's seen. Chances are they're next."

CHAPTER 27

DALLAS

On the north side of hill-less, soulless Dallas, beside an eight-lane freeway, sat a drab, two-story office park housing six brick buildings with tinted windows and dying trees. The parking lot was half full of cars of half-hearted employees who worked there half their lives. The businesses ranged from insurance adjusting to copier sales to software consulting and were all owned and operated by men and women who gave up on their childhood dreams long ago. In the far corner of Building C were double doors with brown windows, brown handles, and a metal sign that read: "Environmental Health Clinic."

Despite the sleepy look outside, the drab waiting room inside was packed. Men and women of every size and shape looked like they had been ridden hard and put away wet. Some sucked on tubes attached to oxygen tanks. Others slumped sadly on loved ones' shoulders. A few were hunched in pain by themselves. It was depressing as all hell. The dingy linoleum floors and flickering fluorescent lights didn't help. Everyone was here because they had been to countless doctors in numerous cities across the country who could not figure out how to get them well. Some had been sick for months, others for years. All were told they were crazy. Because that's what doctors who were easily stumped told the chronically ill. Most of the people here had lost hope. Many had lost their minds. Prescribed a litany of antidepressants and sleeping medications which only made them worse. This surreal place was their last chance to reclaim their lives. A sort of halfway house to the netherworld. Either you bounced back, or you didn't.

The EHC did things differently. Looked at the body, mind, and spirit in ways traditional Western doctors were not trained. They incorporated unorthodox protocols introduced from Eastern, Indian, and Mexican medicine, and any other medicines in the world that worked. They operated outside the box for which they occasionally found answers and were often ridiculed. As a result, they could not bill traditional medical insurers the customary way. So not only were the people in this room fighting for their lives, but they were also battling bankruptcy to pay for their care out of their own pockets with what money was left after prior practitioners milked them dry.

Bam! The front doors blew open and a team of suited FBI agents tornadoed inside, flashing badges and issuing calm. It was a strange, dichotomous procedure for which they were trained. A slender, attractive, auburn-haired agent in her thirties named Lily Miller spoke sternly yet quietly to the frightened clerk at the desk. "Lily Miller. FBI. Where is Dr. Walter Dunn?" Stunned, the poor woman pointed across the room to a door in the corner.

Down the hall, the agents flushed past room after room of wide-eyed doctors and nurses and patients and clinicians startled to see a team of what looked like Secret Service agents stomping through their regularly scheduled program.

"Where is Dr. Walter Dunn?" asked Lily, badge ablaze, to a jaw-dropped black nurse.

"In his office, I suppose," she said without an air of reverence.

"Where's his office?"

"Past room three. In the corner."

The army of agents drew their weapons. A couple of nurses gasped. The agents pushed through the door not bothering knocking and surprised the bejesus out of mild-mannered Dr. Dunn, a tall, lean fellow in his sixties with curly grey hair, reading a file at his desk.

"Good heavens!" he exclaimed.

"Dr. Walter Dunn?" asked Lily.

"Yes, what is this about?" he chirped.

"I'm Agent Lily Miller with the FBI. We have reason to believe you may be in danger."

CHAPTER 28

LILY

Upper-crust neighborhoods were a dime a dozen in Dallas. And the suburb of Plano was host to a whole slew of them. Draining the life out of the water system to keep their plush grass green in the low desert was commonplace. Edged driveways twisted past transplanted trees to stucco mini-mansions with two-story hickory decks and waterfall-fed swimming pools. At 5355 Highland Drive, two black SUVs sat at the curb. Six stoic suited agents patrolled the innards and exterior of the expansive home looking for any sign of malfeasance.

At the kitchen table made of refurbished wood from an early 1900s barn door sat Lily Miller with Dr. Dunn and his lovely wife, Gaylen, a grey-haired beauty with drawn features which belied her sixties age. She fashioned herself a painter, and her minimal peaceful watercolors hung on the walls. Lily shared the bureau's concern. Dr. Dunn's name appeared on a long list of medical practitioners Martin Livingston had seen in the last thirteen years. The list was diverse, the locations erratic, stretching from Los Angeles clear across the country to Sarasota, Florida. Federal agents were reaching out in every city to every doctor the killer had seen, taking every precaution they could to prevent anyone else from becoming his next victim. Dallas was further west than the remaining cities, and thus their immediate concern as Livingston's much-ballyhooed death march appeared to be headed east.

Photos of Livingston had been pulled from the web and distributed widely by the FBI. A few printed copies were laid on the table before Dr. Dunn and his wife. Lily asked question after question of the good doctor, pushing him to recall any details he could of his former patient. But it had been nine years since he had seen Livingston, he had seen thousands of patients since then, and the withered file before him did little to trigger his fading memory.

It seemed Dr. Dunn was a patient of environmental illness himself, poisoned by chemical toxins in the water outside his former town of Lincoln, Nebraska years before. He, his wife, and their twelve-year old daughter, Meredith, lived downstream from a processing plant whose vats of insecticide ran off into the local basin, inadvertently poisoning sixteen families. What followed was a horrific onslaught of symptoms affecting the nervous, endocrine, and lymphatic systems, including malaise, fatigue, migraines, nosebleeds, shortness of breath, intestinal discomfort, internal bleeding, jaundice, coughing, brain fog, and, well, memory loss.

"I don't remember him. I'm sorry."

"His file says you met with him five times over six months."

"That's often the case. Patients come looking for answers. They get them or they don't."

Gaylen took her husband's hand caringly, helping settle his tremors.

"Did you find any?" Lily persisted.

Dr. Dunn twisted a file on the table with a heavy breath, and quickly perused his illegible handwriting, which he himself had trouble reading.

"Patient presents with . . . symptoms of autoimmune encephalitis . . . dizziness, disorientation . . . shortness of breath, low-grade fever . . . prolonged fatigue, flushed skin, nervous ticks, pale nails . . . and jaundice . . . congruent with long-term exposure of a toxic substance."

He flipped the page and found his recommendations.

"Patient was prescribed antivirals . . . steroids, along with ProAir, homeopathic remedies of garlic complex, ginseng biloba, valerian root, and Bach remedies of aspen, mustard, and walnut. Put on bed rest, high fluids, and recommended for intravenous bi-weekly sodium chloride drip."

Lily stared. "That sounds like a lot," she said flatly.

The doctor shrugged. "He had a lot."

She looked perplexed. "How do you know what works?"

"Trial and error."

An hour later, as the sun set, Lily sat in the driver's seat of the SUV outside the Dunn house talking on FaceTime with Dent who reclined on his bowed bed in his humdrum motel room back in Culver City. His open suitcase and dirty clothes lay spread beside him. It was evident by his casual nature he knew Lily well. And evident by her tone she was jaded by the experience.

"Are you sleeping?" she asked.

"I'm relaxing," he lied.

"You haven't changed a bit."

"I smoke less. I drink more."

"It's a wonder you make it through physical each year."

"I'm fun to be around," he said.

"Oh, I remember."

"You used to be fun too, you know."

"Eh. That was a long time ago," recalled Lily.

"How'd it go with Dr. Feelgood?"

"Fine. Typical. Couldn't remember the suspect."

"It was a while ago. You got eyes on him?"

"Yeah, we're locking him down now," she said glancing toward the house.

Inside the Dunn home, FBI agents checked windows and doors, cued the security system in the kitchen, and stepped outside to patrol the grounds. Except one last agent who walked down the dark hall upstairs past happy framed photos of the family to the master bedroom at the end. He knocked politely on the door.

"Come in," said the doctor.

The agent peeked in, found Dr. Dunn in a white T-shirt, sitting up in a white canopy bed reading a Carl Hiaasen novel.

"Sorry to interrupt," said the agent. "Just wanted to make sure Mrs. Dunn was in here."

Gaylen stepped out of the bathroom in a satin robe drying her long curly hair. "I'm right here," she said.

"Great," the agent said. Then promptly drew his weapon from his holster. The Dunns' eyes widened. Before they could yell . . . *Zip! Zip!* Two darts zipped quietly from the agent's gun. One in the doctor's chest. One in his wife's. Their eyes glazed and they collapsed. The agent stepped slowly into the dim light. His features were sharp. His voice familiar. It was the killer who filled Handsome Dan full of maggots in Tucson. And whose face appeared in the photos on the downstairs kitchen table. *Martin Livingston.* Only now, his face was covered in a fake mustache, his head adorned in a black wig, and his FBI uniform rented from a costume house.

Outside the home, the feds surfed their phones unknowingly, peed in the bushes, and snored in the second SUV while Lily continued her conversation with Dent in the first one. She was smiling now, his usual charm wearing her down.

"What are you doing in a motel?" she asked.

"I'm looking for a new place."

"You're homeless."

"You're sleeping in a car."

She laughed. It was his favorite part about her. Her laugh. And it was a breath of fresh air from his current situation.

Scattered on the bed before him were dozens of photos of each of the deceased victims provided by Sanjay and Shayna. Wide shots, and close-ups, featuring gory details of their untimely demises. Blood, skin, bruise, and bone. Organs and limbs ripped and shredded by blades and maggots and dryers and saunas. Dent's eyes roamed them freely, looking for clues he hoped he'd been missing.

"Are you alone?" Lily asked.

"Rub it in."

"I would if I could."

Now Dent was smiling too.

In the Dunns' bedroom, different story. Livingston wound a clear large plastic bag around the doctor's head and tied it tightly about his neck with black electrical tape. The doctor gasped awake, hunting for breath. He found his wrists and ankles bound to his bed posts, a familiar red ball clamped in his mouth, and his dear wife unconscious on the floor.

"Don't worry," said Livingston. "I won't hurt her."

Dazed and confused, the doctor sighed with relief, as if though the man towering over him could be trusted.

"*You* on the other hand . . . ."

In the motel room, Dent pressed Lily for updates on her life, both utterly unaware of the horrors transpiring inside the Dunn house. "What's your story?"

"Unhappily married to a man beyond reproach," said Lily.

"Sounds boring."

"It is."

"Have you suggested a little role-playing?"

"I have. He suggested I get therapy."

"Poor bastard. Doesn't know what he's missing."

Upstairs, Livingston paced back and forth before the bed of Dr. Dunn, whose weary eyes strained to follow the killer back and forth.

"You met with the agents, so you must know who I am."

Dunn could only blink back.

"But I bet you're wondering why I chose you."

Staggered breaths flared from the doctor's nostrils.

"Treat 'em and street 'em. Isn't that what you say?"

Dunn's breaths drew plastic, his oxygen grew less.

 "You give us drugs. You take our money."

Dunn's muscles tightened and tugged, but it was useless.

"But you don't know what works, what doesn't."

The doctor choked and gagged and turned blue.

"That's why they call it medical *practice*."

In the SUV outside, Lily loosened her blouse and let down her hair. Memories of being with Dent allowed her to feel alive again. She bit her bottom lip.

"I miss those days."

"Me too," said Dent.

"Maybe our paths will cross again."

"I hope so."

She closed her phone with a grin. And so did he.

Upstairs, Livingston whispered to Dunn in his raspy voice. "How do you feel?"

The doctor's eyes rolled back in his head.

A rush came over Livingston. "Awful, isn't it?"

Dunn inhaled the plastic.

"Unable to breathe?"

His breaths grew fewer.

"Wishing you were dead."

Until there were no breaths left.

Outside, two agents climbed into the SUV with Lily. Their shifts were done.

The engine started and they drove slowly away.

CHAPTER 29

BROOKLYN

If you ever needed a good deal on heroin, you used to go to Red Hook, the dark, dank, crime-infested nook of Brooklyn south of the world-renowned Brooklyn Bridge. Riddled with gangs, drugs, shootings, and lootings, it was the poster child for bad luck and bad decisions. And then, all of a sudden, it seemed to change. It wasn't thanks to the mayor or the governor or the city council. It was good ol' fashioned capitalism. Manhattan plain ran out of space for anyone making under $150k a year. So, the lesser-thans headed east to the nearest brother borough. But soon that filled up too. The nice parts anyway. Brooklyn Heights. Cobble Hill. Park Slope. So, folks began to bleed into the rough spots . . . like Red Hook. There, commuters could get a real steal on a two-bedroom for $600k and still make it to Soho in under thirty minutes on the F train. Ironically, they had to if they had any shot of working a job that would enable them to afford their home. Per usual, the brazened, the bold, the adventurous—the LGBT—led the way on the new frontier. Slowly but surely, they staked their claim on dilapidated brownstones and condemned cafes, rehabbing blocks from the ground up with tips and tricks gleaned from HGTV. Before you knew it, graffiti-covered storefronts were painted in pastels and anointed in daffodils. Brownstone steps were pressure-washed and filled with handsome men and women wearing stylish Equinox workout gear and drinking foamy, heart-topped lattes. Once the coast was clear, the yuppies moved in with their golden retrievers and their baby strollers. Full-blown gentrification ensued with Starbucks, Massage Envys, and West Elms. In no time flat, most of the original brick and mortar built by our hardworking, blue-collar founding fathers was mowed asunder.

The last glimmer of the old world anywhere were the pubs. The few and mighty dotted corners and alleys here and there like historical landmarks. At the end of Fisk Street near Baxter Park sat O'Malley's, the least innovative name for a bar with the least innovative décor on the island. Everything about it wreaked of Dublin. The barstools, the barflies, the bartenders. Filled with age-old oak and low-watt lighting, you had to let your eyes adjust when you walked in, which lent itself to everyone looking better than they felt. Old timers yearning for the old days and young timers yearning to be relevant held court in tall, wood-backed booths with real leather seating. It may have been musty, but it was authentic.

In the early afternoon, the place had patches of lonely drunks and hungry salesman equally eager to drown their sorrows. At the end of the bar nursing a wine spritzer from a straw and reading *The New York Times* was Pac-man, an odd sight in his stretchy bike pants and scraggly dreadlocks. But he was paying full rate, so no one minded. That was the thing about New York. Everyone was equal under the eyes of Lady Liberty as long as you paid your way.

"Read your own paper much, do ya?" said the barkeep in a thick Irish brogue. Mark dried heavy beer mugs with a weathered old rag. Bespectacled and vested with grey strands eking their way up his burns, he was the most affordable therapist for miles.

Pac-man didn't peer up. Just methodically circled postings in the want ads with a red felt-tip marker.

"Not reading, hunting," he said.

"Thought you had a job."

"Not for long."

"What'd you do?"

"I don't have the stomach for it."

"For *writing?*"

"I'm a crime writer. Hard to write crime if you can't take crime scenes."

Mark nodded with understanding. "What are you looking for?"

"Maybe something with quiche. Or balloons. Maybe kittens."

Mark chuckled. "They write about that stuff?"

"Not writing. Baking. Blowing. Herding."

"You say that as though you have a choice in what you do."

"I don't?"

"You're a writer, brother. That's not something you choose."

"It's not?"

"It chooses you."

"You know this because . . . ?"

"I know people."

"Bartending chose you?"

"It did."

"There wasn't anything else you wanted to do?" asked Pac-man.

"Sure. I had dreams, designs on a bigger life. But I don't get to say. *He* does," Mark said nodding upward.

Pac-man glanced upward. "You don't think we make our own fate?"

"We can try. That's when life gets rough. Full of bumps and depression and cancer."

"There are no bumps on the right path?"

"There are. But He helps us through those."

Pac-man sucked down the rest of his spritzer, then slammed it down like a tough guy.

"You're right."

"What?"

"This is where you belong."

Mark held out his hand. "That'll be fifty bucks."

Pac-man grinned.

"Get ya another?" Mark asked.

"Not sure I can afford it."

Mark smiled and stepped away to get him one anyway.

On the bar, Pac-man's cell phone vibrated. It said "FBI GUY." He looked at it for a second and hesitated. Then hit the mute button and flipped it over, ignoring it. Then his phone buzzed with a text from FBI Guy. He flipped it back up. It read: *Malcolm X. Got a tip for ya. No maggots.* Pac-man grinned, looked at Mark by the refrigerator, and reflected on his words. The barkeep popped the top on spritzer two and returned to the end of the bar with a fresh glass. But Pac-man was gone. All that was there was fifty bucks laid atop the want ads.

CHAPTER 30

THE BABYSITTER

There was a knock at the motel room door. Dent rose from the bed and peeked through the hole. He bowed his head, dumped a breath, and reluctantly opened it. Melody stood in a dark suit and pointy heels talking on her cell phone a mile a minute, allegedly doing some kind of business deal with somebody important in northern Portugal. At her side stood Riley with sad eyes and a heavy frown wearing a pink dress that she hated holding a blankie she loved.

"Hey, Butter," said Dent with a smile.

Melody covered the speaker long enough to insist, "I need you to look after Butter." It wasn't uncommon for Melody to spring last-minute demands on Dent. It was the way of the narcissist. Everyone, they assumed, was at their beck and call.

"Hi. How are you?" said Dent sarcastically.

"I have to fly to Minneapolis."

"You could have called."

"I tried. You were on the phone."

He figured she was right. Dent glanced over his shoulder at the photos of dead bodies spread over his bed.

"Little busy at the moment."

Melody scoffed.

"You see, Riley? Big Daddy doesn't want to see you."

Riley stared at Dent. He rubbed his temples.

"Give me a minute."

He closed the door, hid the files, bid Melody a not-so-fond farewell, and let Riley inside. He knew doing so left him open to incrimination, but he would do anything for Butterball.

The New York Times newspaper landed on SAC Parker's desk at FBI headquarters. The front-page headline read "THE #1 KILLER HITS ARIZONA Written by: Lyle Packard." Parker turned three sheets of red and swung open his glass door in a reptilian fury.

"Where the hell is Dent?!"

He knew Dent was the only one who knew what happened at Canyon Ranch and leaked it to his new friend in New York. The article spoke in detail about the unorthodox fire at the illustrious resort and how management had gone to great lengths to cover it up. Miss Ramona nearly had a stroke when she saw it, called her boss, who called his boss, who called their senator, who called the FBI director in Washington, who called the regional director in Los Angeles, SAC Parker.

"I'm going to kill that son of a bitch!"

Sanjay and Shayna and Charlie looked up from their stations. But none of them had a clue where Dent was.

On a cement wall beside a frozen yogurt shop, Dent and Riley sat side by side eating single-scoop cones. His was chocolate. Hers was too. She loved Dent and always got what he got. Some dripped onto her little pink dress.

"Man down," said Dent. He leaned over and wiped it off, but it still left a stain.

"Your mom's gonna have a conniption," said Dent.

"Con-nip-tion," repeated Riley. "What's that?"

She was young but smart.

"A hissy, a tizzy, go crazy," explained Dent.

"She has a lot of those," said Riley.

That made Dent laugh out loud. Something she often made him do.

"I bet," he said.

His few moments alone with her were the best moments of his whole miserable life . . . free from her mother, bureau bureaucracy, and his dark thoughts.

His cell phone rang. It read "DICK."

"Shit," said Dent.

"Shit," said Riley.

"Don't say that."

"Why not?"

"It's not right."

"You said it."

"I'm an adult."

"So."

Good point, he thought.

"Just don't say it in front of your mother."

"She'll have a tizzy?"

"Exactly."

The elevator doors opened on the fifth floor of FBI headquarters and Dent strolled out with Riley at his side. Heads turned, lighting up with smiles seeing the grizzled Dent walk into the highly secure area with a little blonde girl in a pink dress.

Charlie's eyes lit up and she smiled ear to ear.

"Butterball!" she exclaimed floating over to greet them.

Dent properly introduced them.

"Riley, this is Charlie. Charlie, Riley."

Charlie bent down and extended her hand. Riley shook it like a big girl.

"Hello!" said Charlie. "Nice to meet you!"

"You too," Riley managed, a little overwhelmed by it all. She was clearly not used to so much attention. Certainly not from strange adults in a strange place with strange computers.

"Dent!" barked Parker from the back.

Dent looked to Charlie. "Can you . . . ?"

"I got you," she said. And took Riley's hand.

"Riley, why don't you come with me? We'll have fun!"

Riley smiled and followed Charlie, but her eyes watched Dent as he lumbered half-heartedly toward Parker's office in back.

"What in God's name are you doing? You know you can't bring a kid in here," Parker said.

"She's five. I don't think she's a risk to national security," Dent replied.

"We have rules here, protocols."

Parker knew Dent had no patience for either.

"You wanted to see me?"

Parker lit into Dent over *The Times* article, condemned him for putting the bureau at odds with politicians. Especially since he so badly wanted to be one. Dent was used to blow back from breaking regulations. He ducked what he could and let the rest slide off his back. It was the only thing that kept him sane in an insane line of work. After puffing like a freight train for eight minutes straight, Parker drew his engine to a stop and got down to business. The killer had struck again. In Dallas. Right under their noses. Dent's eyes widened.

"Don't worry. Agent Miller is fine."

Dent raised a brow. *How'd you know?*

"There's not a lot of things I don't know about my agents."

It's one of the things Dent admired and despised about him. He was thorough.

"That's five murders in ten weeks. Washington is up in arms. The White House is getting questions left and right from the press. And we have no answers."

"We have a few," said Dent.

"A psychopath stalking doctors is not much to go on."

"It should put the non-doctors at ease."

"It doesn't." Parker lifted a file off his desk.

"This sick bastard saw forty-five medical practitioners in seven states over thirteen years. That we know of. Who knows what other nutritionists, pharmacists, psychics may have ticked him off!"

Dent blanched at Parker's use of the word "bastard." That was a lot for him.

"We're doing our best to get to them all," Dent said.

Parker threw the file down on his desk for emphasis.

"I don't want them. I want *him!*"

Dent turned, but something stopped him in the doorway.

"Begs the question though, doesn't it?"

"What's that?" offered Parker.

"Did craziness make him sick or sickness make him crazy?"

Parker eyed Dent as serious as could be. "I don't care. And neither should you."

At Sanjay's computer station in the bullpen, Riley sat on a desk swinging her high tops, playing Fortnite. Her little finger clicked a mouse rapidly, blowing up zombies. Sanjay, Shayna, and Charlie cheered her on. "Left, left, left! Shoot! Shoot! Shoot!"

"It's a wonder we get anything done around here," said Dent rolling up behind them.

"She's a natural," said Sanjay keeping his eyes glued to the screen.

"Little young for recruitment, isn't she?"

"Start 'em early I say," said Shayna.

Dent looked at her. *Who are you?*

"Special Agent Dent McCreary, this is Shayna Gold, IT," said Sanjay.

"You're the one who helped with the math on this?"

"Yes sir," said Shayna sprightly.

"Alright, you can stay."

She grinned. She liked him. Everyone did. Well, almost everyone.

"What's the latest?" Dent asked Sanjay.

Sanjay glanced at Riley, reluctant to talk shop in front of a five-year-old.

Charlie grabbed a pair of headphones off the desk. "Hey, Riley, put these on. They're awesome."

Riley affixed them over her ears. She smiled. Earmuffs she didn't have to hold up herself. And now she had Fortnight in Dolby sound.

"That's cool!" Riley said a bit too loud.

Shayna drew her finger to her lips.

Riley nodded and whispered. "That's cool."

Sanjay smiled and twisted the computer screens with maps and stats and photos from Riley's view to show the others.

"We've pulled Livingston's addresses, isolated the ones from the last thirteen years."

A map lit up with red lights in all the cities where Livingston struck: *Los Angeles, Bend, Salt Lake, Tucson, Dallas.*

"Same as the murders," said Dent.

Sanjay nodded. "Yep."

"What are these?" asked Charlie pointing to a few green lights.

"Nashville, Atlanta, Tampa," said Shayna.

"He lived there too?" asked Dent.

Sanjay nodded.

"Christ. He's seen doctors there?"

Sanjay nodded again. "But no murders."

"Yet," said Charlie.

"We've got teams on the ground in each, contacting the doctors he saw," said Sanjay.

"He a traveling salesman, this guy?" asked Dent.

Sanjay shook his head. "He is, was, a screenwriter."

"A screenwriter? Of what?"

Shayna pulled up a link to IMDB, the Internet Movie Data Base, revealing Livingston's film credits. Horrific posters of grotesque killers accompanied each.

"Horror movies. Zombies, vampires, monsters . . . axe murderers," she said.

Beside them, Riley blew up zombies in the video game with wide-eyed glee.

"Terrific," said Dent.

"Explains his creativity," said Charlie.

"And means," said Shayna. She angled one of the screens so they could see the list of films.

"*Death March, Back in Black, The Killer Cometh 1, 2 and 3.*"

"I loved that movie," said Dent. "Well, the first one."

"That's just the beginning. He's written fourteen films with a cumulative worldwide gross of eight hundred million," said Shayna.

"You're shitting me," said Dent.

"These are all old," said Charlie, scrutinizing the list of films.

Sanjay nodded. "They were all written before he started seeing doctors. Before he got sick, evidently."

"We know what was wrong with him?"

Sanjay shook his head, pulled up Livingston's medical files. "He tested for everything under the sun: diabetes, HIV, thyroid, mono, Lyme, cancer . . . nothing was conclusive."

"Maybe there was nothing wrong with him," said Charlie.

"Hypochondria? He see any shrinks?" asked Dent.

"Here and here," said Sanjay pointing to Bend and Atlanta.

"Got a current address for him?"

Sanjay and Shayna looked at one another.

"What?" asked Dent.

"It's . . . near Washington."

Dent muttered "Rey-Rey."

Sanjay nodded. "Parker made us give it to him."

"Shit!" said Riley a bit too loud, getting taken down by a zombie.

They all looked at her. She looked back. *What?*

CHAPTER 31

WASHINGTON

A thin sliver of cumulous clouds floated across the light blue sky of the nation's capital. The White House, the Capitol, and the monuments shined like superstars in a *West Wing* redo. Important men and women in dark suits and long skirts hurried up and down white steps like busy bees building a hive.

At 935 Pennsylvania Avenue Northwest stood the headquarters for the Federal Bureau of Investigation, the cathedral of law enforcement in the United States. The heavy concrete edifice ran eight stories high and eight stories deep. The first two levels beneath ground were isolated meeting rooms and storage vaults loaded top to bottom with highly secure data. The rest were underground parking. All of it surrounded by three feet of cement. If there was going to be a tornado, hurricane, or zombie apocalypse, this was the place to be.

Leading the march of a small team of strong G-men across the shellacked parking lot to a white wall of black sedans was a revved-up Rey-Rey. He had three cups of coffee. His adrenaline was high. And he was proudly sporting his black Ray-Ban aviators, even though he was four floors underground.

"Tito, you're with me!" he said to a young, handsome, Hispanic agent walking eight feet from him. Tito rolled his eyes, knowing his supervisor fed on power like swine on slop.

"Copy that," said Tito sarcastically.

Rey-Rey was not always a douchebag. Growing up as the youngest of five in a humble home in upstate New York laid the foundation. Never were there enough rolls on the table, enough cereal at breakfast, enough time in the day. As a result, he had to fight tooth and nail for scraps and attention. The youngest and smallest of the batch, he seldom won out. His father worked nights for the city water department, so his mother was left to contend with "the animals," and she had little time to referee the brood. Plentiful beatings from his older siblings left Rey-Rey bruised inside and out. He never sought the therapy he so richly deserved, so he left home at eighteen for community college at Farleigh Dickinson and stumbled into the FBI on a wing and a prayer. Everywhere he went, he left a wake of alienated peers, professors, and professionals. He rose by the little-heralded Dilbert principle. That is, he kept getting promoted so those below him would not have to work with him anymore.

Rey-Rey was partnered with Dent by the New York bureau chief because she thought they were equally abhorrent. The two were just short of their one-year anniversary when they came to blows. Dent had worked undercover for eight months in narcotics, and Rey-Rey was his outside contact. The case was painstaking on both sides, but Dent was the one in the field. When the consortium of cocaine dealers Dent infiltrated suspected him of working for a rival cartel, he wanted out. But Rey-Rey insisted he remain. Without a bust on tape and drugs in hand, the perps would walk. After all, drug dealers had the highest-paid lawyers on the eastern seaboard. One thing led to another, and rumors flew it was Rey-Rey who blew Dent's cover. On a rainy night on the North End, bullets and bloodshed decorated Davio's Ristorante. Dent took two in the abdomen. Rey-Rey got off without a scratch. Until Dent got out of the hospital. Then he kicked the living shit out of him on the fourth floor of the parking garage of the DC federal building.

"Let's get out of here!" said Rey-Rey emphatically, in a car in the parking garage.

Tito hit the gas and led six black sedans up the ramp, pouring into the streets of DC, flashing their dashboard blues. Two SWAT trucks roared into the street behind them. The black parade roared south on Twelfth Street and swung east on I-695 around the city to hightail it up the back road to Pikesville. Once en route, Rey-Rey's phone rang.

"Reynolds!" he answered in the coolest voice he could.

On the other end was Dent, standing with Sanjay, looking up at a wall of video monitors overhead featuring a series of satellite images of Livingston's Pikesville home. It was a pleasant four-bedroom, two-bath ranch at the dead end of a quiet street on the outskirts of Baltimore. Each house had an acre to itself. Some had pools, some swing sets. It was a quiet, mild-mannered community where no one would expect a serial killer to live.

"Where you at?" asked Dent. He didn't bother introducing himself. He knew Rey-Rey knew his voice. And that his former partner was relishing the hell out of being a step ahead of him.

"Well, well," said Rey-Rey. "Call to get in on the action?"

"Wanted to make sure you didn't fuck it up."

"Like you did Dallas?" jabbed Rey-Rey.

"That wasn't exactly me," replied Dent.

"It was Lily. And you taught her everything she knows."

"She was unlucky."

"Luck is half the game."

"So say the lucky."

"You've had your share, my friend," said Rey-Rey.

"I think you make your own luck," replied Dent.

"So say the arrogant."

Dent grimaced, just like old times. "You haven't changed a bit."

"Why change perfect?"

"And you call me arrogant."

Dent was unnerving Rey-Rey too.

"Did you call for a reason?" he said.

Dent got down to business. "Don't Code Two this guy. He's smarter than you think."

Code Two was tech talk for *silent entry.* It meant sneaking up on the assailant.

"He'll never know what hit him," said Rey-Rey.

"He's methodical, intentional, prepared."

"So are we."

Dent rolled his eyes. He knew there was no arguing with him. "What's your ETA?"

"Twenty-five minutes."

"You on Blue Force Tracker?"

"Alfa-Bravo, Seven-Niner, Delta-Zulu," said Rey-Rey looking at his onboard screen. He didn't mind giving his coordinates. He wanted Dent to see him beat him. And everyone else as well. Sanjay punched the code into a keyboard and live satellite imagery of Rey-Rey's caravan came up on the screens overhead.

"Take it slow, will you?" said Dent.

"Just sit back and watch how it's done, my friend."

That was a dig, and it burned. In their line of work, it was all about being in the game. Not on the sideline watching it on TV. *Click* went the line as Rey-Rey hung up.

Sanjay peered at Dent. "Confident fellow, isn't he?"

It would be just his luck, Dent thought, that he would have done all the groundwork, tracking the perp, seeing and smelling the bodies, only for Rey-Rey to get the collar.

Across the fifth floor, Dent spied Charlie and Shayna returning from the bathroom with Riley bouncing happily between them. Only now, she was sporting an oversized, grey, standard-issue FBI sweatshirt swiped from a third-floor equipment room.

Dent and Sanjay smiled as the girls approached.

"You're one of us now, I see," said Dent.

"F-B-I." Riley said proudly.

"I surrender," said Dent putting up his hands.

CHAPTER 32

PIKESVILLE

Passing the sign into Pikesville, "Population: 33,387," Rey-Rey and the caravan cut the blues and dropped their speed. They were now trying to sneak up on the serial killer who had eluded authorities in five states. Whoever took him down would have their face on every news show in the northern hemisphere. Maybe even the talk show circuit. Athletes dreamed of touchdowns. Agents dreamed of takedowns. And this was the Super Bowl.

In Los Angeles, Charlie perused Livingston's movie titles on IMDB. Shayna flipped through his medical files on FHIR. And Sanjay ran searches on Livingston's neighbors on MLS. Word had leaked on the floor the madman's apprehension was imminent, so staffers were migrating their way. The room bristled with anticipation, everyone peering up at the overhead screens and murmuring tactics.

Dent tried to bend Riley away.

"C'mon, Butter. It's time for you to go."

"I wanna watch," she said.

"This ain't PG, baby."

"Mom lets me watch," she said as if it were Disney Channel.

"No, she doesn't," laughed Dent.

Melody was petrified that Riley watching anything on television might trigger an epileptic seizure in her. Not that she had the disease.

Just that her great, great, grandfather on her mother's side did, so Melody was concerned watching anything pixelated might one day trigger it in her too. "Your mom would have my head if she knew you were even here."

"I can keep a secret," she said with earnest eyes.

"Dent," said Charlie, rescuing him from his predicament.

"Don't move," Dent warned Riley. He pointed two fingers at his eyes, then at her like Deniro in *Meet the Parents*. "I'm watching you."

She grinned big and planted her butt in a swivel chair.

Dent stepped over to Charlie. "What's up?"

"Look at this," she said pointing to the IMDB screen. The fifth movie down on the list was called *The House of Ill Repute*. The poster was dark with a bright moon, a black cat, and a four-bed, two-bath ranch at the end of a dead-end street.

"Look familiar?"

Dent peered at the surveillance screen above. *It was the same house.* His eyes widened. Suddenly, the FBI caravan careened into the frame, cruising down the street straight toward it.

"What's it about?" Dent asked briskly.

Charlie read the movie summary quickly. "In a small town, a young woman named Marguerite McCall ran a halfway house for former prostitutes trying to start their lives over."

As the FBI sedans and trucks skidded to stops on the screen above, live audio piped in overhead with the strike team's walkie-talkie feed.

"Alpha Team Bravo," said the SWAT leader.

"Alpha Team Bravo," called other members arriving.

"Copy, Alpha Team, standby," answered Rey-Rey.

Satellite registered no movement in or out of the house in the last two hours, but that didn't mean it was empty.

Agents quietly exited their autos and drew their weapons.

"Keep going," said Dent to Charlie.

"But the madam knew the first thing the women needed to get back on their feet was money."

On the screen, the SWAT team and agents encircled the house, armed with a battering ram and flash bombs.

"Alpha Team in position," said the SWAT leader.

In LA, everyone tensed beneath the screens, watching like opening night at the drive-in.

"Keep going," said Dent.

"Little did the Johns know that the madam of the house had something else on her mind," read Charlie.

"Alpha Team, go. Alpha Team, go," said Rey-Rey.

"Revenge," said Charlie.

"Alpha Team moving," said the SWAT leader.

"No, no, no," said Dent.

"For all the men who had crossed the women to finally get what they deserved," read Charlie, sweat beading her brow.

Dent grabbed a microphone on the console to try and stop the siege.

"Rey-Rey!" he gasped. "Stand down!"

"Go!" said Rey-Rey.

"Go, go, go!" said the SWAT leader.

BAM! The doors of the house were breached. The teams converged inside. One of the members promptly tripped a thin steel wire stretched across the front hall with his shin and . . . *KABOOM!* The house exploded in a massive fireball turning night into day on the dead end.

Dent and Charlie and Sanjay and Shayna and the rest of the FBI floor watched in abject horror. Motionless. Until hearing Riley utter "cool" from where she watched it all behind them.

CHAPTER 33

LIVINGSTON

A thousand miles from Pikesville in a dimly lit room in an undisclosed location, Martin Livingston drew a yellow solution from a small glass vial and injected it into his long arm. He swooned as it swept through his veins like it was ordained by the gods. On a crisp, clean granite kitchen counter beside him sat a silver iMac computer monitor with four grainy black-and-white video feeds with timecode. Somehow, he managed to tap into the FBI surveillance cameras in Pikesville and watched the whole operation unfold just as Dent had in the bullpen.

Beyond the screen were floor-to-ceiling windows spanning a wall that overlooked the restless waves of an ocean crashing onto a broad beach beyond tide-grassed dunes. This place was far from a diabolical lair. It was, in fact, a beautiful, high-end condo in an upscale seaside community. A hand-painted bowl filled with fresh fruit of every shape and color was centered on a long wood table in the immaculate dining room. Silver Keurig and espresso machines bookmarked the counter between stainless steel appliances in the kitchen. The piano tinkling of George Winston echoed faintly from an eighty-two-inch LG TV mounted above a seldom-used stone fireplace in the open living room fit for *Architectural Digest*. Bookshelves were filled with tomes young and old, authored by horror masters, special effects wizards, and holistic medical gurus. On the wall was a painting of the United States with raised textures indicating mountain ranges. Small red flags were stabbed into familiar cities coast to coast: Los Angeles, Bend, Salt Lake City, Tucson, Dallas.

Livingston plucked a blue flag from a ceramic bowl full of different colored flags and stuck it in Maryland. Then stepped back to admire his work as though he were the artist himself. Whatever people may have said about the Number One Killer, he was a meticulous, detailed perfectionist. And he was not alone. Splayed out on a white leather couch in the living room was a ten-year-old yellow Labrador named Frodo, no doubt coined after the lovable character from *The Lord of the Rings* charged with saving Middle Earth. Frodo was Livingston's best friend, his only friend, really, faithful to a fault and snoring up a storm.

There was a knock at the door, and Frodo perked up, his ear flipping funnily over his head. He grunted once with amusement, not alarm. He was no guard dog. Livingston spun on his stool and rose casually to answer the door. He wore his typical household wardrobe, baggy black sweatpants that tapered at the ankle and a grey heathered T-shirt inscribed with NYU. He opened the heavy oak door and found the Amazon guy.

"*Señor* Randall. How you today?" asked the chipper young Hispanic driver with a thick Puerto Rican accent. He couldn't have been more than twenty-five and was as eager a beaver could be. A dream employee who drank Jeff Bezos's company Kool-Aid and had every intention of rising up the proverbial ladder. He went by Hector. He slid Livingston a heavy brown box, never knowing what his real name was or that the boxes he brought, nearly daily, were filled with the tools of the trade Livingston needed to kill.

"Evening, Hector. Late one, huh?"

You couldn't blame Hector. Livingston seemed so incredibly normal when he wasn't torturing people. Down the road, well-respected psychologists and psychiatrists would debate in panels and papers whether Martin Livingston had a multiple personality disorder. But he did not. He had a mission.

Frodo greeted Hector with customary wags and licks, and Hector rewarded him with a customary treat. "Hola, Frodo!" he said. The truth was Hector was one of the few people Livingston and Frodo saw on a regular basis.

"How's your dad?" asked Livingston.

"Good, gracias. It was just sprain, not break. So, he back at work."

"Glad to hear it."

"Gracias." Hector backed away with a wave. "Have good night."

Livingston lifted the box and stepped inside. "You too."

And that was that. Just like always.

A moment later, Livingston dragged a grey-handled razor blade across the tan tape of the brown box, cracking it open like a kid on Christmas morning. Inside the box was another box. This one white and sealed tight. Livingston pulled it carefully from the bubbles of foam that surrounded it and placed it on the kitchen table. He popped the sides of it with the blade. His eyes widened, his pulse quickened, and a thin grin curved on his lips. Picking up on his master's adrenaline, Frodo perked with anticipation himself, his paws tapping on the hardwood floors.

"Look what we got, Fro."

From out of the box, Livingston drew just what he needed for his next victim . . . one of four shiny, white gallon jugs labeled "hydrofluoric acid."

"Just what the doctor ordered."

Pleased with his delivery, Livingston carried the box downstairs to the garage where a shiny, black Ram pickup truck sat. Beyond it was a lone closet door with a padlock. He keyed it open. Inside stood a menagerie of chemical containers. His brows furrowed with trepidation. The big man held his breath as though the mere sight of the potions would make him dizzy. Then set the new box inside and sealed and locked the door before finally exhaling. Whatever it was about that room terribly unnerved him.

CHAPTER 34

THE CONNECTION

A weathered basketball *smack-smack-smacked* in the paint on the court on the north end of Circle Park in Carlsbad, California. In the middle of a heated game of five-on-five sweaty marines was Colby Lewis, Charlie's love muffin, shucking and jiving with the best of 'em. Muscles churning, heart pounding, Colby fake-pumped, faded away, and shot. *Swish!*

"Way to go, baby!" Charlie yelped from the bleachers.

Colby winked at his fiancée the way he thought cool guys did. She blew him a subtle kiss. He loved her for a lot of reasons. Mostly because she loved him. But she was also cute, kind, clean, and had a job of her own. He didn't really know what she did at the FBI. Pushed papers for all he knew. Research, statistics, perhaps. That was their deal though. Not to bring their work home with them. That way their time would be their time and not anyone else's.

A few bleachers down sat the rest of the flock of girlfriends or wives or lovers of the rest of the players, gossiping about hairstyles and skin ointments and TikTok. But Charlie sat alone, in her pink sweatpants, hoodie, and Nikes, looking over medical files in a manila folder.

Martin Livingston's records had been condensed for review. Looking for combinations and contradictions was what Charlie lived for. Lord knew Dent wasn't going to read them. She slurped on a Diet

Coke through a red straw as she flipped through the pages. One after another. Until something caught her eye. She paused. She read. Her eyes narrowed. Slowly she ran her finger down the page listing Livingston's symptoms in Salt Lake. Her lips moved as she read, something she wasn't particularly proud of but meant she was onto something. She murmured when things started coming together.

"Patient . . . describes . . . recurring . . . sensation . . . eaten alive . . ."

Her jaw dropped. "What?" she said aloud.

Smack-smack-smack went the basketball on the court.

Charlie sat up straight, thumbed through more pages.

"Tucson . . . Tucson . . . Tucson . . . ."

She found it.

"Symptoms."

She ran her finger down that page, then stopped cold.

"Patient . . . complains . . . low grade fever . . . burning sensation . . . ."

Laughter erupted from the girls nearby over some banality.

Charlie scrambled faster through the pages to Los Angeles.

"Patient . . . presents . . . acute dizziness . . . ."

She looked up, her face paling as it all came together. The victim in Salt Lake died being eaten alive. The Tucson victim by heat and fire. The Los Angeles victim tumbling in a dryer. Her breath left her body. Martin Livingston was killing his victims in ways he suffered under their care. She didn't have to look at Bend and Dallas. But knew the symptoms there would show some semblance of a sword through the torso and the inability to breathe. Something she was having a little trouble with herself at that moment. The basketball *smacks*, the giddy laughter, and zooms of traffic all built into one surreal cacophony. Finally, she grabbed her files, her purse, her phone, and bolted from the bleachers, leaving her love muffin standing alone at center court wondering where on earth she was going.

"Charlie?"

CHAPTER 35

THE HANDOFF

Dent and Riley sat side by side on a bench in a park in Newport Beach looking out at the setting sun. Her little feet swung back and forth as usual. Her backpack beside her. Her eyes teary.

"I don't wanna go."

"I know, Butter."

"Why can't I stay with you?"

"That's not how it works."

"But I don't wanna go with mom."

"I know, baby. But we can get together again."

"That's not what mom says."

"Yeah, I know, but . . . here we are, right?"

There were so many things Dent wanted to say to Riley that he couldn't. Not at five years old. Not that was appropriate. Or that she would understand. Maybe one day when she was older. Until then, he had to take the high road. Clearly not his specialty.

Melody's burgundy BMW screeched to the curb twenty yards behind them, convertible down, techno blaring. Years of being overshadowed by her siblings left her yearning for attention that she would take where she could get. Dent and Riley reluctantly rose to greet her midway in the grass. Melody swung her keys from a leather leash like a cocky gunslinger.

"You got her a sweatshirt," she said of Riley's new bureau swag.

"It was more comfortable," replied Dent.

"You're such a Disney dad," she said with a guffaw.

Dent didn't laugh. Melody didn't care.

"Did you have fun with Big Daddy?" she asked Riley in little girl vernacular Riley didn't require.

"We had froyo!" said Riley.

Melody rolled her blue eyes. "You're spoiling her."

"Somebody has to."

Truth be known, that's why the two of them didn't work. Melody was attractive, brilliant, successful, and exciting, but Dent simply couldn't take how she treated Riley, how she used Riley to manipulate him, and, despite his training, how he couldn't change Melody to save his life. Or Riley's. He bent down to say goodbye to her, never really knowing if it would be for the last time.

"I love you, Butter."

Melody tightened, angry Dent had not said those words to her in eons. Riley threw her little arms around as much of Dent as she could.

"I love you too," she murmured into his chest.

Dent melted as always.

"You know, if you loved me half as much as you loved her, we would be married now."

Dent rose beside Melody ready to go a few rounds but was saved by his buzzing phone. It read: CHUCK. He knew it was important. She only called if it was.

"I got to take this."

Melody jumped at the chance to deride him.

"Oh, look who's busy now."

Melody grabbed Riley's hand. "Come on, Riley. Big Daddy is too busy for us," she said, half-dragging Riley toward her car. Riley looked longingly back over her shoulder. Dent wanted to tell Melody he wished she would get hit by a train. But instead, he just bid farewell.

"See you soon, Butter," said Dent.

"No, you won't!" said Melody. "She'll be with Tim."

Tim Witherspoon, aka Tiny Daddy, was Riley's biological father who Riley liked less than her mom. That was the challenge Dent faced, being the island between two storms with no say as to which way the wind blew. Melody never referred to Tim as Riley's father. Never wanted to admit she bore the child of a peasant. He was actually in auto part sales, but to Melody, they were one and the same. Every month the two would arrange for Riley to fly back and forth between California and Georgia where Tim lived. It was a lot for anyone, especially a five-year old.

"You're an evil woman," called out Dent.

Melody plopped Riley in her car seat in the convertible.

"You hear that, Riley? Big Daddy thinks mommy's evil," she said cackling like Cruella de Vil.

Dent simply stewed. "Some things never change." A tear streaked down Riley's cheek.

VROOM! Melody roared off into the not-so-busy street as though she had somewhere important to be.

CHAPTER 36

THE ONES

"I know what the ones are!"

"What?" asked Dent.

"The ones! I know what they are," said Charlie.

She slammed the *Hippocratic Corpus* on Sanjay's desk in the bullpen at FBI HQ. The ancient book's dusty pages were opened to page thirty-six.

"The Hippocratic oath," she said pointing to a translation from Greek atop the page.

Dent bent the book's cover back to make sure it was real.

"Where'd you get this?"

"The library, downstairs."

"We have a library?"

Sanjay and Shayna curled their chairs into the conversation.

"Next to the laboratory," said Sanjay.

"I knew about that," Dent joked.

"He's torturing his victims in ways he felt," Charlie said.

On a high-tech mainframe, Sanjay pulled up the symptoms Livingston reported to the dead doctors beside those doctors' causes of death. Ran his finger between the columns.

"Maggots . . . maggots. Burning . . . burning. Stabbing . . . stabbing."

Shayna chimes in. "He's trying to teach them a lesson."

"Or everyone else," said Dent.

The notion washed over them.

"Explains the public displays of the bodies," said Charlie.

"What are the ones though?" asked Dent.

"Here," said Charlie spinning the book. She dragged her finger across the page as she read. "I swear by Apollo the Healer, by Asclepius . . . and by all the gods and goddesses . . . that I will carry out . . . those regiments which will benefit my patients according to my greatest ability and judgment . . . and I will do no harm or injustice to them.'"

"*Primum non nocere*," said Sanjay.

They looked at him.

"First do no harm," he translated.

"Rule one," said Charlie.

"You know Latin?" Shayna asked Sanjay.

"I was prelaw for twenty minutes," he said with a shrug.

She nearly swooned.

"Little hypocritical, isn't it?" asked Dent.

"How so?" said Sanjay.

"He's harming a lot of fuckin' people."

"Just the ones who caused him harm," said Charlie.

"Or could cause harm to others," added Shayna.

"That's why there are only five," said Sanjay.

"Five?" said Dent.

"Victims. He saw forty-five docs, right? Only five died."

"What makes you think he's done?" asked Dent.

"I don't. But I don't think he's backtracking," said Charlie.

Charlie points on the map. "Look. He started in Tucson, right?"

She traces a blue line across the screen from one city to the next in the order the murders took place. "Los Angeles, Bend, Salt Lake, Dallas. He saw multiple doctors in each of these cities. The effort the killings require, the planning, the resources . . . ."

"He would take care of business while there," Shayna said.

"A logical serial killer," said Dent.

"Jives with what we've been hearing," said Sanjay.

He pulled up reports from local FBI agents in every city he's struck with photos of Livingston's acquaintances.

"Agents Swann, Barnes, Miller have interviewed friends, family, coworkers of Mr. Livingston in every city he's been. They all say the same thing."

"Quiet? Neat? Kept to himself?" said Dent wryly.

"More than that. Organized. Practical. Thoughtful, even."

"What kind of thoughtful person shoves a sword up a woman's ass?"

"The kind that thinks he's saving others from her pain."

"Great. A medical vigilante," concluded Dent.

"Just a matter of time before the press figures this out," said Sanjay.

They knew once word broke the killer was hunting doctors, it could give every other disgruntled patient in America the idea to follow suit. That's all they needed. Copycats.

"Where's next?" asked Dent.

"He's headed east," said Sanjay pointing to the screen. "That means Nashville."

"Good," said Dent. "Let's see if we can keep him from killing anyone else."

CHAPTER 37

THE BATHTUB

A white van backed up to a loading dock at Lowe's Lawn & Garden. Overwrought daddios were packing their SUVs to the brim left and right with honey-do-list supplies, hoping to keep their mommios on an even keel. Hourly workers in proud blue aprons helped when they had to. That's the beauty of the hourly wage. You get paid whether you do anything or not. There was no beep to the van. It was just a rental picked up for thirty-nine dollars a day from U-Haul. The irony was renters needed the back-up beeps more than most. They had no idea what they were doing.

Two hungover college kids in jeans and tees and boots and requisite vests pushed a pallet on a dolly to the edge of the dock where the van parked. On the dolly was a heavy white acrylic bathtub, larger than most, made to spec for master bathrooms of overpriced condos.

From the driver's side door emerged Livingston, eyes down and hoodie up. A bit of an odd sight for an eighty-five-degree day. He almost didn't see the forklift motoring by. He stopped on a dime, his eyes spread wide. Not from nearly being run over by the four-ton hi-lo, but from what it was carrying: boxes of chemicals. Almost involuntarily, he held his breath until the lift passed . . . just as he did in his garage closet.

"How ya do, Mr. Flowers?" said the taller kid, Jake, shaking Livingston from his daze. He knew Martin Livingston by face but not by his actual name. Only his pseudonym.

"Uh, fit as a fiddle," said Livingston. "How's accounting?"

"Not my favo," he said in rad college vernacular. "The professor's bof."

"Bof?"

"Aw, boring old fart."

"Ah. Well. Not sure Seinfeld could make accounting interesting."

"Who?" asked Jake.

"Never mind," said Livingston, feeling older than he was. "That for me?" he said, eying the tub.

"Bet. The Empava 2000, top o' the line."

"Greato," he replied.

Livingston was not your average serial killer. Not that there was such a thing. He was, in fact, polite, remembering people's names, family, classes. He was for all intents and purposes . . . a people person. "Thanks, Jake."

"Aim to please. Hey, how'd that pulley work out for ya?"

Livingston stalled, then recalled he bought the pulley he used to hoist Inga's hefty frame onto the bridge in Bend here.

"Just fine."

Buying the supplies Livingston needed to kill miles from where they were used helped him elude law enforcement. Driving instead of flying did too. And only pseudonyms for authorities to run through a database. Years as a screenwriter, crafting antagonists with devious modus operandi prepared him for using alter egos to duck police and press. As a writer, he had to stay two steps ahead of his audience, anticipating their expectations and flipping them on their head. That was what he was born to do. Or so he thought.

It wasn't Livingston's plan to get sick. He moved to Hollywood with grand aspirations. To write. To direct. Wed a starlet. Pop out a tyke. And move to the nearby mountains. He would venture into the smoggy den of the LA basin only when required. But he learned things don't always work out like you plan. God, Satan, who have you, has their own plan. And whoever it was wins. Period. Fighting the flow makes things difficult, makes you anxious, makes you depressed, makes you, well, sick. And he had quite enough of that. After years of seeing doctors to shake a condition no one could diagnose, he let go. Of all of it. Obviously, Hollywood was not where he belonged. But that begged the question: *Where did he belong?*

No one could understand it unless they went through it. What it's like to be ill for a third of your life. For no one to know what's wrong. For everyone to think you're crazy. What was worse were the doctors who didn't care. Gave it the old college try but, in fact, made things worse. Administering treatments or therapies that made him feel he was spun in a dryer, stabbed by a sword, or eaten by maggots. So, in the dark of night in pain-ridden loneliness, it dawned on him. *His new mission.* To see that any doctor who caused him pain would never hurt anyone else again. And that every doctor who learned of their fate would think twice before prescribing so much as an aspirin. No hurrying through assessment to make it to the golf course, no short shrift on tests before scurrying off for cocktails. His intention was to make their deaths so horrific, so public, they could not be swept under the rug. And that was the hardest part for the authorities hunting him. He didn't care if he was caught, incarcerated, or died in a hail of gunfire as long as his message was heard.

"Must be some church," said Jake.

"What's that?" said Livingston, his tone shifting.

"The church you're building," Jake said friendly enough. "The pulley for the cross, the heating unit for the loft, this fine-looking bathtub. Must be a sight!"

His words reminded Livingston of the lies he told.

"Oh yes . . . it's for the pastor's quarters, out back."

"Well, sure like to see it when it's done-zo."

Livingston nodded and climbed in the cab.

"Bet," he said.

Livingston dropped the van in gear and drove off as calm as could be. What he actually intended to do with the bathtub an utter mystery.

CHAPTER 38

REDONDO BEACH

Dent drove his Buick south on Sepulveda Boulevard trying to circumvent traffic on the 405 Freeway. But there were no more shortcuts within a hundred miles of Los Angeles. Everyone knew them all. Every road everywhere was packed every day with everyone thinking they were getting the best of everyone else. But traffic was the least of his worries. Haunting him were the visions from Pikesville. The explosions. The screams. The static. Investigating something somehow, someway connected to the killer from days gone by gave him little release from the pain, but he had to do something. So, he and Charlie had set sail south for answers. He peered in the rearview mirror. The empty child seat with Fanta grape stains stared back. He bought it to whirl Butterball around the South Bay while he and her mother were dating. It kept him from being ticketed for endangerment of a child. He kept it hoping she would wind up in it again. He flipped the mirror up, so he wouldn't have to see it.

"You miss her," said Charlie.

"I just dropped her off," he deflected.

"I mean . . . you miss her . . . in general . . . generally."

Dent didn't bother answering. He knew she knew.

"It's understandable, you know? The bond of a child with a parent, even a surrogate parent, is beyond . . . words, beyond . . . comprehension."

Dent peered at her.

"You know this because . . . ?"

"Oh, I've read books."

"You've read books."

"Sure. We do, did, deep psychological profiles on the parental condition in training."

"The condition?"

"Are you going to repeat everything I say?"

She vexed him.

"I'm just making sure I'm getting it," said Dent.

She waxed on.

"We studied it to understand the lengths people would go to for their children. It combines two of the most powerful aspects of the human psyche: protection and survival. Especially when the parent . . . or enmeshed parent . . . sees the child as an extension of self."

Dent knew she was talking about him but didn't really care.

"You've given this some thought."

"Oh yes."

"For professional purposes."

She knew he was talking about her now but didn't really care.

"We're going to have children," admitted Charlie a little too cheerfully.

"Ya are, are ya?"

"Two. A boy and a girl," she said as if she had any say.

"Got it all planned out," said Dent.

"Well, of course, God is in control. But we have faith he's on our side."

"I'm sure he is," he said sarcastically.

"We want to be married a few years, of course."

"Right."

"Buy a house. A two-two with a porch swing, a fenced yard for the dog," she said with a smile.

"There's a dog?"

"Oh sure. That's how we'll build our parenting skills prior to parenting."

"With a dog."

"Most likely a poodle. He wants a big dog. I want a small one. We'll compromise. Which is . . . a poodle."

"Got a name picked out, I suppose."

"Tuggles," she said with a smile.

"Cute."

"Thank you."

"What if God has a different plan?"

"What?" she said, not really understanding the question.

"I mean . . . ya know, this God of yours . . . what if he has a different plan for you and Mr. Chuck?"

"Ha! Colby would simply blow his lid if he heard you say that. He is going to be a *sergeant* soon, you know."

"My mistake. Sergeant Chuck."

"Ha!"

Dent liked that he could make her laugh. It made him feel . . . fatherly . . . in a *dad joke* kind of way. Which, on second thought, made him feel old, which made him feel bad.

"I think God wants us to have what we want . . . as long as, you know, our desires are in line with his teachings," said Charlie.

"God wants you to have a poodle?"

"He wants us to have a family. 'Children are our reward.' Psalms 127:3."

Dent raised a brow. "You know all the chapters?"

"The important ones," she said with a shrug.

"There are unimportant ones?"

"I'm more of a New Testament girl."

"What's wrong with the old one?"

"It's too BC for me," she said in bible school speak.

"BC."

"Yeah. Jesus . . . he didn't say those things in the old version."

"Moses . . . he doesn't count?"

She looked at him as serious as could be.

"Moses ain't no Jesus."

Dent steered the Buick off the main drag onto 190th Street, a well-trodden thoroughfare connecting the revitalized town of Redondo Beach with the rest of the outside world. This was the last bastion of Los Angeles before the well-to-do snuck their way up to Palos Verdes.

"Why did you want to come here?" asked Charlie.

"It's where it all began."

"It was fifteen years ago."

"It doesn't matter. According to Sanjay, this is where Livingston was living when he saw the first doctor he killed. Maybe there's some explanation, ya know . . . for what got him started."

For all her smarts, Charlie knew she was still a rookie, learning daily, if not hourly. And although Dent didn't know it, she requested to partner with him. Word was he was the best. And one thing smart students know is to seek the best teachers, regardless of their personality.

Bam! Dent pulled the Buick onto the curb of a humble but pleasant South Bay street. Traditional, 1970, one-story ranches were interspersed with three-story condos. City restrictions had prevented developers from building anything higher. The idea was to keep the community quaint. What it did was add to the sprawl.

Dent and Charlie climbed out before a white, stucco, cookie-cutter townhouse embattled with stains from rain on the ocean side. It wasn't exactly old, but it wasn't new either. Raised black metal numbers read "4706." Dent eyed a scrunched piece of paper in his hand. On it was scribbled the address "4706 Speyer Lane."

"What is it?" asked Charlie.

"It's a condo."

"So."

"So, it's supposed to be a house."

"Maybe it's mistake."

"Sanjay doesn't make mistakes."

A little Asian woman walked down the sidewalk toward them with a fat cat on a leash. They say people look like their pets. Whether they chose pets who looked like them or morphed into looking like them over time was one of life's great mysteries. Either way, this lady and her cat were dead ringers. Who was walking who—also a mystery.

"Excuse me. I'm looking for a house here, '4706,' " said Dent.

Before she could respond, her cat hissed at Dent. He winced.

"There no house," she said with a heavy accent that sounded hiss-like itself.

"Yeah, I see that. But there's supposed to be."

"There no house!" she spat, apparently angry that he asked.

Hissy cat hunched its back. The woman pulled him back with her leash. Good thing, because there was a fair chance Dent would have drop-kicked the furball across the street.

"Great," he said even keeled. They drove halfway to Mexico to nothing but a dead end. He turned back to the car, angry. But Charlie didn't. She tried a different approach.

"Excuse me, ma'am."

The woman huffed.

"This condo. How long has it been here?"

"Too long! Their friends, they park my side!"

"Right. When did that start happening?" she asked.

"Too long! Too long!"

Dent leaned on his car and lit up a cig.

"Ma'am?" said Charlie more pointedly.

She mumbled something rude in Chinese.

"*Ma'am!*" Charlie flashed her ID.

The woman may not have spoken much English, but she knew what "FBI" meant.

"Ai-ya!" she exclaimed. It wasn't clear if she was illegal, housed them, or hired them, but she changed her tune quickly.

Dent's phone rang. He glanced down. The screen read: DICK. He sighed.

"How long?" Charlie continued with the woman.

Dent silenced his phone.

"Ten year!" said the woman. Charlie raised a brow.

"What was here before?"

"A house! Here," she said pointing.

"Thank you," said Charlie holstering her ID.

"Do you remember anything about the man who lived here?"

All she could muster was "Bad house."

Dent peered up, knowing the waning moments of questioning were often when the nuggets came.

"What do you mean? What happened here?" asked Charlie.

"It go boom!" she said motioning with her hand.

Charlie bent back like she felt the blast.

"Boom . . . like exploded?"

"Boom . . . with truck . . . with shovel!"

"A bulldozer?" said Dent.

"Ya! Bull truck! Bad house."

Somewhat content, Dent glanced down at his phone. What he found turned him white.

"Fuck me," he said a tad too loud. Charlie and the lady glanced his way. The woman was confident she wanted no part of it. She and hissy cat quickly waddled away.

"What is it?" asked Charlie.

Dent simply held up his phone. She stepped forward to see. On the screen was an article in the Washington Post about the massacre in Pikesville pinning responsibility squarely on the shoulders of the lead investigator of the serial killer case, *FBI Special Agent Dent McCreary.*

"Oh no," said Charlie.

Her Quantico training had taught her the importance of anonymity. It was more than just humility, respect, integrity. It was a requirement of the job to slink in and slink out of investigative situations unnoticed, uninterrupted, and unscathed. Honestly, the photo did him no favors either. Not only was his ashen mug now plastered all over the internet for all of mankind, but the chosen pic was a candid snapshot posted by an old army buddy on his Facebook page after an impromptu run-in with Dent at a bar years earlier. There was, as usual, no smile on his face or joy in his heart.

In an instant, Dent knew this would make his job exponentially more difficult. He was a solitary sort to begin with, and now he would be one of the most recognized—and condemned—men in the country. Who and how and where and why someone would have leaked this information to the press was beyond him. The thought of it all swept over him like a tidal wave.

"I'm screwed."

His mind swirled, his eyes glazed. And suddenly everything got a little dark. He reached for the pills in his pocket, but lost his balance, spilled the pills on the pavement, and landed against the side of his car before Charlie caught him. Her eyes stunned and scared.

"Dent! Dent! Are you okay?"

"What? Yeah. I'm fine," he mumbled.

But clearly, he was not.

CHAPTER 39

THE HEART

Patience was not Dent's forte. Part of his Aries birthright, he told himself. And others. Waiting on anyone anywhere got under his skin and it showed in the way his jaw clenched, his brow furrowed, his breathing slowed. Waiting in waiting rooms was worse. Then, he was surrounded by other waiters engaged in their own fidget fest which made him more conscious of his own. The last place he wanted to be now was waiting on a doctor. But his little swoon on the sidewalk mandated it by his superiors. Reclined on static wool seats around him were a handful of other patients with heart issues. Overweight blue-hairs with heart monitors, pacemakers, and low morale. Surely, he did not have to be here. He was younger. Fitter. Virile, for God's sake. And he had a job to do.

"Mr. McCreary," said a young Black woman who looked three weeks out of a two-year med-tech program.

Christ, they get younger and younger.

"Right this way." She showed him into room three, took his vitals, and asked him to undress, which, for some reason, made him feel uncomfortable. Once she left the room, he was left to his own devices. The walls were covered in medical artwork and labeled diagrams of a thousand things that could go wrong with the body. Blockages and leaks and fissures and bleeds. It was enough to give anyone anxiety, let alone heart patients. Dent stripped down to his skivvies and put on the apron which closed in the back, which meant it didn't close at all. It was a dainty, vulnerable act for a man, especially one of Dent's testosterone level. His feet hit the cold linoleum floor, prompting him to quickly sit up on the examination table. With little rest the last few days, he decided to lay back and close his eyes. At least he could wait in peace. Drift off into some forgotten memory of days of yore. Until . . . .

"Hello!" In walked a pint-sized Indian woman with a big brain and no heart. Ironic for a cardiologist, Dent thought. Doctor Vishra graduated top of her class from, well, everywhere she went. Elementary studies in Madurai. Boarding school in London. Undergrad at Emory. Med school at Vanderbilt. Residency at the Miller Family Heart, Vascular & Thoracic Institute in Cleveland. Her stripes left little room for dispute. Still, Dent was Dent.

"Why you no take your medicine, Mr. Dent?" she said in her strong, pitchy, Indian accent that years in the states had somehow not eroded.

"I take it. Sometimes."

"Why not all the time?"

"It makes me feel bad," he said.

"How bad? How is it bad?" she barked at him.

"I don't know. I feel shitty when I take it."

"Shitty how?" she said not missing a beat.

"I don't know. Shitty-shitty, bang-bang. Like icky inside."

"Icky how?"

"Like someone strung me up to a car battery," he said.

She made a note on her iPad.

"Your blood pressure is 150 over 90. It no good. You must take your medicine. We try three kinds now. You no like any!"

"I don't wanna take it."

"You almost nose-dive today. On the sidewalk! You don't want it?"

He grimaced.

"There lots of medicines. Everyone take something. If you don't take one, it can lead to all these things," she said pointing to one of the foreboding charts on the wall. "Heart disease, heart attack, aneurysm, stroke. You want to have stroke?"

Dent soured. He had heard this all before. He just wasn't motivated.

"You still smoke, drink, bacon, salt?"

"A little."

"You exercise?

"A little."

She shot him a glance beneath her glances.

"I run after people."

"Avoiding stress?"

"Define stress."

She frowned.

"American Heart Association says you should do forty-five minutes of cardio five days a week. You do that?"

"Who does that?" he asked.

She held up her tiny hands. "Don't shoot the messenger. You pave a dark path for yourself. You no know. I see them every day. ER filled with people like you!"

"Well, I don't feel shitty when I don't take the medicine. I know that."

"You just used to living with HBP," she said shaking her head. "You tough guy. You have to toughen up! Let your body get used to medicine."

Suddenly it dawned on him. Just how and why Livingston had taken to offing his doctors. The poking, the prodding, the scrutiny, the criticism was one thing. But the sheer audacity for someone to condemn him for what he might be feeling was mind numbing. There was no way for Doctor Vishra, or any doctor, to know how he felt on a particular medicine. Even if she took them herself. Everyone's body was different.

"We try carvedilol. It good drug! No side effects. No matter metabolic rate."

"Alright. Whatever you say, Doc."

Her fingers danced on her iPad, and his script was on its way to a pharmacy.

"Come back see me six months. You stick to medicine this time!"

A few minutes later, dressed and humiliated, Dent slinked from the office like a punished student from the principal's office—knowing he had little-to-no intention of making any of the changes she had suggested. After all, if the new blood pressure medicine really worked, why should he? Bacon was the work of the Gods.

CHAPTER 40

THE LOFT

A knob turned on a heavy door inside a brick loft on the third floor of a converted warehouse in downtown Los Angeles. Sanjay slinked into his cultured lair with clanging keys and a brown bag of Chinese food. Wandering in doe-eyed behind him was Shayna, peering about like a kid in a candy store. Not only had her charm and hard work landed her a dream job at the FBI, but now she was in the home of their prized IT guy. Their plan was to work late together over dinner. Her plan was to get Sanjay on his back and make him her bitch. She seemed innocent enough. But she was not. Deep-seated daddy issues and an unhealthy dose of *Fifty Shades of Grey* had bred in her a hunger that could not be quenched by any normal relationship. She needed to be scolded, spanked, punished. Sanjay was clueless.

"Do you have anything to drink?" she asked, turning for the frig.

"Oh, um, I think so," he said, unsure how to answer. It was, after all, nighttime, after work, at his place. And she was a few years younger.

"There's iced tea, LaCroix, orange juice, some oat milk. Not that . . . you want oat milk with your Chinese food." He was clearly uncomfortable.

She was not. "Do you have anything stronger?"

"Um, well, there's a wine-rack in the dining room. A bar with the harder stuff beside it."

She swung right past the wine to the liquor with a spring in her step, opened the cabinet and her eyes lit up.

"Now we're talking."

She lifted a bottle of Smirnoff Vodka, quickly checking the flavor and volume. Unimpressed with its peach taint and meager contents, she plopped it back down. Then a full bottle of Seagram's 7 reached out to her.

"Do you have any pickles?"

Sanjay paused opening the Chinese food.

"Pickles?"

"Well, pickle juice."

"With Chinese food?"

"No, silly. For the whiskey."

"Ohhh," he said as though he should have known. He opened the frig and filed through the shelf.

"Let's see . . . ketchup, mustard, probiotic, capers?"

She shook her head. In the back, he finally found . . . "Pickles! I don't know how old they are." When he turned back, she was looming closely behind him, whiskey bottle in hand.

"Let's see."

She took the bottle, opened it, and took a whiff, letting the scent fill her soul. "This'll do."

An hour later, the dining table was covered with laptops, files, photos, food cartons, and fortune cookies. Each of them had two short glasses before them: one with whiskey and one with pickle juice. The whiskey bottle was nearly empty, the pickles long discarded. What was left of the pickle juice was the chaser.

"Ready?" asked Shayna.

"Another?" replied Sanjay.

"We have to finish the bottle."

It was obvious he was tipsy. He didn't drink often. And five or six shots of whiskey was something he hadn't done since, well, never. His shirt was loose, his face flushed, his hair askew.

"Well, guess we can't leave that little bit. That would just be rude."

"Yes, it would," she said.

Shayna was drunk, but she was a happy, sexy drunk. The alcohol brought her to life, it brought out her wild side. He leaned over for the whiskey bottle, and she kissed him. It took him by surprise, but he liked it. He pulled back as though he had done something wrong. But then realized he hadn't and kissed her back. She grabbed him by his shirt and pulled him to her chest, knocking the whiskey bottle over. It rolled for the table's edge. He reached for it and knocked over the pickle juice. She reached for that and knocked over the lo mein. Before they knew it, they were falling in a tangled mess of booze and food to the hardwood floor. But neither one cared. They tugged and tore at each other's clothes . . . excited, passionate, ferocious . . . until Sanjay's phone *rang*.

"Leave it," she said, pushing it skittering away.

But it caught Sanjay's eye as it slammed into the wall. The screen read: *DENT*. Sanjay closed his eyes to ward it off, but it rang again. Slowly, reluctantly, he began to pull away.

"No!" she said as though it were a command.

But she was not his commanding officer.

"Sorry," he said. "It's Dent."

She sat up, lustful and unkempt like a lion ready to attack.

He slid to the phone on the floor and hit answer.

"Hello, Agent McCreary," he said peering back at Shayna.

In his dingy hotel room in Culver City, Dent was packing a beat-up suitcase. On his phone on his paisley bed was an awkward moving image of Sanjay's face with Shayna, half-clad, behind him.

"Working late, are ya?" said Dent wryly.

"Oh yes," said Sanjay a little emphatic.

"Looks like it's going well."

It was then, on the floor of his loft, covered in lo mein, that Sanjay realized Dent did not call him on his phone. He called him on *FaceTime* and could see everything. Mortified, Sanjay quickly fumbled the phone around, so the camera faced his direction.

Dent smirked. "Don't worry, amigo. Glad she let your hair down." Sanjay knew better than to cast a lie for the country's top profiler. He probably sized them up the minute he saw them together.

"What can I do for you?"

"Parker's got me going to the service . . . in DC. Can you help Charlie?"

That's why Parker phoned Dent earlier. He wanted Dent to represent the investigation at the agents' memorial who died in Pikesville. And by "represent," he meant take the heat for it. Parker would no doubt be there himself to press the flesh, but with Dent in attendance, Parker could deflect condemnation for its failure Dent's way. It was purely Machiavellian. But that's how Parker rose to power. Politicking. And everyone knew it.

"Of course," said Sanjay. "Whatever you need."

Resigned to fate, Shayna calmly rose and began cleaning up. Sanjay tried to wave her off, but she paid him no mind.

"The house in Redondo. It was destroyed. Years ago," said Dent.

"Oh. Wow. Why?"

"That's what I want you to find out."

"No worries. We got you."

Across the loft, Sanjay watched Shayna quietly let herself out. His face sunk as the door shut. On the other end of the line, Dent saw it and heard it.

"Don't worry, Sanj. She'll be back."

Dent's words gave him peace. But then it occurred to him he might not want her back. He wasn't sure he could handle her.

Click went the line, leaving Sanjay all alone in his loft.

Snap went Dent's suitcase. He grabbed his jacket, his cigs, his keys, and headed out the motel door for the airport.

CHAPTER 41

THE FUNERAL

The flight into Washington reminded Dent of all the things he hated about the place. The pomp and circumstance. The traffic and construction. The whip of the wind off the Potomac, the eternally grey skies. And the irony of white wealth stepping over black poor to appeal for equality. For some reason, Dent couldn't remember the good things. Certainly, there must have been some, but that's not how his brain worked. That made him good at his job, of course, but a horrible partner, for work—and life. He never married, which astounded most, until they got to know him. *Ohhhhh*, they would say. Who wants to hitch their saddle to Captain Misery? He was the best at getting in the darkest reaches of people's minds, which included his lovers, which, for some reason, they never seemed to warm to.

In the back of a rumbling cab, Dent popped two pills to keep his heart in check. He knew where he was headed was sure to get it pumping. *Bam!* The taxi hit a pothole. One of a million in Washington. The pills tumbled to the ground. He bent to pick them up and . . . *bam!* Hit his head on the seatback in front of him. The cabbie rattled out something condescending in Arabic he didn't think Dent would understand. But after three tours in Afghanistan, the former intelligence officer surely did.

"*Kunt mae walidatik tawal allay,*" Dent responded calmly. His command of the language shot the cabbie upright in his seat. That or

Dent's reference to his being with the cabbie's mother the night before. The immigrant's eyes shot to his rearview mirror. Dent was obviously not an ordinary American. In fact, the only "infidels" that could speak a lick of his native tongue were military. Dent casually pulled back his coat revealing his Glock. The cabbie swallowed hard and didn't say a word the rest of the trip which, unfortunately, left Dent to his own demons.

Dent was not a fan of funerals. Funerals made death real. The rest of his work felt like a movie to him. Or a TV show. Or a video game. But all those crying eyes of all those left behind at cemeteries made him hurt inside in places he didn't even know existed. He couldn't explain it. He lost a grandparent or three from old age, a cousin from overdose, a few friends in the middle east, and saw a smorgasbord of corpses in homicide. But all that he was able to keep at bay.

It was the death of his dog that left him broken inside. When he was ten, his cocker spaniel, Buffy, followed him across a frozen lake to school. It was a shortcut his mother swore him not to take, but at ten years old and late to class, rules were more suggestions. The ice broke and Buffy went under, so Dent did too. He dove in the ice-cold water trying to save his best friend. His only friend, really. After three minutes, fishermen pulled out a hypothermic Dent, but Buffy never came out. The army therapists said detachment was a common coping mechanism for his collective pain. So was alcohol. An even blend of both kept Dent on an even keel most of the time. But it all lurked inside him somewhere just itching to come out.

The cemetery was filled with hundreds of people in black. The tone was somber, the sky misty. Grey tombstones decorated pale green grass. Dozens of chairs were set out by groundskeepers for the mourners, but they had not anticipated the number in attendance. This was not an ordinary funeral service. It was for five agents of the FBI who had died in the line of duty hunting the most notorious serial killer in recent times. Politicians and press were there, family and friends, and seemingly half of the Washington bureau. Some of which Dent knew, all of which knew him. By reputation. By rumor.

And by the fact he was the special agent in charge of hunting the sociopath responsible for killing the men and women they were now burying. Dent was never one for small talk, even on the good days. And today was not a good day.

"Dent!" called out SAC Parker from a gaggle of balding brass. Among them was the Washington bureau chief who sent Dent packing to the west coast a few years earlier. Montgomery was his name. An African American gentleman who was bold and brilliant but untrustworthy as they came.

"Well, look who it is, the man of the hour," he said.

"Monty," responded Dent, which always pissed Montgomery off.

The brass shook their heads. None of them particularly cared for Dent, or his disregard for authority, but they couldn't argue with his record. The fact it was being tested now more than ever gave them some *schadenfreude* pleasure.

" 'Proud people breed sad sorrows,' agent," said Montgomery.

Montgomery's jab was accentuated by the word "agent," because he knew Dent never warmed to it. He still considered himself a soldier. Agent came with a bureaucratic connotation that never felt right. But the title came with the job and the job came with a paycheck.

"I told Rey-Rey not to go in that house. He didn't listen."

They knew he was right. It was all on record. But they needed a scapegoat, and Dent was the lowest hanging fruit.

"He was a stubborn sonuvabitch, that's for sure," said a broad-shouldered, silver-haired gentleman entering the fold.

"Agent McCreary, you know the director," said Montgomery.

By director, he didn't mean of any branch or office. He meant *the* director of the entire Federal Bureau of Investigation. Everyone gave him space.

"Only by reputation, sir."

His name was Walter Daltrey. Like Dent, he earned his stripes on the battlefield, but returned to the states and attended law school, worked his way up the ranks until being appointed director.

"McCreary. Good to finally meet you," he said.

"Dent, sir," Dent said with military-like respect.

"Glad you're on this," he said which surprised Dent. After being hounded by everyone else on the ladder, the last person he expected to know him, let alone respect him, was Daltrey. But that was Dent's experience in the military, management, anywhere, really. The ones at the top were not the backstabbers. It was the ones clawing to get there you had to watch out for.

"Thank you, sir."

"Any new intel?"

"We painted Nashville, Atlanta, Tampa. Alert authos, pressed press, ran stats. Hope to root 'em toot sweet, sir," said Dent.

Daltrey didn't blanche at the military jargon. But his underlings did. They knew time in battle forever bonded men, and they hated that Dent and Daltrey spoke the same language.

"Very well." He turned to Montgomery. "Monty, see if you can keep your folks on a rope, eh? Don't knock in anymore doors unless Dent's on site, understood? I got the president on my back, half of Congress blowing up my call sheet, and five dead agents' families to console."

Montgomery stewed beneath the surface. Dent didn't dare gloat. But it felt good to know that someone—anyone—thought he was the best man for the job. Let alone his boss's boss's boss. But with that acknowledgement also came responsibility.

"And Dent. No quarter," said the Director.

"Copy that, sir."

Gunfire erupted into the air as marines from nearby Quantico Station performed a twenty-one-gun salute in honor of the fallen. Smoke spun from echoing rifles, mixing with the mist, shaking the mourners. All eyes were on the riflemen, except one person.

In the back of the gallery in a herd of trees, dressed tastefully in black, behind sunglasses, mustache, beard, hat, tie, and umbrella was Martin Livingston. He was there watching Dent. Studying his every move, his gestures, his emotions, as writers were wont to do. They were, after all, the consummate analysts. It was this attention to detail that allowed him to kill without a trace. The great Chinese philosopher Tao Te Ching said "Those who know, don't talk. Those who talk, don't know." So too is this for writers. They save their power for the page. Or something else.

Sensing something, Dent craned toward the cluster of mist in the trees.

But Livingston was gone.

CHAPTER 42

THE PARTY

The bass was thumpin'. Rocking the rafters of the infamous Sigma Chi fraternity house on the south side of campus at the not-so-illustrious University of South Florida. USF was the fallback plan for those "less inspired" college students who didn't quite have the grades, scores, or means to get into a real college. And the twenty-odd lads inducted into Sig Chi through double-dog dares and twenty-four-hour drinking binges were far from the cream of the crop. Lord knew they were not growing up to be doctors or lawyers, but everyone on campus knew they threw the best parties—ragers that started at sundown and didn't end until sunup. Anyone who was anyone clambered to get inside. But the Tampa fire marshals had long been onto them and stuck the house with enough fines that the front door was now eternally manned by the biggest dog in the frat to halt capacity at 180. This semester, it was Duke Embry who everyone called Big D. Not so much for his six-foot-four, 300 lb. frame but for the reputed girth of his mighty cock which had sent more than a few girls running from the house in terror.

"Big D!" called a familiar voice. It was Jake from Lowes, riding high on a two-week paycheck direct deposited earlier that day into his Wells Fargo account. It wasn't big money, but it was enough to keep him in ramen soup and Count Chocula for the week and Colombian

Gold and Bud Light on the weekend—staples of any true frat rat this side of the Georgia-Florida line.

"My man," said Big D, greeting Jake with the secret handshake only brothers knew.

"What ya know?" said Jake, corralled by three of his dormmates eager to get inside and strike out with girls too rich and smart to hook up with them.

"Aw, ya know, same ol'," bemoaned Big D. It was the typical fraternity fraternizing that held the collective depth of a petri dish but allowed wayward young men to feel they belonged to something bigger than themselves. Big D nodded approval and the wide-eyed foursome marched through the tall oak door with eyes aflame.

Inside the party, Jake and the boys twisted through the gyrating dance floor filled with scantily clad coeds shaking their moneymakers in skirts too short and heels too high. *Legs had power*, the girls told themselves. And tickets to a better life. Ideally, one with a gated community, Mercedes hatchback, and beach club membership. The band was a cross between young Lenny Kravitz and old Metallica, cranking enough wattage to blow the roof off the Amalie Arena. The lights were low, the temperature high, and smoke wafted up the stairs like a vape convention. Jake's counterparts careened toward the keg, the standard first stop of every warm-blooded male, but Jake had to piss like a racehorse—the shots from a dorm room pre-party welling up to his eyeballs. Up the stairs he went, past freshmen making out, a sophomore passed out, and a junior out of his mind on cocaine. He shook his head with a grin.

"God bless America," he mumbled. And then a lump formed in his throat.

Coming out of the bathroom at the end of the hall at the top of the stairs was the one and only Valerie Mitchell. Beautiful, blonde, coy, and svelte, but it was her smile that stopped traffic. And Jake fell for her the moment he saw it. Born the same year, the same month, the same week, Jake was sure they were destined to live and die together. That is until, in the blink of an eye, she broke his heart his freshman year. After a litany of promises during slow walks, fast food, and study sessions, she split around noon on a cold October day. One moment, she was in the back of his Chevy Blazer saying she would go with him anywhere, and the next she was packing her bag like the law was en route—which, come to think of it, they could have been.

Valerie, or "Val" as she liked to be called, was a mystery in motion. Raised on a farm in the middle of nowhere, her father dropped dead when she was fourteen, leaving her with abandonment baggage; her mother passed away from Alzheimer's, filling her with early onset fears; and the bad boys that tried to fill in the gap left her with more issues than *National Geographic*. To compensate, she would stick and move, stick and move, running from one guy to the next, never sure if she was coming or going. Police picked her up in Daytona Beach after she ran away on spring break and tried to have their way with her themselves. The bastards got more than they bargained for. A boot to the balls, incisors to the palm, and Lee Press On Nails clawing their eyes out. Thanks to a voyeur video by a motel maid taken from a second story landing, Val was quickly released with an apology from the DPD, a bus ticket home, and a check that would pay her way through college at USF.

Little of the young beauty's backstory was relayed to lovestruck Jake on his and Val's first dates, so he stumbled hook, line, and sinker for her. At first, there was no sign of her multiple personalities. But when he forgot her birthday, she nearly bit his head off. It was but one of her identities that reared its head over the years to protect her from the slings and arrows of outrageous fortune. *Val, Valerie, Valkyrie, Valentina,* and *Viper* were all at her unconscious disposal. Fortunately, or unfortunately, for Jake, the volume of Sutter Home rosé coursing through her frontal lobe this evening had her in a fun and frisky mood.

"Jakey!" she exclaimed a bit too loud and drew to him like a moth to a flame. Unsure if she was brandishing a shank or not, Jake stood frozen and wide-eyed until she melted into his body and gave him a soft kiss on his cheek. "I miss you!" she purred.

Jake breathed a sigh of relief. She seemed to be in her right mind, but then alcohol brought that on. Sobriety was when her thoughts wandered into the dark.

"Uh, nice to see you," Jake said shakily, the pieces of his fractured heart aflutter.

"Are you with anyone?" she asked pointedly.

"Uh, just the guys," he managed.

"Well, you're with *me* now," she said taking his arm in hers.

Whether he was too smitten to put up a fight, or too afraid of what she might do if he did, Jake acquiesced, following her dancing down the hall. *Bam!* They crashed through the door at the end, slinging jackets and boots like Walmart shoppers on Black Friday. They kicked their way past strewn flannel shirts and beer cans in the room and collapsed on a messy brown futon. Before he knew it, Val had him flat on his back with his Levi's to his ankles. She climbed atop him like a rodeo rider ready to tame a stallion. The bass from the band shook the floor beneath them, the volume from a big screen blared CNN, and Val's emotional croons rang over it all. Crazy women did have their perks, he thought. Just as young Jake was about to release, Livingston's face plastered across the tv screen with the text: *The Number One Killer at Large.*

"Holy shit!" cried Jake, sitting up, inadvertently tossing Val to the floor with a *thump.*

"What the fuck!" she exclaimed, cast aside.

But Jake paid her no mind. His eyes were glued to the man on the tv who he knew only as . . . "Mr. Flowers!"

CHAPTER 43

THE BAR

Whenever Dent was summoned to Washington, he stayed at the same place. A quaint, eight-bedroom inn on the south side of town and a ten-minute ride from the bureau. The rooms were nothing special, the view was for shit, but the bar in the basement was perfect. It was dark and brown and burgundy—the shades pulled, the chairs leather, the bartenders female. There were plenty of speakeasies off the beaten path in Washington for senators and aids to have hush-hush meetings over brandy, but this one, they didn't even know about. It was a place the feds stashed informants, management was on the dole, and the doormen packed semi-automatics. Suffice it to say, whatever happened in this inn with no name stayed in the inn.

Dent sat on his usual stool at the end of the bar, nursing a gin and tonic. Business travel always made him lonely. If Charlie were with him, it wouldn't be so bad, but she was not. If the bartender were prettier, it wouldn't be bad either, but she was not. So that left Dent longing for the home he didn't have and the family he never had. He thumbed through his phone to occupy his mind, but that only yielded photos of better days. *He and Butterball at the zoo with lions, at the circus with clowns, at the fair with cotton candy.* There were no photos of Melody. He wiped them when she went around the bend. Just the sight of her would make his brain hurt. He took a sip of his drink and mustered the nerve to call.

"I'm in a meeting," answered Melody coldly.

"No, you're not," he said flatly.

He knew her better than anyone, and she hated him for it.

"What do you need?"

He didn't need anything. But that was her way of controlling the conversation.

"Can I talk to Butter?" he asked.

"You don't want to talk to me?"

She knew he didn't but still held a torch for him and festered the idea of them reconciling.

"She around?" he asked.

"She's with her father . . . in *Georgia*," she said with disdain. It was a chapter of her life she just assumed forgotten. Her meeting Tim in a bar one drunken night in graduate school led to a one-night stand that led to a baby that led to an acrimonious relationship that led to a barbaric custody battle. If Melody had not been ordered by the court of Fulton County to return Riley to the state for quarterly visitations with Tiny Daddy, she would never set foot in the state again.

"Hope he's being good to her."

"He's never good to anyone."

He knew she was right. He had seen it for himself. Tim yelling at Riley in a parking lot when he was dropping her off to her mother. Of course, he knew abused children grew up to be abusive parents, but that gave him little sympathy. Adults have a responsibility to work out their own issues. Dent wanted to take his trusty Louisville Slugger to the son of a bitch but knew that would not have been a good look on his CV.

The phone went *click*. The conversation was done, leaving Dent feeling emptier and alone than he did before.

The door swung open in the bar, allowing a sliver of daylight and patter of rain to slice through the darkness. Down the steps came the silhouette of a young man with dreadlocks.

"What the hell?" Dent said squinting to make him out.

"That how you greet your mama?" said Pac-man.

"That's how she greets me."

"That explains a lot."

Pac-man sidled up beside Dent at the bar.

"What ya drinkin'?"

"G and T."

"Didn't take you for a spritzer man," he jabbed and peered to the bartender. "Jack n' Coke, please."

She whirled away to make it.

"Drinking on the job, are ya?" said Dent.

"I'm a writer. We're expected to drink on the job."

"Explains your writing."

"You read it?" he said with surprise.

"Not slinging tips to any ol' hack."

"Touché."

They toasted. They drank.

"How'd you find me?"

"Wanna find a drinker, go to a bar."

"You tailed me. From the service," Dent deduced.

"You ain't the only investigator, ya know."

Dent nodded in acceptance.

"Sorry about your boys," said Pac-man.

"Thanks. They weren't exactly mine."

"Pretty dumb to crash a house of a guy who evaded the law in five states."

"That's what I told 'em."

"That on the record?"

"Not on your life. How am I supposed to be your deep throat if you go quoting me?"

Pac-man winced at the use of "deep throat," peering about wryly.

"Watch where you're throwing that, Holmes. People get the wrong idea."

Dent grinned. He liked Pac-man just fine. A journalist, nonetheless. Go figure.

"Well, I got something for you."

Dent raised a brow. "Oh?"

Pac-man unfolded a crumpled napkin and laid it on the bar. On it was scribbled a phone number with an "813" area code.

"Florida?"

"Kid in Tampa. Says he thinks he saw your boy."

"In Tampa?"

"In Lowes. Buying a bathtub."

"A bathtub. Get video?"

"They ain't pulling video for press. That's all you."

Dent pocketed the napkin.

"Why'd he call *you*?"

"He call you, you keep it secret. He call us, we make him famous!"

Dent rolled his eyes.

"You know . . . it's all about *likes* these days," said Pac-man.

"Why you givin' it to me?"

"What comes around goes around."

Dent grinned.

"I take back all the bad things I said about you."

"Shit, I'm a prince, homey."

Dent held his glass high. "To the interwebs."

"To the interwebs," said Pac-man.

Clink went their glasses.

CHAPTER 44

THE FUN GUY

Lowe's Companies, Inc. was thrilled to be issued a court-ordered warrant from the Federal Bureau of Investigation. The twelve-page document not-so-subtly insinuated the most notorious killer in America was using their Florida flagship as his personal toolshed. After an army of lawyers scoured the nooks and crannies of the paper, they finally relented, providing Sanjay and squad with what they requested. Video of the loading dock revealed it was indeed Livingston beneath the hoodie buying a thousand-dollar bathtub. Receipts showed one Marvin Flowers as the buyer. Receipts from the rental van showed Nicholas Baxter as the renter.

Once information poured in, Sanjay let Shayna handle it. She was on top of her game, and he had other fish to fry. Namely, helping Charlie get to the bottom of whatever happened to Livingston's house in Redondo Beach. The separation of duties allowed him and Shayna to divide and conquer, as well as have much-needed space. Her trying to Mr. Grey his ass on the floor of his loft and him blowing her off like a tumbleweed did not sit well. She was all business now. And he was all apologetic. It was gross, honestly, seeing Sanjay suck up to her. And for Shayna, it wore the sexual allure right off.

Her newfound work ethic did breed results, however. The APB on the homogeneous van destined for points unknown returned hits from security camera footage at a truck stop in South Carolina, a Burger

King drive-thru in North Carolina, and a toll booth in Virginia. But she wasn't the only one looking.

Miles away, a lowly intern combing news footage on the fourth floor of CNN in Atlanta recognized Livingston standing in the back of the FBI funeral ceremony in Washington. She promptly reported it to her producer, who reported it to his boss, who reported it to the head of the network, who gave the greenlight to broadcast it worldwide. The FBI director blew a gasket. He himself was not but forty feet from the killer. *Did no one expect the motherfucker to attend?*

The next thing Dent knew, his cell was blowing up with calls from around the globe. Singled out as lead investigator on the case, he was now the laughingstock of the civilized world. Cable News was having a field day pitting his photo against Livingston's. "Grudge Match" animation broke out with the killer outwitting the lawman. Chat groups exploded with rails and riffs against him and the bureau.

Dent had been semi-famous before. In the early 2000s, he helped prevent an assassination attempt on a senator. When allegations of sexual harassment reared with a certain southern governor, Dent's infamy quickly subsided. He figured it would again as soon as something bigger hit the headlines. Until then, however, his life would suck—more than usual. And make his hard job even harder.

Charlie, on the other hand, different story. She could fly below the radar. She was not in Washington. She was not in the news. And was currently headed to Van Nuys, California, a worn and weathered suburb of LA's seedy Simi Valley. Papers filed with the City of Redondo Beach fifteen years earlier revealed Livingston's house on Speyer Lane had been condemned. A lawsuit filed by Livingston's attorney at Forbes, Perry & Maxwell showed the reason being a single cause: *mold toxicity.*

Aspergillus. Cladosporium. Trichoderma. Stachybotrys. All were categories of fungi that, left to their own devices, were innocent enough. They grew every day around us everywhere. The problem was when they moved *in* with us. Left unchecked, they could wreak absolute havoc on the immune system, which allowed allergies to develop to everything, including, ironically, mold. And the more mold one was exposed to, the less the body could defend against it. It was what healthcare practitioners called the *toxic load*. A ruthless cycle of disease that ravaged every system of the body. The worst part was most doctors had no idea how to fix it. Especially fifteen years earlier. You really had to be immersed in its study to even have a clue.

Eugene Burnsley was just such a man. Raised on an apple farm a hundred miles south of Seattle, Eugene had seen his share of mold. His family had little money for discretionary expenses, like insulation, so when the rains came, they came hard, and so did their ramifications. Leaks in the roof bred water damage in the ceiling, behind the walls, and in the foundation of his rickety wooden house. Dark black mold formed across the walls, cobwebbed in the bedroom corners, mildewed in the cracked windows. His father died of asthma, his mother of aneurism, his sister of suicide. Despite his upbringing and circumstance, Eugene was somehow as upbeat a fella as they came. In fact, everyone knew him as *The Fun Guy*. His neighbors thought he was nuts. The truth was he was just happy to be alive.

Eugene was the only person who inspected Martin Livingston's Redondo Beach house before it was demolished. His reports were thorough and respected. He loved what he did for a living, and it showed, even now in the three-bedroom shithole he was inspecting on the wrong side of the tracks in the gang-ridden part of Van Nuys.

"Hello?" said Charlie, knocking on the screen door. The paint was chipped, the screen torn, flies buzzing.

"Come on in!" Eugene called cheerfully from within.

Charlie hesitated. She wasn't sure she wanted to touch the door handle, let alone go inside. "Um, well . . ."

"I'm in the back!"

She knew if Dent were there, he would already be inside. She dumped a breath, wrapped a handkerchief around the door handle, and let herself in. The screen door fell with a slap. The house was empty of inhabitants, but their soiled belongings and torn furniture remained scattered. It looked like a crack house because it was a crack house. There were bullet holes in the walls, blood on the carpet, used syringes in the couch. Dirty clothes, fast-food wrappers, and empty beer bottles laid everywhere. Cats had scratched and clawed and shit the whole place. It was, in a word, disgusting. Charlie covered her mouth from the smell with a handkerchief. Then flipped the cloth around, remembering she had used the inside of it to open the door.

"Back here!" called Eugene.

In the master bedroom, Eugene had ripped up the corner of a chocolate brown carpet between an empty rusted keg, a broken four-drawer dresser, and an unmade waterbed.

"Hi!" he said way too cheerily.

Charlie stood stiff in the doorway. Eugene was a shell of a man at fifty-five, slender, pockmarked, bluejeaned, and booted.

"Grab that side, will ya?"

Charlie raised a brow. *What?*

"Go on, it won't bite."

She angled to the corner opposite Eugene.

"Here?"

"Yeah, just grab it, and pull when I say."

"Um . . ."

She bent at the knees like her father taught her and grabbed the uprooted corner of the carpet.

"Ready?"

She shook her head no.

"One! Two! Three!"

He pulled, so she pulled, and the carpet wrenched from its rusty nails, revealing dark, wet floorboards, and an army of ants skittering for cover. The stench caused Charlie to cough.

"Never get used to it, huh?" said Eugene echoing Duvall's words from *Apocalypse Now.*

"It's disgusting," said Charlie.

"That's nothing. Look at the rug!"

The underside of the carpet revealed a horror show. Hundreds of black mushrooms grew out of the fabric. Charlie nearly puked but instead swallowed whatever came up to be ladylike, which made it worse.

"It's okay, sweety! Let 'er rip, if ya need."

She dropped the carpet thumping back to the floor and ran out of the room.

A minute later, she was sitting outside on the steps, catching her breath, and sipping from a water bottle—presumably washing down whatever she curdled up. Her eyes were watering, her lips quivered.

"Nothin' like being in the belly of the beast!"

Eugene stepped out beside her and took a deep sniff of fresh Los Angeles air.

"How do you do that?" she asked.

"Ah, it gets easier after a while."

She couldn't imagine.

"Why do you do that?"

"To help people," he said as though it were obvious.

She shook her head with disbelief.

"Same as you, I reckon," he said.

To each their own, she thought.

"What can I do ya for?" he asked.

"Your office said you were the one who inspected the Livingston house in Redondo Beach. Was his this bad?"

"Oh, Lord no," he said.

She sighed, somehow relieved.

"It was much worse."

She peered at him. He looked a little moldy himself.

"His house was one of the worst I'd ever seen. Stachy was caked all through the attic, the crawl space, behind the walls, under the carpet. It's a wonder that house didn't kill him."

His words struck her odd.

"It doesn't make sense. He is . . . was . . . meticulous . . . neat."

"Ah, well, honey, neat has nothin' to do with it."

He took a seat beside her like they were old pals. She slid back a bit as though she were giving him room, but in truth, she was afraid he might get her a little moldy.

"What do you mean?"

"His house was moved."

"Moved? What do you mean moved?"

"I mean it was moved. From Hollywood to Redondo."

"How do you *move* a house?"

"Depends on the house," he said with a guffaw. "A flatbed eighteen-wheeler is the easiest. Cut the house in half, if ya have to, and take her on two trucks."

"I don't understand."

"Houses not built on the ground they stand on are ripe for the pickin'."

Now she understood less.

"Sorry, it's an old apple orchard sayin'."

She wondered if he was half crazy himself. He reeled it in.

"If the foundation is not laid properly, it allows mold to seep in every crack and crevice. And in a moved house, there are a plenty. And once it's in, boy howdy, it spreads like wildfire!"

"And it makes people sick," she supposed.

"Oh, cancer comes a callin', that's for sure!"

The extent of Livingston's ordeal began to wash over her.

"He was renting the house, is that correct?"

"Oh yeah. Sued 'em for half the tea in Texas."

"Did they pay?"

"Well, they didn't. But the insurance company sure did. We were subpoenaed to present our findings."

"May I see them?"

"I don't know why not. Missy from the office can get 'em for ya."

Charlie forced a smile for him, figuring he didn't get many.

"Thank you . . . Mr. Burnsley."

"Oh, call me Eugene," he replied as though he'd made a friend.

"Eugene."

"But everyone calls me *The Fun Guy*. Get it? *Fungi?*"

She got it. Tried to smile again. But couldn't.

CHAPTER 45

NASHVILLE

Everyone had a dream. What they wanted to be. What they settled for. Nashville was filled with a million of those stories. The waitress who became a singer. The singer who became a waitress. It was all a roll of the dice. Which is why the locals called it "Nashvegas." Well, that and to make themselves feel cool.

Whoever was in charge of city planning here got it right. They put the football stadium on one side of the river. The hockey arena on the other. Between them was a hundred honky-tonk bars featuring the best musicians in the world. Tourists poured in from all over the country looking to shake their groove things. Streets were filled with pretty bachelorettes wheeling party bikes and drunk frat boys hooting and hollering at them.

Keeping it all in check was the overworked Nashville PD. Like the citizens they were sworn to protect, every cop in Nashville had a story. Mildred Hunt was a little overweight for a police officer. Still, she squeezed her 190 lb., five-foot-four frame into her patrol uniform five days a week, strapped on her heavy belt, and holstered her .45 ACP. She wasn't always a big girl. Like many young women with stars in their eyes, she came to the great state of Tennessee to break into the music business. It was a lot closer to her hometown of Opelika, Alabama than the Big Apple.

Mildred learned to sing in the church, and sing she could. Belting hymns of "In Christ Alone" and "How Great Thou Art," she could raise the mighty roof of the church and make handkerchief-waving parishioners feel Jesus himself. Armed with the protection of the Lord and guided by the Holy Spirit, Mildred set out for Nashville to share her God-given talent with the world. No one told her country music was no place for Black folk. It was never said out loud, of course. Not in this day and age. Instead, it was quietly understood. Not until Charlie Pride did anyone even consider letting a Black man perform at the Grand Ole Opry. And that was only after the NAACP pitched a fit. Darius Rucker was among the only other brothers they let in the place, and that was because he headlined the whitest band in America—*Hootie & the Blowfish*. It wasn't that the executives from the music labels were opposed to signing Black artists, it's that their audience was. Of course, they didn't mind a few "soul sisters" spouting doo-wops in the background, but the bulk of small-town country fans just plain did not want to see any "negroes" center stage.

Mildred landed a gig or two backing up Shania Twain in the nineties, but it was no way to make a living. They were pay-per-show scenarios with the checks barely enough to cover her gas to the gig and dinner going home. When she got knocked up by the poor preacher of a small church on the eastside, she had to find a job that would help support the family. Pressure from the city forced the NPD to open its door to minorities. The job came with bi-weekly paychecks, full benefits, a uniform, and a career Mildred's grandma could be proud of. She was inducted at twenty-five years old, promoted at twenty-eight, and landed her own patrol car by thirty. The other perk of the job, Mildred soon learned, was cops never had to pay for meals at restaurants. Owners were happy to have them there to ward off trouble and smooth over hiccups with the health department. Everyone loved Mildred at the greasy spoons and Donut Inns, the late-night diners, and all-you-could-eat smorgasbords. As a result, she put on a few pounds.

It was a little after 9:00 p.m. CST when Mildred got the call. An APB on Livingston's white van with Florida plates had been found in an alley behind the football stadium at Vanderbilt University. Law enforcement always kept a lookout for abandoned vehicles, but Nashville had made it a priority since some nutbar with overdue phone bills tried to take out the AT&T building with a homemade bomb. The only thing he had managed to take out was himself—in a white van.

Mildred drew her cruiser to an easy stop and squeezed from the door. Her blue lights swirled over the van twenty yards away. Curious coeds hung from dorm windows to watch the action below as Mildred called into her shoulder-mounted radio.

"Central, Alfa-Bravo-Niner, 11-24 at Vanderbilt University, confirm."

The radio called back.

"Alfa-Bravo-Niner, 11-24, GPS lock on PC7, Twenty-Sixth Avenue South. Back up en route, over."

Mildred was never one to back down from a fight. And she sure didn't need a man to make her feel safe. Since her training had instilled the importance of immediacy, she put her right hand on her weapon and moved slowly toward the van. The windows were tinted and dusty, the wind cool and whispering. Some drunk college girl screamed from a windowsill, "You go, girl!" Mildred rounded the side of the van toward the driver's door, careful to keep her distance. Her heart pounded and her breath quickened.

"NPD! Step out of the vehicle!" she shouted.

There was no response.

Carefully she drew her weapon—which she was taught to do only if she was prepared to use it. She inched toward the van, her eyes riveted on the driver's-side window. She tried to get a glimpse of any movement from the sideview mirror, but it was too dark inside to see.

"Step out of the vehicle!" she shouted again.

Still, there was not a sound but the din of traffic in the distance and echo of a baseball game on a dorm room television. She peeked in the van window, but could not see a thing, gripped the door handle with her chubby hand, and yanked it open with a squeak. But no one was inside. The seat was clear of debris and the dash was dark. Mildred exhaled and moved around to the rear of the vehicle as the dormitory audience grew. She could hear air support coming in the form of a McDonnell-Douglas 500E helicopter and sirens angling closer on the streets, but neither were there yet. *POP!* She flung open the back doors of the van, expecting the worst. But it was empty too. Whoever was driving this van was long gone. And so was their bathtub.

CHAPTER 46

DR. SMILEY

Wheels down at Nashville International Airport came at the crack of dawn. Dent hated mornings, and he hated to fly. So, having to get up early to catch a flight was right up there with getting a root canal. His grumpy attitude was grumpier than usual. And that was saying something. Having his ass chewed out by management the night before didn't help.

The requisite parade of black sedans met him and a handful of other agents on the tarmac as they descended the steps of the Gulfstream. Bureau reinforcements had been installed given the case's newfound notoriety. Simply put, the director did not want to be embarrassed again.

Livingston had met with three different doctors in the Nashville area a few years earlier, and the agents were there to cover them all. This was their first, and maybe only, chance to catch Livingston in the act or, with any luck, before he acted. Too many times Dent had gone to the ends of the earth to take down a sociopath only to have him wriggle free of consequence from inadequate evidence. Catching them red-handed was the surest way to see the bastards fall next to, of course, putting a bullet in their head.

The doctors were spread across the city. One was a chiropractor in crowded Green Hills. Another, a nutritionist in upscale Brentwood.

The last, an ENT in outlier Franklin. Six SUVs took to Interstate 440 like a convoy headed to battle, peeling off in pairs at different exits to meet local law enforcement at each of the doctors' homes. This early, the physicians would not have left for the day unless they had a sadistic love for CrossFit. If so, the fleet of feds would converge on the gym like piranha scaring the living daylights out of the overachievers.

Any physicians suspected of attack had been notified by authorities for their own safety. But not everyone heeded such warnings. *It won't happen to me. I took jiujitsu in college. I trust in the Lord.* Humans had a knack for rejecting the obvious. And doctors were the worst. Smarter than most, richer than some, and vain as the day was long, they did as they wished, ignoring the rules imposed on the rest of those to whom they administered their sorcery.

Since Charlie's study of Livingston's medical files showed his wrath focused on those doctors where he reported the most pain, Dr. Kevin Smiley's house was where Dent was headed. Smiley was an ENT by trade, a surgeon by craft, and father of three. His undergrad studies at William & Mary, medical school at Yale, and residency at Vanderbilt made him one of the nation's top artisans of myringoplasty and stapedectomy.

Two of the kids were already at school when the FBI arrived. The youngest was home with an ear infection. The sprinkler was going. The lawn manicured. The house enormous. Franklin PD had already secured the premises and stationed two cruisers on the street. A grey-haired, grey-goateed Smiley and his overly pleasant wife met the entourage in the driveway as though they were greeting guests for a cocktail party. She in a sweater, he in a sweatshirt.

"Dr. Smiley?" asked Dent as they approached.

"Kevin," offered Smiley with a friendly hand.

"Dent McCreary, FBI. Sorry about all this."

"Better safe than sorry, I suppose. This is my wife, Gail."

"Hello!" she said with an exuberant smile. "Would y'all like to come inside?" She raised her voice an octave at the end of her sentence like southern ladies do to sound nice. It wasn't necessary and bewildered the northern-reared Dent.

The innards of the house were something out of *HGTV Dream Home*. All those shows seemed to do was knock down walls that builders went to great pains to erect. Everything was open to everything else. The living room, the dining room, the kitchen, the study, the foyer, the den. It was like a Soho loft hidden inside a southern colonial. The furnishings were modern and white. The paintings were originals. The pillows matched everything. Tastefully framed bible quotes hung on the walls as guiding lights. *"Psalms 27:1 The Lord is my light and my salvation." "Psalms 118:24 This is the day which the Lord has made."*

Seated in the kitchen at the marble counter beside the little boy with the sniffles was Charlie. She had been there for an hour already and asked every question Dent could imagine.

"Well, look what the cat dragged in," said Dent.

"Can't let you have all the fun," she replied.

He was happy to see his young protégé. She brought a spark to his sparkless life.

Charlie and Gail had become quick friends. Coffee cups had been refilled twice. Muffins had been half-eaten.

"She's eatin' us out of house and home," said Smiley with a grin.

Dent liked Smiley. In another life, he thought they could have been friends. But not now. There was too much to cover and not enough time.

"What was wrong with Livingston?" asked Dent.

"Well... a lot of things. Undiagnosed sleep apnea, gastroesophageal reflux, chronic candida, depression for sure. Untreated, they compound one another. What we treated him for most though, well . . . *tried* to treat him for, was chronic invasive fungal encephalitis."

That rang a bell for Charlie. "Fungal encephalitis?"

Smiley nodded. "His scan showed one of the worst I ever saw. Fungal infections are difficult to detect . . . and eradicate. So are bone infections. He had both. Slowly eroding his skull."

Dent's jaw dropped. "He had a fungal infection in his *head*?"

"For ten years . . . by the time he got to us."

His words weighed on Charlie. She had seen the mold in the crack house in California, and even though Dent had read Charlie's report on the flight in, it wasn't the same as seeing it, smelling it, breathing it.

"How do you treat that?" asked Dent.

"Carefully. Primarily with intravenous loads of amphotericin B via PICC line."

"What's a PICC line?" asked Charlie.

"We insert a small catheter into the patient's vein in his forearm, run it up through his shoulder to his chest to his heart. It then pumps the medicine evenly through the body."

"Jesus," said Dent.

"That works?" asked Charlie.

"It can. But it takes a while. The patient has to hang a drip bag for an hour a day, every day, for weeks, or sometimes months."

"Sounds awful," said Charlie sympathetically.

"It is," agreed Smiley. "But for many, it's their last stop. The worst part is tolerance. The side effects can be brutal. An emotional rollercoaster of depression, anxiety, hallucinations, nausea, vomiting, headaches, chills, sweats. Some patients say it feels like acid is being pumped through their body, burning them from the inside out."

Charlie and Dent exchanged a look.

Gail noticed. "What?"

Dent admitted "Mr. Livingston bought a bathtub. We found the van it was transported to Nashville in, but not the bathtub itself."

"Oh, my Lord," said Gail knowing his MO from the news. "He tortures the doctors, right? In ways he felt?"

Neither Dent nor Charlie had the heart to nod.

"Don't worry," said Charlie. "We have your home surrounded. You'll be fine as long as you stay here."

"No problem," said Smiley. "Until tonight."

Dent raised a brow. "What happens tonight?"

"I have a gig."

Smiley smiled. Dent did not.

Outside the house, more FBI agents arrived. And not just a handful like Texas. *FBI agents had died.* So, dozens of blue-jacketed, yellow-insignia'd, gun-toting "gung hos" patrolled the grounds. All of them triple-vetted with identification to confirm their identities. A black bulletproof SWAT truck positioned itself at the end of the driveway. Sharpshooters set atop the house. K-9 units spread out with German shepherds. Neighbors walked, biked, and drove past, gawking with displeasure at the commotion. In a neighborhood like this, no doubt many a neighbor would phone the authorities to quiet such a hubbub. *But who were they going to call?* This was the FBI.

The irony was the mass deployment was exactly what led Livingston to the property. He set up outside the local FBI field office in East Nashville early that morning on a nondescript, non-rumbly, non-labeled motorcycle. His grey helmet's tinted visor disguised his face from being seen. His leather jacket blending in with the swath of cow blanketing the town's musicians. The license plate bought on eBay as a collector's item. He simply followed the FBI convoy that he created to the good doctor's house at a safe distance. Idling past the home, one thing became abundantly clear to him. He would not be taking Dr. Smiley there. But then, that was never his intention. He grinned beneath the polycarbonate mask that no one could see. And rode off casually down the road to prepare for whatever was next.

CHAPTER 47

THE GIG

Like nearly everyone in Nashville, Dr. Smiley played a musical instrument. A red '77 Fender Stratocaster to be exact. In fact, the reason he chose Nashville to do his residency was not because of Vanderbilt Hospital's prestigious program in rhinoplasty but because it was in the heart of Music City. Smiley didn't mind missing work. Patients could wait. But there was no way he was going to miss playing music. He would blame it on his bandmates whom he didn't want to let down. Truth was he just loved playing guitar. It's the one thing that kept him grounded, made him whole, and replenished his soul. His Strat was his *Rosebud*, the iconic McGuffin from *Citizen Kane* that reminded him who he was. So that's what he called her.

Dent read him the rote over canceling the show, but the good doctor would have none of it. His arrogant dismissal of authority seemed nearly equal to Dent's which, of course, Dent appreciated. If the FBI was concerned for his health and welfare, they could cover the club with as many agents as they wanted—as long as they paid the cover charge.

The band loaded in from the alley behind Layla's, one of Nashville's penultimate watering holes for fostering new talent. Like Smiley, the guys in the band were not new. They were all in their fifties with real jobs, but they were new to the strip. If they had their way, they would be playing old-school rock n' roll—Springsteen,

Seger, Cougar, Petty. But the bars on tourist-centric Broadway were required to play country—new country at that—McGraw, Chesney, Aldean, Urban. The band drew the line at Luke Bryan. They had some self-respect.

By ten o'clock, the joint was jumping, the band was rocking, and the bar three rows deep. Dent, Charlie, and four other agents had checked into their hotel rooms at the nearby Holiday Inn on West End and dressed in street clothes to blend in. Jenny on the Block, as she liked to call herself, ran the place with confidence. Not that she needed to work at all. She was the fifty-year-old wife of a successful songwriter who crafted a few Garth Brook's hits in the nineties. That gave them more than enough money to live on, and their kids, and their grandkids. But Jenny wanted—no, needed—something to get her out of the house, to give her purpose, and to make her feel alive. She parked her $80k Infiniti out back with the delivery trucks to hide it from the patrons and wore ripped jeans, a flannel shirt, cowboy boots, and a trucker hat to fit in. She was the long-ordained den mother of Layla's. So much so that even the regulars thought she was Layla herself.

"Callie! The gun is empty!" she called over the noise.

Charlie's head snapped from her Shirley Temple at the end of the bar. But Jenny only meant the bar's soda gun was out of CO_2. A spry young blonde named Callie swung into the bustling kitchen of burly cooks to retrieve another. Watching her pass, Charlie couldn't help but think they could be in each other's shoes if fate dealt them different cards.

Boom! The drummer hit the kick drum with the force of dynamite and the band dropped into a rousing rendition of "She's Country." Standing beside the stage, the sound rattled Dent's brain like mortar fire, taking him back to a time and place in the Middle East he just assumed forgotten. He shook it off best he could and kept focused on his mission . . . keeping Dr. Smiley alive. The doc wasn't half bad on guitar, Dent thought. But didn't think he should quit his day job.

"Can I get ya anything, sweetie?" asked a cute brunette waitress in cutoffs, converse, and Lynyrd Skynyrd halter top. Dent grinned. He could have used a lot of things at that moment but knew none of them would be appropriate coming from her.

"I'm good, thanks."

"Name's Becca. Just holla," she said with a sexy smile and sashayed off into the crowd tray held high.

Jenny, Callie, and Becca were the belles of the ball in this honky-tonk turning heads and breaking hearts at every turn. They held the drinks, the tabs, and, thus, the power. Outside the bar was a different story and they knew it. It was no easy feat standing out in a town of the prettiest women in the country, so they made the most of every moment at "the office."

A drunk redneck, with a Coors in hand, spotted Dent, elbowed his drunk friend beside him, and whispered, thinking he recognized the grizzled dude from the news.

"Hey . . . hey man . . . you that fed? That shitty fed?"

Dent barely looked back. Because across the crowded bar through the smoky haze and gyrating dance floor, something caught his eye. A big man in a grey hoody beneath a black jacket a little too warm for the local weather. Agents were trained to see things everyday people didn't. And this was a Class A example. The man headed down a back hallway toward the bathroom. Dent whispered into a wireless microphone hidden in the wrist cuff of his coat.

"Red Team, got a bead on a suspect, heading toward the back. Grey hoodie, black jacket." In an instant, Charlie peeled away from the bar in that direction. The other agents angled before the front and rear doors, all of them armed and alert.

Charlie greeted Dent in the narrow brick hall in back. Weathered graffiti and band posters covered the wall. A few short-skirted debutantes gossiped before the women's room, and a drunken frat boy stumbled from the men's. He got one look at Dent and ducked out of the way. At the end of the hall was an exit door with a fire alarm. Charlie gently pushed it to see if it worked and it *rang*. She pulled it closed. Dent tugged on a storage closet. It was locked. Now they knew the suspect was in one of the two bathrooms. Together they drew their weapons.

"Ready?" he asked.

She nodded somewhat confidently.

"Go," he said, not giving her time to think.

They pushed into their respective rooms.

In the women's room, Charlie found a couple of girls doing makeup in the mirrors and moved toward the stalls.

In the men's room, Dent found a skinny man doing a line of coke at the sink.

"Fuck off," Dent said flatly.

The man quickly did, coughing as he went.

Charlie bent down to look beneath the three stalls to see which were occupied. One had red high heels on a slender woman's manicured feet. The other stalls appeared empty.

Dent pushed on the first of his three doors quietly. It opened and no one was there. Charlie pushed on her second door, and no one was there.

Dent *tap-tap-tapped* the barrel of his gun on the second door in the men's room and no one replied.

Charlie squeaked open her third door in the women's and found the stall empty.

BAM! The last door in the men's room flung open in a heap and the man in the hoodie roared out like thunder driving Dent crashing into the wall. He grunted and lost his grip on his gun. It clattered to the tile and the man rushed out of the room.

In the bar, the suspect barreled through the crowd, swinging into Becca, knocking beers from her tray onto the redneck. "Sonuvabitch!" he called out.

"Suspect's on the move!" Dent barked into his wrist mic.

The agents swung into the crowd as the redneck took a swing at the suspect. "Asshole!" But he clocked another guy by mistake and all hell broke loose. The tables emptied and arms flew. Dent and Charlie poured into the frenzy. Soaring bottles hit the stage, and the band wound to a discordant stop. The suspect snuck past the bouncers coming inside to restore order and out the front door onto Broadway. Until *WHACK*! He was struck with a baton across his midsection with the force of a bear and landed flat on his back in the middle of the sidewalk.

"FREEZE, FOOL!"

It was Mildred. God love her. Now pointing her .45 in the man's face, her eyes aflame, and all 190 pounds of her heaving with venom.

Dent and Charlie spilled from the bar and caught up, quickly assessing the situation.

"Are you okay?" Charlie asked her.

Mildred just nodded, her grip firm on her gun.

Dent pulled back the hoodie on the perp. It was a red-haired fella with bloodshot eyes and a cold sore on his lip. Not Livingston.

"Shit!" said Dent holstering his sidearm with anger.

He slammed the guy against the sidewalk by his jacket.

"Where is he?!" Dent barked in his face.

"I don't know . . ." the redhead tried to say.

BAM! Dent slammed him harder.

"Where is he?!" he yelled.

"I don't know, man!" he said with tears in his eyes. "Some guy just paid me to distract ya."

Dent and Charlie's eyes blew wide. They craned to the bar window, seeing the band had gone on break amid the ruckus. They burst past the bouncers into the frazzled room. Dent grabbed the drummer by the elbow at the bar. "Where's Doc?!"

"I don't know, man. Think he went out back to get some air."

Dent raced through the kitchen and flung out the rear door into the alley. There, he found one of the burly cook's white aprons on the ground. And one of the loading trucks gone.

CHAPTER 48

THE SEARCH

Helicopters crisscrossed the Nashville skyline, spotlights swirled like a Luke Combs concert. Police barricades cordoned off the wild bustle around Layla's. Cruisers sat on every corner with lights flashing. Television trucks lit up wide-eyed reporters making the most of the dire situation. Uniformed officers directed traffic around the mayhem best they could, but it was damn near impossible. This time of night, the streets were filled with people. Drunk people at that.

Compounding matters was that giddy bargoers had put everything on social media. Facebook and Instagram and TikTok and Snapchat were all aflutter with posts of the barfight, the takedown, and Jenny on the Block boasting the infamous Number One Killer was "in the house." She thought it would bring exposure to the bar but was too shortsighted to see it was all the wrong kind. Rednecks in pickup trucks with shotguns and pit bulls roared up around the haunt like a wild west posse ready to round up an outlaw on the run. Rumors were flying that Reba McEntire had offered a $10,000 reward for Livingston's apprehension, but no one could substantiate it.

Behind the club, an FBI mobile field office had been set up in the back of a black eighteen-wheeler loaded with automatic weapons, computer monitors, video surveillance, and techies on headsets. Now that the operation had unraveled, every FBI officer within a hundred miles converged on Broadway. They were easy to spot. They were the ones in suits.

In the alley, Dent was harried as ever, coordinating massive efforts between Nashville PD, Davidson County Sheriffs, and Tennessee State Patrol. He knew losing Smiley was on him. He followed protocol. Had four on the floor. The doors covered. Police notified. But none of that mattered now. *He fucking lost him.* The one doc he actually liked was gone, whisked away by a maniacal sociopath who had little remorse for killing—*no, torturing, then killing*—five other doctors west of the Mississippi. Maybe the fact Smiley was successful at diagnosing what ailed Livingston would have the madman go easy on him, Dent wondered. Then again, one thing his years of investigation had taught him: *Never apply logical thinking to illogical people.*

"Where is he?!" screamed a woman pushing through the throng in the alley.

It was Gail, Doctor Smiley's polite wife. Though she wasn't feeling very polite at the moment. Within minutes of her daughter notifying her that her sister told her that her friends saw her father was missing on TikTok, Gail blew a gasket, jumped in her silver Range Rover, and roared down Hillsboro Pike through tourist traffic to the chaotic scene of the crime.

"Where the hell is he?!" Gail's voice no longer lifted an octave but stayed steady, low, and loud. She wasn't looking for her husband. She knew what happened to him. She was looking for Dent. And spied him in a meeting at the foot of the steps of the FBI truck, and charged like a determined rhinoceros, her finger pointing like its malevolent horn.

"You!"

Dent glanced up, prepared for the oncoming assault . . . when Charlie swept into her path.

"Mrs. Smiley! We're so glad you're here."

Charlie's sweet-speak totally disarmed Gail, if not utterly confused her.

"We need your help," said Charlie.

"What?"

Gail glared at Dent but turned instinctually to Charlie who promptly led her way.

"We can't do this without you."

Dent breathed a sigh of relief. *Damn that Chuck.* She was turning out to be quite the partner. Off to the side, she lobbed questions at Gail about her husband's habits and hobbies. Soon Gail's anger segued to sobs as the gravity of the situation dawned on her. Charlie certainly hoped for a nugget of knowledge that might lead them to find her husband before he was killed. But mostly she was keeping her from the command center so Dent and the others could do their job.

At HQ in LA, Sanjay ran his fingers over his computer keyboard like Liberace, trying to do what he could to help. He managed to lock into global satellite imagery of the club at the time of the abduction and watched helplessly as a man was ushered out the back to the rear doors of a delivery truck. In the dark of night from thirteen thousand miles above, it was hard to tell if it was, indeed Livingston or Smiley, but it was enough to convince Sanjay to follow the truck's trajectory from downtown east. Tracking video from an earlier timeline seemed like time travel to Sanjay. He could enter GPS coordinates anywhere in the world and, within seconds, zoom into that locale at any point in time within the last thirty days, then slide the timeline backward or forward as needed. He sped things up as fast as he could, following the truck stopping and starting at lights and signs, hoping—no, praying— the good doctor would still be alive when he caught up to them in real-time.

Shayna had run the plate. At least, what they could make of it. All they had to go on were a few foggy digits in shadows that looked like "GR" and "1." But frankly, the G could have been a "0" and, well, the "1" could have been an "I." Come to think of it, the "R" could have been a "B." Nevertheless, Shayna ran every possible combination of seven digits with those variables and, within eight minutes, came away with a vehicle matching the delivery truck's description rented earlier that day to one Sheldon Beach. A quick search on Intelius revealed Mr. Beach as a character in one of Livingston's films. Another search proved that all his rental contracts used names of characters from his films. Easier for him to keep his story straight, they concluded.

"Got him!" belted Sanjay. Shayna's heart jumped. Her ego was still bruised from his slight at the loft, maybe her thigh as well, but the adrenaline coursing through Sanjay's body in the glow of his computer screen seemed to get her all hot and bothered again.

Shayna rolled up behind him in her chair. "Where?"

He did a doubletake at her. "Um, uh, well, there." He was happy, if not surprised, she was still into him. Or at least the case. Either way, he was glad she was beside him. On screen, the GPS showed the truck was getting onto I-40 East.

Shayna's chest heaved with excitement. "It's freaky, isn't it? We're here, in an office, in LA," she said, gesturing around. "And everyone . . . out there . . . a million miles away is . . . counting on *you*." Her finger pressed on his chest.

His heart jumped. But he played it coy. "Well, it's the tech really. You just have to know how to use it." He hit return on the keyboard, and the trace on the truck raced downline to the mobile task force.

"That's it?" she asked.

"That's it."

The radio on his desk squawked to life. Tennessee State Patrol was notified. And choppers and cruisers swung to the east en masse in one of the largest manhunts in the state's recent memory.

Shayna looked like she wanted to fuck Sanjay right there, and this late at night, she could probably get away with it. The office was nearly empty but for a few late-night staffers manning computers in the back. The shimmering lights of the city out of the sprawling windows somehow made everything more romantic. *Wham.* She thrust his lean body against his computer console.

"Wh-wh-what are you doing?" he managed.

"What I should have the other night," she said steadily.

Sanjay swallowed, glancing around. "Here? Now?"

Without a second thought, Shayna reached up her skirt and dropped her panties to the floor. Wildly aroused, he began unbuckling his belt. *Just desserts*, he thought, for a job well done. The two tore off each other's clothes smack dab in the middle of the computer station.

"Sanjay!" Dent barked from the speaker.

Sanjay didn't budge this time.

"You should get it," said Shayna.

"Screw 'em," Sanjay said surprisingly.

Shayna moved for the microphone on the console herself. "Go for LA Base."

"What happened? We lost him!" Dent yelled over the speaker.

Sanjay peered at his computer screen seeing the truck had somehow *disappeared*.

"No—no—no—no." The color drained from his face. His mind spun. There was nothing that could impede the agency's satellite state-of-the-art camera technology. Except for, well, clouds.

"Seattle of the South." That's what the tourists called it. Nestled smack dab in the middle of the Gulfstream, Nashville bore the remnants of nearly every storm that sprung from the Gulf of Mexico. Louisiana, Arkansas, Mississippi, and Alabama were hit the hardest by the fronts. But no matter what beach a hurricane, tropical storm, or light sprinkle landed, they all seemed to find their way to Nashville—as if they knew that was where the afterparty was.

"Where'd he go?" asked Shayna half-dressed.

The storm over middle Tennessee made Sanjay's job exponentially more difficult. Random cargo trucks did not carry little black boxes with transponders like commercial airplanes, and there was no cell phone yet to trace. Beneath the clouds, Livingston was a ghost. Sanjay knew the capabilities on the ground were limited and people were counting on him. Suddenly his eyes lit with an idea. He flipped off one screen and flipped on another.

"Working on it!" exclaimed Sanjay.

"What are you doing?" said Shayna.

"Going to ground." Sanjay typed furiously, his eyes glued to the screen, his mind on the mission. "We lost our eye in the sky, but we can try and track him from ground cameras."

A flutter of video feeds popped onto Sanjay's screen like bubbles atop a boiling pot of water. Each one zoomed in on images of trucks here and there in greater Davidson County.

"Now that we have the vehicle description, model, and license plate, we can try and find it remotely by street cams in the area . . . beneath the clouds," said Sanjay.

A few agency workers passed through the far end of the office floor.

"You should probably button your pants," she said, buttoning her blouse.

But Sanjay had bigger fish to fry. In the Tennessee countryside, tracking the van was like looking for a needle in a haystack, bobbing between available, permissible, building-mounted video systems. A bank here. A warehouse there. And all through a rising rain. Sanjay did his best searching, searching, searching, until . . . .

"There!" shouted Shayna.

The truck soared past a stand-alone post office on a two-lane street in a one-horse town.

Sanjay keyed the radio. "Got 'em!"

"Where?" Dent asked.

"Headed east on Andrew Jackson Parkway!"

"Send it," said Dent.

Sanjay pressed return and the tracking coordinates were sent instantly.

In Nashville, Dent nodded to a TSP captain. The big man got on the horn to his troops and eyed a computer monitor in the surveillance truck.

"All units, be advised, suspect one headed east on AJP, approximately two miles east of the I-40 split."

This time, Sanjay was not taking his eyes off the truck on his screen, flipping between feeds of streetlight ground cams . . . *third street . . . fourth street . . . fifth street . . . .*

Until his screen went blank.

"What? No—no—no—no . . ." he said, standing over his computer.

"What?" she asked.

"He's gone!"

The problem was the county line. Local voters promptly rejected the increase to their taxes to provide street-wide security surveillance, deeming it the unpatriotic work of the Democrats. "Big Brother," they bemoaned. "We'll handle it ourselves," they boasted. So, the last Sanjay saw of the truck was it rumbling across the tracks on Lebanon Pike.

Bam! He slammed his fist on his desk, rattling his mouse. "Damn it!"

In Nashville, Dent pulled his headset off and looked up from the map over the swarming mass in the alley. The press, the police, the public. And poor Gail, now crying like a baby in Charlie's arms. To compound matters, the rain was beginning to move in on them too. This was not how this day was supposed to go. He hung his head with defeat, veins pulsing in his temples. He drew his heart medication from his pocket and tossed one in his mouth. Picked up somebody's half-empty bottle of Mountain Dew and chased it. Because a straight shot of caffeine is the best thing to chase blood pressure medicine. All was lost. Again.

CHAPTER 49

THE STRIP CLUB

"The Bible Belt" was a term used loosely around the South. It was slung this way and that whenever or wherever it behooved the person slinging. For the Bible-thumpers, it was a badge of honor, to hail from the bright side of the moral right. Like belonging to the country club or living on the Upper West Side. For the heathens, it was a line drawn in the sand. An imaginary border separating good from evil. Like the 38th parallel or the Mason-Dixon. Regardless of which side one resided, there was a wealth of fine, and not-so-fine, low-lit "dancing establishments" patronized by men. Mind you, there were plenty of women, too, but they were largely employees.

The Slippery Slope was like Las Vegas. Whatever happened there stayed there. And a lot happened there. It was the hot spot for lowlifes looking for love in all the wrong places. Night after night, truckers and bankers, bakers and thieves would wander through the door into the stank and stickiness of the rose-hued lounge filled with old paisley chairs and Formica-topped tables. Old beer signs hung half-lit on chipped walls. Bad '80s rockers crackled from worn '90s speakers. Epcot was the DJ most nights. A straight-up send-up of the token brother on *Starsky & Hutch*, Huggy Bear. He wore brass shades and diamond rings, a gold vest, and two-tone shoes.

"That's right, that's right, fellas, don't be shy!" he belted into the microphone. "These ladies are hot, hot, hot, and ready to dance the night away for you." It was the lamest of pimp pitches and why Epcot was destined for a lifetime career of gyration narration.

Two redheads straddled poles to Pat Benetar's "Hit Me with Your Best Shot" with the enthusiasm of sleepy tortoises. A handful of other once-pretty girls rode laps of dollar-tossing patrons across the smoke-filled room. Ordinances carried little weight outside of Nashville.

Ox was the nightly bouncer here and no one dared mess with him. At six foot seven and 320 lb., his imposing size was enough to scare off even the meanest of drunks. Meth heads, on the other hand, Lord knew. They all thought they were composed of pixie dust and could walk through walls. Truth be known, Ox was a teddy bear. It broke his heart to break a jaw, but a job had to be done, and rent had to be paid.

In the corners of the bar, old televisions ran local stations sans sound. One showed the storm moving in from the west, the other, the white truck with the kidnapped doctor headed east. No one here paid them much mind, but management thought they were a good idea to pass themselves off as a "full-service" bar. Rumors of Reba's reward had spread to the media. And Billy Ray Cyrus had joined the cause. Most likely to stay relevant. And enjoy the tax deduction.

Bam! The front door flew open, and a good ol' boy in faded overalls, a John Deere hat, and a five-day scruff swung in, eyes ablaze. "Ox! Come quick!"

The big man set down his Diet Coke and lumbered off his ripped stool. "What up?"

The parking lot was a sight to see. Three gals, two guys, a golden retriever, and a ferret were cuddled up frightened behind a blue Ford F-150 armed with handguns and cellphones.

"What the fuck?" uttered Ox stepping out into the drizzling rain.

"Shhhh! Keep it down!" whispered John Deere. He spat a wad of Skoal to the ground and waved at Ox to follow him to join the rest behind the truck. "Stay down!"

Big Ox did his best to duck, but that only reduced him to six foot one without throwing out his back. "What's going on?" he mumbled to the wet group.

One of the girls, nineteen tops, part-time dancer, part-time bulimic, glanced behind her with bloodshot eyes and pointed toward the corner of the cracked parking lot. "It's that truck!" she said with a southern twang.

Ox stood up to see, until John Deere and Miss Bulimia, yanked him back down.

"Stay down!" they said in tandem.

"What truck?" Ox asked, confused.

"From the TV!"

The retriever barked in agreement.

Ox stared blankly. His signature look.

"The Number One Killer? From Nashville?" blurted John Deere.

Ox may not have been a *New York Times* subscriber, but he sure as shit knew about the Number One Killer. It had filled social media for weeks. His brows raised. "How ya know?"

Miss Bulimia thrust out a photo of the truck on Reddit on her cell. "They just escaped from Layla's in a truck like that with that fuckin' license plate!"

Ox peered over the top of the truck bed and, sure enough, through the dark sky and light rain, saw a white truck with the license plate digits matching those on her phone . . . "G, R, 1."

"Sombitch," offered Ox. He slumped back down beside them. "What ya wanna do?"

"Dumbass called the police," said Miss Bulimia elbowing John Deere in the gut.

He grunted. "Well, it seemed smart at the time."

"Why wouldn't it be?" asked Ox.

One of the other girls in a pink tutu who went by Princess rolled her hazy eyes, pet her pet ferret, and spoke with a redneck drawl. "The re-ward, mo-ron"

Ox stared blankly. So, she explained.

"Reba?" Nothing rang a bell.

"Billy Ray?" Still nothing.

"Jeez, Ox! Where the fuck you been?"

"What's with the rat?" Ox asked.

Princess rolled her eyes again. Her signature look.

"There's a re-ward for, like, nine million dollars." Which, of course, there wasn't, but Princess was no math whiz. "And Mushroom is a ferret," she said lovingly.

Ox wasn't quite sure what to make of that. "A what?"

Thump. A sound came from the delivery truck. They all jumped.

"There's someone in it!"

"Holy shit! We're gonna die, we're gonna die, we're gonna die . . ." rambled Miss Bulimia.

"What the fuck?" asked Princess.

In the distance, they heard the faint cry of a police siren.

"Cops," said John Deere.

"Damn," said Princess. They peered at her.

"We ain't gonna get no money if the cops catch 'em."

The thought pressed down on them.

"What ya wanna do?" asked Ox.

"Well . . . we got you, and you're like ten feet tall," said Miss Bulimia. "And Horsemeat and Brad, they got guns."

The quiet guys in camouflage nodded ready.

The dog barked again. Whatever was being planned, he was in.

John Deere grinned. "And a fuckin' ferret."

Swelling with patriotism, Ox uttered the infamous battle cry "Let's roll."

In two-by-two formation, plus a dog and ferret, the motley crew slid and stumbled toward the back of the truck with guns and crowbars high. The truck sounded with another *thump*. But this one louder. The group stopped in their tracks. Rain fell.

"Fuck!" whispered Princess.

The police sirens echoed closer.

Grunts and groans came from inside the truck.

"Holy shit! He's sawin' 'em up right now!" concluded John Deere.

"Do it! Do it!" ordered Princess, clutching Mushroom to her chest.

John Deere nodded to one of the camouflage guys. He gripped the truck handle, sweat beading his face. The others all stood ten feet back weapons raised with trembling hands.

The cops were almost upon them.

"Do ittttttt!" screamed Princess, seeing dollar signs.

Whish! Camo boy twisted the handle, tugged the door, and through the mist they saw . . . .

One of the truckers from the club getting double-teamed by the redheads.

Ox and company stood stunned.

Screech! State trooper vehicles roared into the lot around them one by one by one by one, lights swirling, sirens howling. Ox and John Deere and Princess and company spun dazed and confused like they had been sucked into Alice's Wonderland.

"Drop the guns! Drop the guns!" yelled the police aside their cruiser doors.

Princess dropped the ferret. It landed on its head and took off running.

Clang, clang. Down went the rest of the weapons. The dog barked uncontrollably.

"On the ground! On the ground!" shouted the troopers.

The group dropped to their knees. Except Princess. For some ungodly reason, she took off running after Mushroom, tutu flying in the wind. A couple cops gave chase.

Terrified, the redheads squealed and covered up their pale breasts. The poor trucker who thought he was having the best night of his life suddenly found himself having the worst, buck ass naked, squinting into a sea of guns and lights and spiraling rain.

Wham! Big Ox was pressed hard to the ground by three troopers, pushing his dumbstruck face into a puddle in the pavement. He tried to gurgle something, but they paid him no mind. They were taking no chances with the big man.

An hour later, investigators would learn the truth about what happened. The truck license plate had been switched by Livingston at a gas station earlier in the evening. Ox and friends would be fully exonerated. And Mushroom would be forever free.

CHAPTER 50

THE HILL

The highest hill in the city of Nashville was known as Love Circle. Rising fourteen hundred feet above the Vandy enclave Hillsboro Village, it was the go-to spot for teens and non-teens to make out. There's no doubt many a Davidson County high schooler lost their virginity in backseats on the cement drive that circled the hill. But it was the view above the road that brought folks out day and night to see the sights. From up here Nashville seemed so peaceful, simple—astounding really—that it could breed so much longing and legacy.

By 1:00 a.m., the rain had cleared. By 2:00 a.m., so had the lovers. Just a blinking light atop a lone cell tower locked behind a barbed-wire fence. Which is why it was odd fifteen-year-old Shelby Nichols and her girlfriend hiked to the top with a blanket and backpack. They were already high and aiming to get higher, giggling like the stoner runaways they were.

"What is that?" Shelby's girlfriend asked.

Squinting to see through the darkness, they saw in the middle of the grassy knoll what appeared to be . . . a bathtub.

"What the hell?" said Shelby.

Slowly they approached the large acrylic tub, their glazy eyes and hazy brains trying to compute.

"It's a damn bathtub."

"Hell yeah. Let's take us a dip."

As they neared, their sneakers brushing through the grass, they soon saw the tub was full of some kind of liquid.

"How'd this get up here?"

Closer and closer they neared.

Until Shelby's eyes blew wide, and she screamed at the top of her toke-filled lungs.

Face up, floating in a pool of bloody, thick, hydrofluoric acid, was Dr. Smiley. The skin of his naked body eaten away. His bones eroded into milky nothingness. And the empty black sockets that once held his eyeballs pointing up at the bright stars in the night sky.

CHAPTER 51

THE PRESIDENT

Phones rang all over Washington. And in an age when text was tops, that was saying something. No one liked to hear anyone's voice anymore. Least of all four in the morning. But the AMA, the APA, the AHA, and every other medical association north of the equator was livid. The heads of each were blowing up the phones of every senator they bribed on golf courses coast to coast, year after year. Senators woke committee members, they woke the speaker, she woke the chief of staff, and fuck it all, he woke the president. The soft-spoken bastard was no gem to be around at teatime, let alone before he'd had his Wheaties. He'd grown accustomed to getting a knock here and nudge there when foreign powers thirteen time zones ahead had their panties in a wad over nuclear threat but could not fathom why someone on his own staff would have the gall to bother him, his wife, and their cat, Cuddles, when something in America went south before dawn. *Could it not wait until after goddamn breakfast?* Suffice it to say, the president woke the director of the FBI, Walter Daltrey, who, up until that very moment, had been a fan of Dent.

"Yes, sir. Yes, sir. Yes, sir," Daltrey said into his confidential Satcom line beside his bed. Accustomed to outranking most in Washington, Daltrey suddenly found himself on the flipside of an ass-chewing from his superior. "We'll get to the bottom of it, sir. Yes, sir. Yes, sir." *Click* went the line. The president was gone. The director, the former two-star general of the third armored tank division of the US Army, was about ready to requisition the National Guard, if need be, to put an end to the ethereal Mr. Livingston.

In Nashville, the chaos had subsided. No longer at stake was Doctor Smiley's life. He was a pile of goo. The missus was well on her way to a nervous breakdown, and the killer long gone. Love Circle had been newly christened the Devil's Tower thanks to the press. News vans were stopped by police barricades on Acklen Avenue. But network choppers swarmed like hungry buzzards overhead before the FBI could get the air space declared an emergency. Subsequently, video of the tub, the goo, the cops, the teens, the whole kit and kaboodle, were now all over the world. People wanted the footage taken down like videos of the twin towers falling but would have little luck. The hill was lit up like a pinball machine with the red and blue and white flickering lights of police cars, ambulances, fire engines, FBI SUVs, and CSI wagons. No one had been called to ID the body because there was no body to identify. Dental records and DNA traces would all come in time, but even those would be a Pythagorean theorem for coroners.

By the time Daltrey's calls got to Music City, Special Agent Montgomery had landed with a hoard of FBI brass and a sore ass himself from the phone calls. Most of them were about simply whether or not to take Dent off the case.

"He's lost his edge," they said.

"He's a damn drunk," some suggested.

"He's over the hill," a few complained.

Everyone agreed Dent should be replaced as lead investigator as soon as possible. But no one had a clue with whom to replace him. He was the only one with the experience, the tenacity, the stomach for the job. Montgomery stormed up the hill with his entourage like they were taking Normandy Beach, ready to make a change. He pushed through the weary throng, eager to kick ass and take names. But there was no sign of Dent anywhere. Or Charlie, for that matter. The two agents who had the weight, and the eyes, of the civilized world on their meager shoulders were nowhere to be seen. It's as if they knew it was coming and simply opted out. The senior FBI officer clamoring for greatness fumed. Veins bulged in his bald black head.

"Where the fuck is Dent?"

CHAPTER 52

SPOONIES

Pancake Pantry was the best breakfast spot in all of Nashville. You would think it was the only one. The line was wrapped around the block every day of every week. It was enough to give all the empty restaurants on the block a complex. Inside, the tables were full, the waitresses overworked. Dent and Charlie sat in a back booth half awake, their plates half-eaten. He had a smorgasbord of cholesterol. She had a muffin. He popped a couple heart pills in his mouth.

"You know, you wouldn't need that medicine if you ate better."

"I thought that's what it's for, so I *can* eat it."

She shook her head with a chuckle as a frumpy waitress in a yellow apron dropped a newspaper on the table. Hair in a bun and frown on her face, she had an opinion on everything.

"This what ya want?" she barked.

It was *The New York Times*. The front page read "#1 KILLER TAKES DOCTOR #6."

The byline read: By Lyle Packard

"Yeah," said Dent chagrinned.

"Helluva way for Nashville to make the front page of that liberal rag, ain't it?"

With that, she wobbled off. How conservatives convinced the working class they were on their side, Dent would never know. Charlie scanned the article.

"Wow. How does he get it all so fast?" she asked implying Dent may have been Pac-man's source.

"How does anyone get anything so fast nowadays?" Dent replied.

The stoner girls had called 911 from their cell phone within ninety seconds of finding the body in the bathtub. Police responded within seven minutes and the FBI were contacted immediately. By 4:00 a.m., Dent and Charlie and a federal forensic team were en route to the mount, collecting evidence Dent knew would go nowhere. Livingston was too clever, too creative, too determined to allow the feds to find what they were looking for. They already had his name and photo for God's sake and still couldn't get a bead on him. He was a ghost.

"He's a spoonie," Charlie muttered, stirring her spoon in her creamed coffee.

"What?" asked Dent.

"That's what they call them."

"A spoonie? What's a spoonie?"

"It's a word they use. The chronically ill. How they keep track of their energy each day."

"That's a thing," said Dent.

Charlie needed to explain. "Let's say you begin each day with ten spoons. If you go to the store, and do your laundry, and you're sick, that may take all your spoons. You're spoon-less. Done for the day."

"And you know this . . .?" asked Dent.

"My granny was sick. For a long time. Nobody could help her. No doctors. She couldn't even move. She was bedridden for years. Rheumatoid arthritis, before they knew what do with it."

"You feel sorry for him," concluded Dent.

"Not sorry. Understanding."

"You saw what he did. In Oregon. Utah. Here."

"He's crazy. That's for certain. I'm just saying . . . something made him that way."

Dent weighed her words, her expression, her posture.

"It's common, you know. For investigators to build a rapport with people they're hunting. Especially female investigators."

She nodded. She knew. And still, she persisted.

"What would you do?" she said, looking him in the eye. "If you were so sick for so long and no one could make you better? And some of those you trusted most made you worse?"

Dent reflected before answering. "I don't know."

And that was her point. But he had his.

"I do know . . . this guy . . . he's got it coming. One way or another. I hope it's us that takes him down . . . but if not . . . something's gonna get him . . . somehow . . . somewhere. You can't dance with the devil and not get burned," said Dent.

"Maybe," said Charlie. "He's smart though. He put time into this, thought, money, effort. I mean, how did he even know we would go after the man in the hoodie. The van from Florida. The house in Pikesville. He knows more about us than we do him."

"Want some more coffee, honey?" said the wobbly waitress passing by with the pot.

Charlie shook her head gently.

"Just the check," said Dent noticing patrons noticing him.

"My way works too, you know," said Charlie.

"Your way."

"You get in the dark side of their heads. I get in the light."

The notion never even occurred to him.

"What if there is no light?"

She smiled as though it were obvious.

"There's always light, Dent. You just have to look for it."

CHAPTER 53

THE GROCERY

A squeaky wheel rolled across the tile floor of Publix store 804. There were over 1,300 of them now infesting the southeast. And no matter the city, county, or state, each one seemed the same. The same green aprons on the same cheery staff. The same fresh produce from the same steady suppliers. The same fluorescent lights shining on the same linoleum aisles. Truth was, that was what people paid for—the consistency. They wanted—no, needed—to know no matter what store they were in, they could find the same ingredients in the same products in virtually the same spots. It was a common ploy by mass marketers to create a uniform experience that gave shoppers a shred of certainty in an uncertain world. When families and friends and health and weather could twist and turn at the drop of a hat, Publix would be there for you—just the way it always was.

Livingston developed a love/hate relationship with food the day his illness began. So, any foray into the grocery was met with trepidation. When his immune system was compromised by toxic mold, it retaliated by thinking everything under the sun was attacking it. Chicken? *Intruder.* Chocolate? *Intruder.* Broccoli? *Intruder.* Soon, his body not only reacted to every food he ate, but every nutrient too. Vitamin A? *Criminal.* Vitamin C? *Outlaw.* Zinc, iron, thiamine? *Evil.* Each entrant to the intestinal tract was met with an army of resistance waging a battle of monumental proportions, which not only dismissed anything of value, but made him feel awful. Eating sugar was like taking poison. Swallowing salt, shooting cyanide. And as any nutritionist knows, nearly everything sold on shelves or served in restaurants possessed, or quickly descended into, one or the other.

The remedy, it was said, was to deny yourself of anything that fell into those food groups, which, of course, made the South Beach Diet look like happy hour at the Cheesecake Factory. Cauliflower, tofu, quinoa, white rice, and egg whites were all staples. Foods so bland and boring, they would readily be cast into a dining room wall by any sane child. And that was just for starters. Even those foods eaten on a regular basis could fall into the opponent's camp by showing up too often in the digestive tract. So even approved foods had to be rotated to not alarm the body. Cauliflower on Mondays. Tofu on Tuesdays. And so on. It was enough to drive anyone crazy—if they weren't already. And that was how Livingston lived—for years. Rotating what amounted to be a diet of cardboard, day in and day out, hoping his intestines would not retaliate, regurgitate, and make him feel worse than the mold baked into his bones already did.

The compromised immune system paid little mind to the route through which toxins invaded. Inhalation was just as powerful, if not more so, than digestion, as was skin absorption. Over the years, Livingston had learned the hard way to steer clear of soaps and shampoos, colognes and deodorants, anything that possessed something resembling a chemical.

Try as he might, it was damn near impossible for him to get through a grocery without a whiff of the monsters on the detergent aisle. That's why he always held his breath around chemicals. When his health was at its worst, he couldn't make it past the Clorox without stumbling dizzily into the Tide and crashing into the Pine-Sol. The place was a virtual pinball machine of toxic militia. So, even now that his body was stronger, he still avoided the cleaning aisle at all costs. Except for days like today. He filled his cart to the brim with enough cleansers to spitshine an army base. Food in front, poisons in back, divided by separate plastic baskets. The young girl at the register almost didn't recognize him.

"Mr. Jenkins!" she exclaimed. "My word. Spring cleaning?"

As usual, Livingston used a pseudonym. How he kept them all straight was a testament to his ability to juggle multiple characters in a story.

"It's not for me," he said flatly, glancing to her tag to remind him of her name. It read Cindy, but he knew she preferred Cynthia. Girls over boys. And Coke over Pepsi.

"I'm sorry," she said. "I shouldn't have asked."

There were strict rules in place at grocery chains not to comment or criticize anyone for the products they laid on the conveyor belt. Donut jokes for the obese or string beans for the spindly could send patrons fleeing to nearby competitors.

"It's okay," he said with an ample sigh. "They're for my mom."

CHAPTER 54

MOM

Daisy Dog ran across the linoleum floor, her little black nails clicking on tile like the Rockettes. With not a care in the world, the fluffy Cavachon hopped on the couch, the chair, and the ottoman before coming to a rest on her cozy blanket beside her stuffed animals before her large window. At ten pounds, twelve ounces, it was obvious this little furball ran the roost.

"Daisy!" exclaimed Donna Livingston as though Daisy had done something she had not been doing every day for the last nine years of her life. "You better mind your manners. Martin will be here soon!"

Despite being left by her husband, battling diabetes most of her life, and overcoming cancer, loud-and-proud Donna maintained the most jovial of airs. Some said it was her youthful spirit at seventy. Others, onset dementia. Either way, Donna was the happiest of clams this side of the intercoastal waterway. A fastidious clean freak, she always had a broom or brush in hand, sweeping and scrubbing every inch of her humble ranch home to keep it spic-and-span.

"We have to tidy up or we'll be in trouble."

Daisy erupted in high-pitched barks that could shatter glass as a black Ram pickup truck rumbled into the drive.

"What is it?"

Daisy spun from her bed and ran to the kitchen door, twirling with excitement.

In the driveway, Livingston climbed from the truck.

"Hi, honey!" said Donna from the open kitchen door.

"Hi, Mom," said Livingston.

Even serial killers had mothers who loved them.

"Hi, Daisy," he said, leaning to pet her as she leapt.

"Got a new one, huh?" Donna said eyeing his shiny truck.

"Yeah, you know. I like to mix it up."

"You sure do. I can't keep up!"

Perks of being a screenwriter, she thought. Necessity of being on the lam, Livingston knew. But Mom didn't need to know his business. He bent into the backseat to grab the groceries he picked up for her on the way over—his usual Sunday ritual.

"Want a hand?" Donna always asked.

"Nah, I got it," Livingston always replied.

Donna called out to Daisy doing circles. "C'mon Daisy, let's go inside."

Per routine, the feds requested local police swing by Momma Livingston's home the week prior, to question her, but the young rookies on duty quickly concluded from her tangential ramblings that she was cuckoo for Cocoa Puffs and reported nothing of value.

"How's that girlfriend of yours?" Donna said as she put away her Clorox.

"She's not my girlfriend, Mom."

"You brought her home for Christmas."

"One time. And she's Jewish."

"I thought you were cute together."

"Yeah, well, she makes everything cute."

"You should marry her."

"I'm not sure I'm the marrying type."

"Well, maybe you should ask her that."

"I'm not sure *she's* the marrying type."

There was no doubt Donna wanted her son to be happy. But what she thought would make him happy—a wife, a child, a family—was something that would make her happy too.

"Be nice to have the pitter-patter of little feet around here," she said with a wink.

He humored her as southern sons were expected to do. Not that you could call Florida the *South*. It was its own planet. A peculiar world that led the country in arrests of tax evaders and psychopaths. How they all found their way to the same place was beyond comprehension. It must have been something in the water—water Livingston had been drinking since childhood.

"She took such good care of you when you were sick, you know. She would do anything for you."

Livingston knew his mom was right. He had dated more than his share of women in his life. Black and white. Young and old. Doctors and lawyers, waitresses and wanderers. Some wanted him for his money. Some for his body. Some for his mind. But only one wanted him for everything.

"How the two of you do long distance is beyond me. Maybe if you were in the same state for more than a week at a time, you could make it work!"

"She's got a job to do, Mom."

"You ask me? Her job should be taking care of you."

Daisy Dog barked as though she agreed. Livingston frowned.

"Maybe if you bought her a diamond ring for Christmas instead of a diamond necklace, she would be."

CHAPTER 55

THE PENDANT

Shayna sat at her desk hacking away at her computer keyboard, her diamond pendant swinging from the gold necklace in her ample cleavage. Since she was tucked away in a cube, her monitors were not easily readable by passersby. Her eyes darted left and right as she scoured the FBI surveillance system on her screens for what exactly the Tennessee office was doing today. And Texas. And Arizona. And Utah. She had all the moves of all the agents on the case at her fingertips. It was, in fact, her job to coordinate their efforts. Little did anyone know, she was doing it first and foremost for the man they were seeking. And steering the rest of the federal posse on a wild goose chase.

Suddenly, she felt eyes upon her. She stopped typing and turned. Standing six feet behind her was Sanjay. Something about him seemed different. He no longer looked apologetic. He looked apoplectic. Charlie's questions about how Livingston knew more about the bureau than the bureau did him got Dent thinking. And one question still plagued him: *Who would have had the means and grounds for leaking his own identity to the press?* He spoke with Sanjay by phone in the morning. Sanjay did some research, combing the network, tracking searches, files, codes, access. Until he was convinced of the horrible truth.

"It was you," he said.

"What?" she asked.

"You know what."

Her eyes darted left and right, seeing several agents form a perimeter around the room, blocking the exits to the elevator and stairs.

"What's going on?" she asked with her doe eyes.

Sanjay began trembling with fury.

"You helped him. He killed FBI agents! How could you?"

The jig was up, and she knew it.

"It's . . . complicated," she said.

Shayna met Livingston in the waiting room at the Environmental Health Clinic in Dallas years earlier. She was there with her father who was suffering from chronic fatigue syndrome. The doctors promised to help him. They could not. But they gladly took his money, his hope, and ultimately his life, Shayna thought. Bitter with resentment, she and Livingston bonded. She was a bit too young for him but had an unhealthy relationship with her father, which lead to unhealthy relationships with men, which lead to Livingston. They shared one uncanny thing in common: They both wished horrible suffering to doctors that did patients wrong. That gave birth to an idea, a plan, and a start date. Along the way, they genuinely fell in love. Donna Livingston was right. There was nothing Shayna Gold wouldn't do for her son, including sleep with other men to achieve their goal.

"There's no way out," said Sanjay. "You're surrounded."

His emotions were all in a tussle. He felt betrayed, not just as a coworker but as an almost-lover. He knew she used him. And that made him feel like an idiot. He trusted her, and that allowed her access to everything. *What did she know? What did she tell Livingston? And when?*

Shayna ran. Not that there was anywhere really to go on the fifth floor of the federal building. Still, she was determined to escape. Given her options, she headed toward the stairs blocked by a single female agent not much taller than her. Little did she know, the young Hispanic agent had trained in her hometown of Albuquerque with the great Holly Holm, the veteran MMA fighter who cleaned Ronda Rousey's clock a minute into the second round in the UFC bantamweight championship. Executing the patented stick and move, the agent easily sidestepped Shayna with her hand outstretched and deftly landed a blow to the chin. The agent was surprised to find that Shayna had simultaneously plunged a letter opener into her gut as she passed. The woman clutched her stomach, gasped once, spit some mucus, and dropped to her knees, eyes wide. The other agents slowed, beginning to comprehend exactly what happened. Never in their Quantico training or water cooler dreams had they suspected their own office would become a battleground, let alone instigated by one of their own.

Bam! Shayna plunged shoulder first into the exit door and disappeared into the stairwell.

Dent was notified of the situation at hand and wondered what in good God's name HR had been smoking when they hired the girl. *Were there not psychiatric protocols in place to root out whack jobs?* Then again, they hired him. Nevertheless, she was in the house. And Dent knew if they could get her to talk, they could find Livingston. *Just take her alive.*

A distressed secretary hiding under her desk anointed with Hello Kitty stickers called 911. The police dispatcher promptly notified her supervisor on duty who quickly notified his regional commander who immediately notified emergency field operations for the local FBI. The irony was the whole telephone tango led back to an office two floors beneath them.

A quick, standard stairwell clearance by armed agents between the first and fifth floors yielded nothing but a bedraggled janitor sneaking a cig break, so the agents began flooding the office floors.

"Move, move, move!" Guns drawn, held high, they cornered left and right as trained, searching through the bustling halls and offices and meeting rooms.

"Clear, clear, clear!" they announced, frightening the daylights out of lifelong agency administrators who had never set foot on a gun range. But Shayna was nowhere to be found. They assumed she would head downstairs to flee the building. But they were wrong.

Wham! Shayna drove her shoulder into the exit door to the roof of the building. But it wouldn't budge. Over and over, she flung her 120 pounds into the steel door. But it was no use. It could withstand the charge of an elephant. No one without a master key was getting out there.

"She's up here!" she heard from below. Her banging of the door had alerted a SWAT member climbing the stairs to the higher floors. Her pulse quickened. Her eyes darted.

What could she do?

CHAPTER 56

THE BIRD

The sixth floor of the Los Angeles Federal Building housed the local forecast center for the US Weather Service. The thinking was from this high up, they could make an educated guess at the area weather by looking out the window in case their gazillion dollars of technology failed. Meteorologists were a quirky group to say the least. Taught and trained fear and theory, they were the go-betweens between the public and God. Maybe that's partially the reason they took to the upper floor of the building as well. So they didn't have to face the constant scrutiny of disgruntled government workers whose kids' birthday parties got rained out over the weekend.

Shayna twisted into the sixth floor lobby like the Tasmanian Devil, blowing past the receptionist in a flurry.

"Excuse me, miss! You can't . . . ." was all the young woman could muster before Shayna swirled through the opening door past a nerdy intern in a polka-dot tie heading for the elevator.

"Who was that?" he muttered. The receptionist didn't know. "Should we call security?" A moment later, a fire alarm sounded through the weather service offices. Heads churned left and right wondering what was going on. *Was there a fire? Was there a bomb? Was this a drill?* And then they saw her.

Darting through the room like a caged animal, Shayna's heart beat a mile a minute. No one was quite sure what to do. Until her face appeared on one of the umpteenth television screens mounted on the north wall of the control center. The caption read "Number 1 Killer accomplice loose." A big Black girl with bouffant curls and flannel jacket screamed when she made the connection. Now people were running for the exit. Shayna bolted for the only room that was not occupied—*the conference room*. She slammed the door, rattling the glass, and wedged a heavy rolling chair under the handle with practiced ease. Curious evacuees peered in at her like a zoo exhibit. Slowly, Shayna pulled a wad of gum from her mouth and placed it on the table. She punched the speakerphone on the conference table and dialed a number far away. Paced back and forth with the lights of LA glittering behind her. Until a familiar voice answered, booming through the room.

"Baby" was all Livingston said. But it was enough to put her mind at ease. He had that effect on her.

"Honey" was all she said in response. And it was salve to his soul.

"I miss you."

"I miss you too."

"We're almost done with this," he said.

"I know," she said. "I can't wait."

"We'll be together soon. Just like we planned."

Boom! The doors from the lobby crushed open and a battalion of SWAT team members in black tactical gear flooded in carrying AR15s, locked, loaded, with fingers on the triggers. Quickly, they honed in on Shayna across the office behind the conference room glass.

"Down! Down! Down!" they shouted to the startled office staff, more frightened by the sight of the masked commandos than the little girl on the phone.

"I love you, honey," she said, tears welling in her eyes.

"I love you too, baby," he replied.

It was the sweetest thing, this love between psychopaths. It just affirmed everything their parents told them when they wondered if anyone would ever love them. *There's someone for everyone.*

The moment Sanjay stepped through the door, the temperature changed in the room.

"Um, do we have to . . . ?" he asked, appealing to the SWAT commander to have his team lower their guns. The commander looked at him like he was crazy too.

"Just . . . please . . ." said Sanjay, his eyes glued on Shayna behind the glass.

Convinced the target was confined, the commando huffed a breath and lowered his rifle.

"Stand down," he said, squelching into his headset. Fanning out, his men reluctantly complied, dropping the points of their guns to eight o'clock position. But their eyes stayed glued on Shayna.

"If I don't make it . . ." Shayna said into the speakerphone.

"You'll make it," said Livingston.

"If I don't . . . I just want you to know . . . that I believed in what we were doing. That we were making a difference. That we would stop . . . suffering."

Seeing her on the phone, the commander nodded to his communications officer who swung to the end of the room where the phone feed connected. Two others moved for the door to the room and jimmied the jam.

"You'll make it!" said Livingston more adamantly.

Sanjay and the other team members stepped closer. Shayna's pulse rose. She didn't have the heart to admit to her love that she had failed him. Failed her father. Failed mankind.

"I'm sorry . . ." she said as . . . *CLICK*. The line went dead, cut by the communications man. Not even the dignity of a dial tone remained. *Just. Dead. Silence.*

Until *bam-bam-bam!* Sanjay knocked on the glass breaking Shayna from her trance.

"Shayna! Let us in!"

She looked for options, but there were none. Just the table, twelve chairs, a video screen, a broken phone, and the view of the Los Angeles skyline.

"Shayna! Let us in. They'll break in. You know that!"

But she would never acquiesce. It wasn't in her DNA. And now, there was only one thing left to do. In one fell swoop, she picked up a conference chair and spun, slinging it crashing through the glass and into the sky.

"Shayna!" cried Sanjay.

The SWAT team raised their guns, unsure exactly why.

"Don't move!" shouted one. "Freeze!" said another. Two tried to crack the door open. But Shayna paid no mind. Instead, she simply climbed onto the air conditioning unit mounted on the wall beneath the open window. The Santa Ana winds blew in around her, whipping her short hair about her flushed face, her adrenaline pumping like a freight train.

"Shayna!" pleaded Sanjay. "We can talk this out!"

But the time for talking was over. She looked down at the street as pedestrians scattered.

Bam! The team members almost had the door open.

"C'mon!" Sanjay yelled to them.

Shayna looked Sanjay straight in the eye, held her arms wide prepared to fly.

"I'm sorry," she said. "I never meant to hurt you."

Bam! The door burst open just as . . . Shayna leaned backward and fell into the sky.

"Noooooo!" yelled Sanjay, his eyes ripped with horror.

Shayna, on the other hand, was finally at peace, soaring through the air like a bird. The thrill of the six-story fall no doubt giving her the greatest orgasm of her whole short life. That is, right until her body hit the roof of a Winnebago parked on the street below, wrinkling the metal, shattering the windows, and triggering the deafening alarm.

Later that night, Livingston snapped awake in a cold sweat in his warm bed. He knew something was wrong the minute the line went dead. He reached his large hand across the empty sheets where she once laid and gripped them tightly in his fist. He missed her terribly, and it showed in his eyes. He could still see her lying beside him with her radiant smile, sparkling eyes, and voluptuous chest. He had flashes of them making love, making breakfast, making plans to incinerate physicians. What they shared was an uncommon and unspeakable bond. *A drive to kill.* That's what got him out of bed, on his feet, and out the door before sunrise. He knew he had a mission to complete. If not for him, for her. Soon he would learn from the news of an unnamed woman who fell to her death in Los Angeles, and it would light a fire in him that could not be extinguished.

CHAPTER 57

ATLANTA

Six Atlanta police cruisers screeched into a small parking lot at full-tilt, lights swirling, lights flashing, like they were auditioning for an episode of *Cops*. The tiny suburb of Dunwoody, Georgia had its share of crime on the outskirts of the ATL, but catching a real-life serial killer was one for the books. The chiropractic office of Dr. Albury Smith was the last place Shayna had pulled up on her computer before she did a back dive out the federal building sixth floor window. And the last place Martin Livingston had sought medical care before he got better.

Once the infection was bored from his bones by enough antifungals to kill a small horse in Nashville, Livingston had to heal the rest of him. If nothing else, so he could get revenge on those that made him sicker. Ironically, it became the driving force for him to get well. Diligent research produced a maverick of a medic with an odd little chiropractic office hidden behind the Mad Italian Sub Shop. What Dr. Smith did from this unassuming place was nothing short of miraculous. Where other doctors stopped, he began using a broad spectrum of innovative and noninvasive holistic therapies. Light, color, sound, smell, vibration, acupuncture, energetic, ultrasonic, electromagnetic, ancestral, moxa, crystals, stones, herbs, supplements, nutrition, reflexology, craniosacral, and, last but not least, the good Lord Almighty.

A staunchly religious man, Doctor Smith would often pray over his patients at the end of his sessions, calling on God, Jesus, the Holy Spirit, and whoever else might be listening to use him as a conduit for healing. It might have seemed strange to those trying to shake an ankle injury, but if you were sick for years and no one else could help you, it was a much-needed balm. Frankly, it gave patients hope where there was none.

A little old woman with a hunched back, grey hair, and gaunt face came hurtling out of Dr. Smith's office into the parking lot, stunning the officers.

They quickly drew their guns, and she shrieked with hands high like she had robbed a bank. Betty was her name, and she was scared out of her cotton-picking mind.

"Don't shoot! Don't shoot!"

The cops weren't sure what to think.

"I'm unarmed!"

A tall officer in charge holstered his gun and stepped forward to escort her to safety behind his patrol car.

"Ma'am, it's okay, are you hurt?"

"No, I'm fine!" She breathed heavily.

"Is anyone hurt inside?"

"No, I'm the only one there."

Puzzled, the officer probed more and sent a detail inside to clear the space. What they learned was that Dr. Smith was on a camping trip with his two young sons to Cooper Creek Campground in the North Georgia Mountains and that there had been no sign of Livingston anywhere. She just didn't know how to act when a handful of police cars surrounded her place of business, and the calls their office received from authorities the prior week had her on, well, edge. Either that or she was hitting the supplements a tad too much herself.

Missing all the fun was Dent and Charlie. They had hoped to be there to secure the doctor but could not be. They were where most of Atlanta was when they were in a hurry—stuck in traffic. Nestled side by side in the backseat of a standard bureau-issued Suburban, they were lost somewhere on the twelve-lane not-so superhighway that surrounded the city called 285.

A phone rang in Dent's coat pocket with the *Nightstalker* theme song. He pulled it out. The phone was pink. The caller's prefix 407. The fed in the front eyed him oddly.

"It's not mine," said Dent.

Dent had told Sanjay to overnight Shayna's cell phone to him in Nashville before they left the Holiday Inn that morning. On it was a list of calls from all over the country, including eighty-seven in the last few months from one number in Florida. Dent could have called it himself but knew that would not have had the same effect. Instead, he waited for Livingston to call Shayna in order to surprise him. It had been hours since Livingston and Shayna were cut off, and it troubled him that he could not get through to her. But he didn't call this time. He FaceTimed.

Dent grinned. Pressed answer. And peered into the phone. "Mr. Livingston," he said.

On the other end of the line *was* Livingston. To say he was stunned to see Dent's grizzled mug would be an understatement. "Oh. Well, hello," he said. He had missed a few days' shave himself. And, also, sat in a vehicle. Only his was parked.

"You look younger in your photos."

"Agent McCreary. You look thinner in yours."

Dent smiled. This was going to be fun.

"Sorry, we missed you in Nashville."

"I had to run. I'm sure you understand."

"Don't worry. We'll catch up to you."

"Where's Shayna?" asked Livingston point blank.

"She had an accident."

The LA office had done its best to keep her plummet under wraps, but it was nearly impossible with social media. Livingston assumed she was dead.

"She was a good girl," he said.

"That's not what my IT man says."

"He was very helpful," said Livingston.

There were few things as exhilarating for a criminal mind expert than to be speaking with a serial killer, except perhaps for a serial killer to be talking with the investigator hunting him. Their words were a verbal ballet of incomparable talent. Charlie sat wide-eyed beside Dent, watching and learning.

"He says you're in Atlanta. We should get together while we're both in town."

"Love to, but I have work to do," said Livingston.

"You know what they say . . . 'all work and no play . . .' " said Dent.

"You're not my type."

"You got to get to know me."

"I have."

The words didn't surprise Dent but sent a chill down Charlie's spine.

Livingston suddenly looked up from his phone.

"This has been fun, but I'm afraid I have to go now."

"I'll see you around," said Dent pointedly.

"Not if I see you first."

Livingston hung up the phone with a *click*.

Dent punched the seat angrily. He was hoping to get more from him than he did.

Livingston peered through the windshield of his truck, seeing what he had been waiting for. Trudging out the front door of a children's daycare with an Asian teacher was . . . Riley. This was where she attended when she stayed with *Tiny Daddy*. And just one of the bits of information Shayna provided Livingston before her untimely demise.

Riley and her teacher were met at the chain-link fence by her father. Tim was a spindly man born with a stick up his ass. He ushered Riley into the back of his pickup truck impatiently and fastened her firmly in her car seat. Out here in Lawrenceville, Georgia there was no shortage of pickup trucks, so Livingston fit right in. Tim started his truck. So, Livingston started his too. As Tim pulled past the row of other trucks of every color and creed . . . Livingston followed.

CHAPTER 58

THE HIGHWAY

Sanjay spent a good part of the day driving the porcelain bus in the office bathroom. Knowing the first girl he had loved in a while was dead was enough to break his heart. Seeing her plunge out the window before his very eyes was enough to break every other organ in his body. Coworkers found him in the back stall in a ball of sweat, tears, and excrement. He had a job to do. And fortunately, or unfortunately for him, no one was as good at it as him.

After a quick bum bath, can of Red Bull, and gym bag makeover, Sanjay was back at his desk doing what he did best. Frankly, having something to do was probably the best thing for him. Working a mile a minute on his computer mainframe, he traced Livingston's phone. As planned, Dent kept him on the line long enough to pinpoint a location. What Sanjay saw on the digital map turned him pale.

"Oh no, oh no, oh no."

Sanjay phoned Dent immediately. They chatted for only seconds before Dent yelled to the driver from the backseat.

"Stop the car!"

The FBI agent looked up in his rearview mirror.

"We're in the middle of the freeway."

"Stop the damn car!"

It wasn't asking much since they were in stop-and-go traffic. The agent hit the brakes. Dent unbuckled his seatbelt.

"What are you doing?" asked Charlie.

"He was at the daycare!"

She looked at him confused.

"Riley! Her father lives here. Shayna knew that. Livingston knows that."

Charlie paled. "Oh my God." She knew Riley meant more to Dent than anything. "What can I do?"

"Find the doctor," he said.

She nodded. "Where are you going?"

"East."

Dent jumped the white wall in the middle of the freeway, his boots landing in the emergency lane. Although traffic was going nowhere fast to the west, cars and trucks were zipping by to the east. Wind whipped around him as they roared past. He put out his hands to stop someone, anyone driving past. But no one was stopping for a lunatic in the middle of the freeway waving his arms like a madman. Honking horns seared his ears as they zoomed by. Finally, Dent had enough. He drew his weapon and stepped into the fast lane, pointing it at the next poor bastard coming down the pike. It was a young punk on a Kawasaki Ninja doing ninety miles an hour. His eyes blew wide behind his mask seeing Dent standing ahead of him with his gun pointed. He hit the brakes and whipped the steering, shrieking across the pavement until coming to a tire-smoking halt inches from Dent.

"Get off," said Dent.

The kid did, frightened out of his gourd.

In an instant, Dent mounted the bike, gunned the engine, and took off toward Riley.

Back in LA, Sanjay's eyes lit up seeing Dent's tracker go from ten miles per hour west to a hundred miles per hour east. He nearly spit up his coffee.

"Um, Agent . . . Dent . . . are you . . . where are you?"

On the bike, whipping down the emergency lane with reckless abandon and fire in his eyes, Dent shouted into his earpiece.

"Where are they?!"

"What?"

"Livingston! Where is he?!"

Getting his bearings, Sanjay quickly locked in on Livingston's phone GPS turning onto a main thoroughfare northeast of the freeway Dent was on.

"Um . . . he's . . . six minutes away . . . well, at your speed . . . five."

VROOM! Dent whizzed off down the emergency lane balls to the wall. Sanjay talked him off the exit and through skidding turns. On the bureau's overhead video monitors, Sanjay had city cameras follow the pursuit—blowing through red lights, hopping on sidewalks, swerving through pedestrians. Cars crashing in his wake, the video feed started to earn a crowd.

"Who is that?" one agent asked.

"Dent," said another.

More agents stepped into the bullpen, placing odds.

"Fifty bucks says he buys a telephone pole."

"Hundred says he lays it down."

Wads of cash hit a desk like a blackjack table in Atlantic City. Drawn by the commotion, SAC Parker stepped from his office too.

"Go—go—go!" shouted a few agents.

"No—no—no!" shouted others.

"Shut up!" belted Sanjay.

He felt like he was playing a video game online and his mother was barking suggestions. On his headset, he was calling the turns quicker now as Dent's blue dot on the screen approached Livingston's red dot.

"Whoa—whoa—whoa! Slow down. You're about to turn," said Sanjay. "Next light, next light! Turn right, turn right!"

Dent hit the brakes, cranked the steering, and smoked the wheels around a curve, just missing a postal truck. A few of the crowd tensed at the sight.

"He should be coming up! Right in front of you! On the right! He's stopping! He's stopping!"

Zooming through a neighborhood, Dent spied a lone black pickup truck turning off the road ahead into a gated parking garage beneath a three-story building. He downshifted, braked, turned, and flew through the automatic gate before it closed.

In the bureau bullpen, the crowd moaned, unable to see what transpired once he left the city streets.

Going too fast to stop in the garage, Dent laid the bike down on the smooth cement and tumbled off as the Ninja crashed into a parked Subaru, sending metal clunking and clattering. After several seconds, he rose painfully to his feet, drew his gun, and leveled it at the man stepping from the pickup truck in the parking space at the end of the garage.

"Don't move!" Dent managed.

The man's eyes went wide. He was Black. So was his son. And both were scared shitless.

"Don't shoot! Please!" said the man.

Limping forward, Dent dumped a breath and lowered his gun.

"Ahhhhhhh!" he yelled with frustration.

The little boy ran into his daddy's arms.

"Please," said the man.

Dent shook his head. "It's okay. I'm a cop."

Stepping slowly closer, Dent peered into the back of the man's truck. Lying all by its lonesome was Livingston's cell phone. He had tossed it into the truck bed as he passed it leaving the daycare, sending Dent and company on a wild goose chase.

"Shit."

Now there was no telling where Livingston had gone.

CHAPTER 59

THE CAMPGROUND

A thousand stars shined in the dark sky over the Blue Ridge Mountains. Huddled around a campfire in a clearing of tall oaks sat Doctor Smith and another chubby dad with a Boy Scout troop of ten. Four green tents dotted the perimeter of the campsite, a white transport van and silver pickup truck sat in the distance.

Smith was a goodhearted fella with a strong, biblical spine and a hearty helping of ethics. So much so, he insisted the ghost stories told were PG. No one would get beheaded, no axes flying, no bloodshed of any sort. To ensure no one wet the bed that night, he was doing the storytelling himself.

"It had been hours and there was no sign of the boys. The storm was coming in and the old park ranger refused to look for them. 'Why not?' asked their worried mother. 'Are there bears up there?' 'No,' said the ranger. 'Something worse!' "

Light from the fire danced around the circle, illuminating the enraptured young faces in a flickering glow.

"The mother trembled," said Smith.

"What could be worse than bears?"

"Sasquatch!" he belted.

In the nearby woods, a branch broke. The kids tensed.

"Surely, there's no such thing!" continued Smith.

" 'Oh, you're not from around here. You don't know!' "

Another branch broke. This time, closer. The kids tightened, peered into the dark woods around them.

"People around here don't like to talk about it," he said.

Slowly the wind kicked up in the woods around them.

" 'Well, what are we supposed to do?' pleaded the mother."

The winds howled louder, blowing trees back and forth.

" 'Nothing.' said the ranger. 'It's too late!' "

With that, a deafening roar echoed from above, a bright light sprayed down upon them, and a booming voice shouted out.

"FBI! Don't move!"

A helicopter hovered over them. From out of the woods came a dozen FBI agents in blue parkas with yellow inscriptions.

A chorus of "FBI! FBI! Nobody move!" sounded from all sides. The scouts stirred terrified, unsure of what to do. In the middle of the pack of feds was Charlie, weapon drawn but at her side. She quickly assessed the situation, spied Doctor Smith, the other father, and no sign of Livingston anywhere.

"Dr. Smith?" she shouted.

He nodded with worry. "What's going on? What's this all about?"

She showed him her badge. "Agent Charlie Norris, FBI. Come with me, please."

Fifteen minutes later, the chopper was gone, agents had secured the premises, and the kids were loading their gear into the van to go home. Charlie stood with Smith beside his truck.

"Sorry about all this," she said.

"Figured we'd be safe up here," Smith replied.

"We can't be too careful. Not until this man is caught."

He nodded with understanding.

"Well, now we have a whole new story to tell!"

Charlie smiled. She had joined the bureau to save a life. And now she felt she had. Doctor Smith was the first doctor on Livingston's list they were able to get to before Livingston did.

Unfortunately, that's what Livingston anticipated.

CHAPTER 60

TINY DADDY

All was quiet in the sleepy neighborhood of Mulberry Farms. The houses were nothing to write home about, but they were more than adequate—one-story ranches with two-car garages. Yards big enough for a dog. Kitchens big enough for a family.

Lilo & Stitch reruns played on a flat-screen TV in the plain living room of Tiny Daddy's brick house he shared with his skinny wife, Carol. Cuddled on a worn couch in her Captain America T-shirt and her blankie, Riley sat sad and alone, unsure what she had done to be flip-flopped between two crazy parents on opposite sides of the country. In fact, the only semblance of normalcy she had known in her five years of living was Dent. And that was saying something.

She heard Carol moan from the kitchen. "Put the brat to bed yet?"

Riley could hardly call Carol a stepmother—even an evil stepmother. She was barely a mother at all. To her, Riley was but a nuisance, a pest, like a gnat that followed her home from a picnic. Truth was, they hardly associated with one another unless Carol shooed her away from the kitchen. And that was just fine by Riley.

Tiny Daddy was a different story. He had to tend to the gnat to keep his wife at bay, so he was constantly counseling and cajoling his occasional daughter, much to her chagrin. He swept into the living room in a white tank and boxers looking worse for wear. His eyes red, his hair disheveled, it was clear he had been drinking less than usual but more than he should. Lord knew most men would be drinking if they lived with Carol.

"Riley! What'd I tell you? It's time for bed," he slurred. He grabbed the remote and flipped off the TV mid-show, enough to send most children into a rage. But Riley was no ordinary kid. She was an old soul, sent to earth for punishment, she assumed.

"Ooookaaaay," she said dragging herself from the couch.

"Brush your teeth. I'll be there in a minute."

She slinked down the hall, dragging her blankie behind her. After a quick brush on a short stool with her Dora the Explorer toothbrush, she wiped her face with a Simpsons washcloth, peed on a Batman toilet seat, turned off her X-Men light switch, shut her door, and climbed beneath her Transformers bedspread. It seemed everything had to be branded nowadays.

Her bedroom was dark and cold and sparse save a couple Billie Eilish posters, who served as her muse. Nothing like five-year olds worshipping a teenager singing jingles about depression. The furniture was clearly second hand, picked up at garage sales and flea markets to make do for a part-time child on a blue-collar budget. It was a far cry from her life in her upscale mother's condo in swanky Newport Beach.

After a few moments of counting the tiles in the ceiling, headlights washed over her room as a blue van pulled in the driveway. She didn't think anything of it. Deliveries from Amazon and UPS and FedEx were as common as a cold these days.

Knock-knock-knock sounded on the hollow front door.

"Who the hell is that?" she heard Tiny Daddy say.

"I ordered some shoes, I think," answered Carol.

She heard Tiny Daddy's bare feet pad to the living room.

"Little late, isn't it?"

The door peeled open. What happened next happened fast.

"What the . . .?"

Pop-pop! Two bullets erupted from a small gun. A body hit the ground.

Riley's eyes blew open, and she sat up, alert.

Carol padded into the living room. "Tim?" She squelched, and then she *screamed*.

Pop-pop! Two more bullets chirped. Another body dropped.

Then the house fell silent.

Riley's breathing quickened, her eyes darted.

Footsteps of a large man in big boots started slowly down the hall. Riley's eyes focused on the bottom of her door where the light shone. She squeezed her blankie tightly. Her door creaked open, and the unmistakable silhouette of Martin Livingston filled the frame. Riley pretended to be asleep beneath the covers. Livingston ripped them back . . . but found no one there. He peered under the bed, but she wasn't there either. Angry now, he flung open the closet door. Nothing but a collection of old stuffed animals. A cool wind blew over Livingston. He turned to find curtains billowing before an open window. He stepped to the sill and peered out. But saw no sign of Riley outside. Infuriated, he swirled in a huff and left through the door he entered. Then stopped. On second thought, he took two steps back and pushed the door closed. Standing behind it, hands by her sides, eyes cemented shut, was Riley. More scared than she had ever been. But not as much as she had a right to be.

CHAPTER 61

EMPTY NEST

The next day, yellow police tape and slack-jawed bystanders surrounded police cars and coroner wagons outside Tiny Daddy's house. Choppers swirled overhead. Detection dogs sniffed fence lines. It wasn't the kind of neighborhood where houses had security cameras, so there was no video footage to view. The only thing the feds had was a nighttime overhead satellite pic that showed the blue van there one minute and gone the next. It *was* the kind of neighborhood where people knew what gunshots sounded like. There was no confusion about firecrackers or backfires. There were four gunshots. Two pairs. In quick succession. And forensics found them all, embedded in the bodies of Tiny Daddy and Skinny Carol.

Walking through the house was haunting for Dent. Not because of the white chalk around the pooled blood around the dead bodies. He had seen plenty of that. This was the first time he was seeing the "other home" of the "other parent" of his Butterball. He had heard stories from Riley, complaints from Melody, but seeing it firsthand was different. Pushing open the door to her room he knew she had been taking refuge in for years gave him pause. To see the warped bed, the paint-chipped walls, the hand-me-down clothes was enough to make him cry. But the worst part was knowing she was gone because of him. He wiped away his tears before anyone saw them.

And that's when he saw it. Sticking out from beneath Riley's pillow was a Little Mermaid diary.

Melody blew a gasket when she learned of Riley's abduction. But didn't blink an eye over Tim or Carol. *Good riddance,* she thought. She would save a mint on lawyers. But Riley was the only child she would ever have. Granted, she was a mistake in the first place, but now Melody saw her, as most borderlines do, as an extension of herself. An appendage. And nothing was more crushing to Melody than having a piece of herself go missing. She left an important meeting with dot-com financiers in San Francisco to take the call. At least, that's what she said. She assumed that would be enough to convince Dent how seriously she took it all.

"I'll get her back," swore Dent on his cell in the driveway of the house.

"You better! Or I'll sue you for everything you're worth!" That was how Melody saw the world. Not by love or loss. But by pain and profit. Even if that person had nothing to lose. *Click.* Melody hung up on Dent, leaving him more alone than he had ever felt in his whole lonely life.

Charlie was an hour north of Atlanta in the upscale gated community of Chateau Elan, nestled behind iron gates in a high-end resort behind a glorious vineyard. It was a place where rich and famous rappers and athletes hid from their adoring fans. It was also a place the FBI hid informants. Charlie's job was securing Dr. Smith and his family there, making sure there was no way on God's green earth Livingston could get to them. U.S. Marshals with bulletproof vests, semi-automatic weapons, and radio headsets were stationed at every door of the house and entrance and exit of the community.

Pac-man got wind of the story from one of his contacts at the AJC, the acronym for *The Atlanta Journal-Constitution.* When he learned about the child being abducted, he knew the gloves were coming off.

Whatever constraints may have been imposed on Dent by the bureau, the law, or society would become *non esset*. He would run around, over, or through whatever he needed to get Riley back. Pac-man wanted to help. He knew people. He called Dent's cell. But there was no answer. He had already gone underground.

Livingston had the wherewithal to change his mode of transportation but no need. At any one time, there were over thirty thousand blue Amazon vans on America's highways. Being inside a truck that looked like one was the easiest way to hide in plain sight. In the front seat, Livingston wore an Amazon jumpsuit, and hat, and drove the speed limit on I-75 South. Behind the metal door in the back of the truck sat a dog cage fit for a rottweiler but currently housing a terrified Riley—curled in a ball with her blankie wondering what on earth she had possibly done to deserve this.

CHAPTER 62

THE DEAL

In the middle of ATL sat a sprawling green oasis of nearly two hundred acres called Piedmont Park. Residential developers salivated over the prospect of turning its botanical gardens, sprawling lawns, and scenic lakes into cookie-cutter communities, but strict zoning laws prevented them.

With his whole world turned upside down, Dent thought it would be the perfect place to get away and clear his head. It was not. Everywhere he looked, children played on swing sets, licked froyo, and ran into happy parents' arms. *"Daddy! Daddy! Daddy!"* came from every direction. His training taught him how to get into the heads of the worst people on the planet. Now all he could think about was what one of them would do to his favorite person on it. He knew he would need all his faculties to contend with whatever came next. The half-empty bottle of Jack in his hand would not help. He took a seat on a bench beside a lake. A bum slept nearby using a coat as his pillow. It occurred to Dent he was but a motel room away from the same.

As an act of attrition, Dent tossed the bottle in the lake with a splash, waking the bum from his slumber. Next, Dent removed his heart medicine and tossed that in too. Now, the bum sat up. Next, Dent tossed his cigarettes. Whatever he was about to do, he was doing stone-cold sober. The bum leaned forward, wondering how he could salvage the sunken items from the water until he saw Dent's gun in its holster. Then quickly rose and left. All alone, Dent sat on the bench and drew one last item from his coat: Riley's diary. He contemplated whether to open it. It was, after all, private. Even if it wasn't, did he really want to know what was rattling around her head? He put it down on the bench beside him. Then picked it up again. Then put it back down. Until finally concluding there might be something inside that could help lead him to her whereabouts. Something seen. Something heard. He opened it and read. The words, written in five-year-old script with worn crayons and amateur sketches, talked of missing mommy, hating Tiny Daddy, and wishing Big Daddy would come and save her and take her away from it all. No doubt she meant from her ho-hum life in Georgia, but the words rang with heightened meaning now. Tears welled in Dent's eyes knowing he was the only hope for his Butterball making it to age six.

The next morning the bright sun rose over tall buildings of the big city. An early-bird street cop found Dent asleep on the bench, his jacket wrapped around his gun as a pillow.

"Hey pal, you can't sleep here."

Clearly, the cop thought Dent was a bum himself. He didn't have the heart to tell him he was a cop too. Or he was just embarrassed. He checked his phone. His ringer was off. There were thirteen messages. From LA, DC, NY, TX, AZ, GA. But none were from where he wanted. Perhaps it would be a FaceTime again. A lone call with a wild demand from a wanted lunatic. He knew Livingston would call him because he had the one thing he wanted. Finally, his phone *buzzed* with a text. Dent looked down. The area code was 941. Dent took a breath and read the text.

"I want the doctor."

Dent texted back.

"You can't have him."

His phone buzzed again.

"I'll kill the girl."

"No, you won't," texted Dent.

"Why not?"

"I have something else you want."

"What?"

What Dent did next changed everything. It was something all his experience had prepared him for. He texted Livingston a photo. And waited. After a long minute, his phone buzzed again.

On it was only an address:

"13208 State Road 72, Sarasota, FL 34241"

Next came a time:

"Tomorrow Sunset"

Dent closed his phone, rose to his feet, and walked away.

In a dark room in a mysterious place, Livingston ran his fingers over his phone screen. On it was the photo Dent sent—of *Shayna*—in a hospital bed. Broken, bruised, and bandaged, but alive.

CHAPTER 63

THE MORTUARY

The sleepy town of Venice, Florida was seldom confused with its illustrious sister city in Italy. Or its arty stepsister in California. For years, it was nothing but a one-horse town for retirees that eventually became a one-car town that, in the blink of an eye, was invaded by forty thousand snowbirds a year seeking asylum from the ice and snow of the great white north. The city was ill-prepared for the onslaught, and as a result, traffic blanketed its sole thoroughfare, Highway 41.

Hurley & Sons was the mortuary on the north side that buried the dead of the upper crust. Passed down from father to son, business was booming. It wasn't rocket science. *Where better to open a mortuary than a town with a mean age of ninety?*

Jimmy Hurley was the younger of the brothers taking over the company from their father who already had more than enough money to retire. Jimmy had yet to net his own nest egg, however, and was determined to trump his big brother in sales. So, he thought nothing of it when Martin Livingston wandered in off the street, inquiring about children's coffins.

"Don't you worry, Mr. Wilson. We've got the best in town," he said. "Oak, mahogany, cedar, you name it." But Livingston wasn't interested in the best. In fact, he wanted the cheapest.

"We're Jewish," he lied.

Jimmy knew orthodox Jews took no pride in fancy departures. In fact, the humbler, the better. Whether the customer was Jewish or just plain cheap, Jimmy didn't care. There were three other patrons waiting.

"I understand," he said in his compassionate voice. "I've got a few out back."

In the warehouse behind the building, the Hurleys stored hundreds of coffins of every shape and size. If the place went up in smoke, they would lose a mint if not for the insurance policy. Jimmy showed Livingston to a dusty row of coffins in the back stacked five shelves high.

"These should suit your needs," he said.

Nothing is sadder than a child's coffin. Seeing a row of them is enough to melt the steeliest of hearts. But Livingston's eyes lit up at the sight. Finally, he arrived at the cheapest coffin available. It sat off to the side collecting dust with rolls of toilet paper stacked on top. He grinned.

"That will do."

CHAPTER 64

THE AIRPORT

Venice Municipal Airport was a one-strip wonder. Eighty miles south of Tampa, it was easy for planes to slip beneath the radar. Private jets of oil tycoons and biplanes of drug runners skipped about ATC like salmon in the fall. Sadly, the airport was best known for serving as a training ground for the terrorists who flew the planes into the World Trade Center on 9/11.

Today, the control tower and ground crew were notified of a special delivery. A Gulfstream G650, property of the well-respected and highly funded Cedar Sinai Hospital in Los Angeles, had been commandeered for medical transport. On the plane-turned-flying-hospital was reported to be one Shayna Gold, the hottie-tottie who plummeted six floors from the federal building in LA and lived to tell about it. Word was, the Winnebago helped. The roof was not as sturdy as its foreign counterparts, so when Shayna's body hit, the roof caved, breaking her fall. She fractured her tibia, femur, two ribs, wrist, and jaw, and ruptured her spleen. She lost four pints of blood before paramedics arrived. One more and she would have been a goner. The fact that the UCLA Medical Center was three blocks away helped save her life. At least, that's what CNN reported that the AP reported that *The New York Times* reported, courtesy of Lyle Packard. How the young reporter continued getting such scoops on bureau operations, no one knew.

Wheels touched down at 9:35 a.m. in Florida. The jet pulled into Hangar Two. The rear door of the plane motored open, and highly trained medical personnel wheeled out a young woman with a brown bob on a gurney sporting a fashionable oxygen mask and IV pump. She was ushered into the back of an ambulance provided courtesy of the Venice Fire Department. In the hangar stood Dent and Charlie and a team of FBI specialists ready to take action.

"I don't know about this," said Charlie.

"It was your idea," said Dent.

"No, it wasn't."

"You said look for the light. This is the light."

"This is *not* light."

"It's as light as this guy gets."

"This is dark. Deceitful."

"You got any better ideas?"

She did not.

Across the tarmac, beyond the fence, local reporters captured the action from a long lens of an expensive camera atop their News Channel 7 news van before the hangar doors closed.

CHAPTER 65

PREPARATION

Watching the news coverage on his television on the wall of his oceanfront condo a few miles away was Livingston. All this show and tell was for him, and he knew it. He had the one thing the FBI's leading mind hunter wanted, *Riley*. Livingston's faithful Labrador, Frodo, lay at his feet as he whipped up breakfast—hot oatmeal with organic raisins, warm coconut milk, and a pinch of cinnamon. He stirred it into a plastic bowl and placed it on a plastic tray with a plastic cup of orange juice and a plastic spoon. As he descended the stairs into the garage beneath his condo, rock music echoed louder. He opened the door to his garage, revealing his Ram truck parked with a tarp over the bed. On a workbench full of tools sat a Bose Portable Smart Speaker blasting Foghat. He pushed past it to a storage closet in the back of the garage and unlocked the door with a key. Inside the closet crowded with tools and boxes sat the locked dog crate. Inside the crate sat Riley, wrapped in her blankie. Her eyes were cried out and her clothes past dirty. Clearly, the music was to drown out any sounds she might make.

"Ready for breakfast?" asked Livingston.

All she could muster was "Your music sucks."

Inside Hangar Two, Dent and Charlie approached the ambulance where Shayna lay quietly breathing through the oxygen mask.

"How is she?" he asked.

"I'm fine," she said ripping off the mask. "Can I get out of this now?"

In an instant, the young woman sat up and yanked the IV from her arm. Then tugged the bandages and special effects makeup off her face.

"This is the worst job ever!"

Without the mask, it was easy to see this was not Shayna Gold at all. It was a pint-sized actress from LA named Mimi Harrington hired to play the role of Shayna Gold who was actually dead as a doornail. Pretending she was alive was merely a ruse concocted by Dent. Any allusion to the opposite in the press was the sole purporting by Pac-man at Dent's behest.

"Can we get my agent on the phone?" pleaded Mimi.

One of the nurses started dialing. Because she was not a nurse at all. She was Mimi's manager. Mimi tore the bob off her head, revealing short-cropped pink locks, hopped from the gurney in the ambulance, and headed for the bathroom to wash up.

"Actors," grumbled Dent.

The others in the room remained. They still had work to do. They were the Hollywood special effects team who made-over Mimi to look like Shayna and were now prepared to do the same with Charlie. Leading the team was none other than Elenie Horvath, the brunette beauty from Beverly Hills whose husband was the first doctor found in the dryer in the laundry mat.

"Thank you for doing this," said Dent.

"Anything to help catch that bastard."

They exchanged a smile.

"You ready?" Dent asked Charlie.

She nodded unconvincingly.

"I'll be with you the whole time."

"I know."

Dent nodded to Elenie and she and her team began to work.

In Livingston's garage, the big man ripped back the tarp from his truck revealing the wooden coffin, pried open the lid, and looked inside.

It seemed so odd to him. No matter what we do in life, where we go, what we achieve . . . we all end up here. How he had not already was an utter mystery to him. He propped his cell phone on a workbench beside the Bose to make a video of his own. Turned on the camera and pointed it at the coffin. Grabbed a ring of keys off the bench and moved for the closet. Frightened, Riley scrunched into the back of the cage as far as she could.

"Leave me alone," she said.

"Don't you want to get out of there?"

Livingston unlocked the gate and motioned her forward.

"No," she said adamantly.

"Sorry."

Livingston flipped the cage upright, and Riley tumbled to the floor in her blankie. She got up to run, but before she could take two steps, Livingston grabbed her shirt. She screamed out, so he slammed her headfirst into the wall, dazing her. He was, after all, a sociopath. Frodo began to whimper. Livingston shot him a look, shutting him up, and marched to the truck with Riley in his hands. He laid her and her blankie in the coffin. Her glazed eyes tried to focus as . . . the lid came down atop her, turning her world near-black. She cried out and pushed on the lid as . . . *bam-bam-bam!* Livingston hammered long nails through the lid into the side panels. Darker and darker the inside of the coffin grew as the slits were sealed. Louder and louder Riley screamed, but no one could hear her over Foghat.

CHAPTER 66

THE PARK

Myakka River State Park was fifty-eight glorious square miles of wetland and wildlife procured and protected by overworked and underpaid park rangers. Tour guides spoke of hundreds of types of flora and fauna here and there, but the only reason people really visited was to see the alligators. No one knew how many there were, but it was enough that each year, a handful of dogs would get eaten. Legend spoke of a mythic gator measuring fifteen feet long and more than a thousand pounds called Big Bertha. No one had actually seen her, but the prospect of a sighting was enough to get thousands of tourists through the front gates each year at six bucks a pop.

Livingston no doubt chose the park as the meeting point for him and Dent because a) it was only twelve miles from his condo, b) closed at sundown, and c) was isolated from everything. His instructions were clear: *Don't be late. Come alone. Bring Shayna.* One out of three ain't bad, Dent thought. He drove the ambulance through the park's west gate past a couple pensive rangers. They knew something was up but were on a need-to-know basis. The FBI thought it better that way so no one would screw anything up.

By now, Dent and Charlie had seen Livingston's video of Riley being sealed in the coffin and watched as airholes were drilled in the sides for her to breathe. In response, Dent punched a hole through the hangar drywall, threw up his lunch in the bathroom, and sawed off the end of the barrel of a Maverick 88 shotgun to accompany his Glock for the trip.

In the back of the ambulance, Charlie sat on the gurney made over to look like Shayna. Bandages partially covered her face, colored contacts made her blue eyes green, and her hair had been cut and dyed. The icing on the cake was Shayna's diamond pendant hanging about her neck. It was Charlie's first time in the back of an ambulance, and being alone was haunting. All around her were glass cases filled with ointments and solutions. But she also had an IV strung to her arm and a mask over her mouth. Why Livingston wanted Shayna back at all was beyond Dent. Perhaps he wanted to kill her for letting him down. Or giving him up. Maybe it was true love after all. Either way, he didn't give a damn. He just wanted his Butterball back. And he knew this was his one and only chance.

In Charlie's ear was a tiny earpiece with a built-in microphone and enhanced broadcast capability. On the other end of the line was Dent, wearing his earpiece, and Sanjay stationed at his console in the bullpen of HQ in Los Angeles.

"Hey there, Charlie, how you doing?" asked Sanjay.

"Great," she said taking in the tinkling instruments around her as the ambulance motored down the main road.

On the bullpen video screens, Sanjay observed the action via cameras hidden inside and outside the ambulance, on body cams on Dent and Charlie, and via satellite from above.

"Remember, you have the syringe in your cast, your sidearm in your sling," said Sanjay.

Charlie checked both to make sure they were accessible. Her gun was loaded with six in the magazine and one in the chamber. The syringe was loaded with enough propofol to knock out a horse.

"Thank you," she said politely.

Dent chimed in from the front.

"With any luck, she won't have to use either."

On the road, cars whizzed by leaving the park for the day. The river paralleled the road, the trees hung over it.

"You gettin' us?" Dent asked.

The video monitors shook with a bit of static, but that's not what Dent meant. The satellite camera was losing the ambulance in the trees.

"Satcom's in and out. Otherwise, we're pretty good."

Sanjay zoomed out on the monitor, revealing the Myakka River in all its glory. One mile wide and thirty feet deep, it ran seventy miles north to south and emptied into the Gulf of Mexico at Punta Gorda. By now, the bullpen had drawn a crowd of onlookers, including SAC Parker, his white shirt unbuttoned at the top, his sleeves rolled to his elbows.

"SWAT teams are on the perimeter, Dent. Don't be afraid to use 'em," Parker said.

A folksy SWAT team leader named Bart responded on the line.

"Red Team ready, Control. Just say when."

Dent peered into the camera pointed at him in the cab. And all he said was "Thank you," which went to show exactly how serious he took the task at hand. There was no wry retort.

CHAPTER 67

THE OUTPOST

Five miles inside the park stood the park's tourist outpost. It was a small collection of cherry log cabins featuring a souvenir shop with gator toys, gator boots, and gator purses. The snack shack offered gator tots, gator soup, and gator skins. Numbered canoes lined the dock beside a boat house for tourists to float among the gators. A fan boat sat nearby to scout for tardy returners. And a few gators themselves sunbathed on the far bank of the river for good measure.

By the time the ambulance crunched into the gravel parking lot, it was near-empty and near-dark. Just a couple ranger SUVs parked for the night and Livingston's pickup parked on the boat ramp. Its back faced the water, its bed covered with the tarp. As the ambulance neared, Livingston stepped around to the back of the truck. He didn't seem the least bit worried, which worried Dent considerably.

"Got eyes on him," Dent said subtly into his microphone. "But I don't see Riley."

Everyone responded.

"Copy that," said Charlie.

"Copy that," said Sanjay.

"Copy that," said Bart.

And then everyone went radio silent.

As instructed, Dent backed the ambulance onto the ramp, so its rear doors were parallel to the back of the truck. The idea was they would make an even trade. *Riley for Shayna.* Once confirmed, they would swap vehicles and depart. No harm, no foul.

Dent climbed from the ambulance and stepped to the rear. Livingston stood waiting, a good five inches taller than him, and staring up at the evening sky without a care in the world.

"We have company, I suppose," he said.

"For insurance purposes," said Dent.

Livingston smiled and looked straight at him. They had seen each other in photos and videos and FaceTime, but being together was different.

"You're shorter than I thought," said Livingston.

Dent was done with small talk. "Riley, can you hear me?" he called.

From the truck bed, he heard "Help me! Get me out of here!"

Dent's jaw clenched. "Let me see her."

Livingston opened the tailgate, revealing the coffin. The blood drained from Dent's face.

"Your turn," said Livingston.

Everyone in LA stood on edge.

Dent opened the ambulance doors. The big man lumbered over and peered inside.

"Shayna," he whispered.

Charlie managed a smile. Which quickly turned to horror. Because behind Dent . . . .

The Ram truck rolled quietly down the boat ramp toward the river.

Dent swung with surprise. "What the . . . ."

In that instance, it became clear why Livingston chose the meeting location he did. *The water.* He knew from Shayna's digging through Dent's files that he had an aversion to water from almost drowning in his youth.

"Get me out of here!" yelled Riley from the coffin.

Dent paled. "Riley!"

"Oh God," said Sanjay.

As the truck sank into the river, the cheap wood coffin twisted from the bed and off into the current. The commotion drew the interest of the gators on the far bank, and they splashed into the river to investigate.

Dent's eyes narrowed on Livingston. "I'll be back for you."

Livingston didn't blink. "Have a nice swim."

Then Dent did something he had not done since he was ten years old. Dove into the water. *SPLASH!* And swam after the coffin.

Content that his plan worked, Livingston set his sights on the ambulance and climbed inside to check on Shayna. "Baby," he said.

"Shoot him! Shoot him!" chirped Sanjay in the bullpen from thousands of miles away. But he knew she wouldn't. She had too good a heart, and in truth, felt sorry for Livingston for everything he had been through. Not to mention, he had no weapon drawn on her.

Under the water, the alligators eyed the coffin in the distance and spied Dent's legs thrusting in the current.

On the surface, Dent swam as fast as he could, despite the years, until finally reaching the floating coffin. He clamped his hands onto the side and yelled, out of breath.

"Riley! Hang on!"

"Help me!" she cried out.

Water poured through the airholes on the side and the coffin was beginning to sink. Dent tried the lid, but it was nailed tight. He eyed the riverbank twenty yards away and began pushing the coffin toward it before it sank. And then he saw the gators.

"Oh, Jesus."

In the ambulance, Livingston ran a hand through Charlie's hair. She shivered at his touch. He kissed her gently, and that's when he knew she was an imposter. He reeled back stunned, eyes wide and angry as . . . *THWACK!* Charlie stabbed him in the neck with the syringe and punched the liquid into his veins. Livingston stumbled backward in horror.

"Yes!" called Sanjay from the bullpen.

In the river, Dent pushed the coffin onto the bank just as the gators reached him. He pulled his Glock from his boot and fired into the first gator. *BAM! BAM! BAM!* Sending it spiraling into the water, a bloody mess for his brethren to feast upon.

In the ambulance, Charlie reached for her gun in her sling, but it wasn't there. Livingston had grabbed it and now had it pointed at her. *BAM! BAM! BAM!* He fired three shots into her from point-blank range. Her body jolted left and right, and her blood splattered across the ambulance's innards.

In the bullpen, Sanjay stood in horror. "NOOOO!"

Parker yelled "Red Team! Move, move, move!"

On the bank, Riley was now drowning *inside* the coffin on the shore.

"Riley! Hang on! I'm coming," yelled Dent.

But there was no response.

With two hands, he grabbed a large rock from the shore and began smashing it down on the lid as water poured out the sides. Harder and harder he thrust, soaking wet and teary-eyed, his hands bleeding, until he finally broke through the wood.

"Riley!" he screamed.

On the dock, Livingston rose from where he fell and pulled the syringe from his neck. Weary and wobbly, he stumbled uneasily for the front of the ambulance.

On the riverbank, Dent pulled a body in a blankie from the jagged hole in the coffin. His eyes glazed over when he peeled back the cloth. The only thing inside was Livingston's portable Bose speaker. He used it to project the sound of Riley's voice he recorded with his iPhone in his basement. Dent dumped a breath of relief. Then swung toward the ambulance with venom in his eyes.

CHAPTER 68

THE GETAWAY

In the ambulance, Livingston punched the gas pedal. It took off with the back doors open, which meant everything in it that was not nailed down spilled clattering onto the boat ramp.

Running along the shore for the dock, Dent found the ambulance disappearing down the road, its white lights spraying into the dark trees and a pile of debris scattered on the boat ramp. A lump formed in his throat when he saw Charlie. His gait slowed, and gently he knelt down and pulled her into his arms. Blood and gasps and tears seeped from her body.

"Oh, Chuck," he said, pulling back her blouse. A Kevlar vest had done its job stopping two of the bullets from penetrating her tiny frame. But the third deflected off its collar through her neck.

"Is she . . . is she . . . ?" was all Charlie could manage through bloody breaths.

"She's gonna be okay," Dent said, half-lying.

But that gave Charlie some peace.

"Ya did good, Chuck."

"I did, didn't I?"

He pushed her hair from her eyes like a caring father.

With a smile, she held up two fingers. Dent knew exactly what she meant. She hoped to save one life as an FBI agent. In her short tenure, she managed to save two.

And then she was gone.

CHAPTER 69

THE SWAMP

A bleary-eyed Livingston drove the ambulance eighty miles an hour down the main road to escape the park. He knew Shayna was dead now, and it fractured his soul. He screamed at the top of his lungs, and it rattled the roof of the cab. Up ahead, he saw the swirl of blue lights of the approaching SWAT teams. Ever determined, he veered off the pavement onto a dirt road, kicking up a cloud of dust along the mighty river.

At the boat house, *CRASH!* Dent punched his bloody hand through the dusty window, reached inside and unlocked the door. Hanging on a hook inside were a set of keys.

VROOM! He cranked the fan boat to life, its long blade spinning at four thousand rpm. He dropped the boat in gear and spiraled away from the dock upriver, its lights searching through a rising fog. He knew stopping Livingston was his only way to save Riley.

In the ambulance, Livingston drove like a bat out of hell to points unknown. Suddenly, headlights appeared in the side mirror from what appeared to be someone racing after him on the river.

On the fan boat, Dent pushed the throttle down, urging the vessel forward at forty-five hundred rpm, knowing it simply couldn't take anymore. Through the trees, he saw the ambulance accelerate ahead. He knew he only had one shot to stop it. He cranked the wheel and drove the boat toward the shore, up the bank, out of the water, through the air, and into the side of the ambulance. *BOOOOM!* The collision of the two speeding objects echoed through the trees. Metal struck fiberglass and gasoline, and the boat exploded, sending Dent spiraling through the air. What was left of the ambulance wrapped itself around a mossy oak. Chunks of flame and steel and glass rained down into the woods, turning night into day.

And then everything fell silent.

Some glass tinkled.

Some debris settled.

Some trees smoldered.

Dent lay half dead in the shallow marsh, his face half-submerged in the dark water. Until *splash*! He shot up, gasping for air. Bloody and bruised, he peered around for Livingston. But there was no sign of him anywhere. He dumped a heavy, wounded sigh. He was hurt. *But perhaps Livingston was dead.* Then, he heard the *sha-crack* of a shotgun being loaded. Dent slowly craned, finding . . . the big man standing over him, silhouette in the burgeoning flames like the devil himself. His body and clothes charred, his face covered in grime, and in his hands—Dent's fallen, sawed-off shotgun.

"For fuck's sake," muttered Dent.

"I only had one more," said Livingston.

"What?" said Dent, out of patience.

"One more!"

"One more what?"

"Doctor! Why couldn't you let me have him?"

Dent did his best to catch his breath. Considered his words wisely.

"Because that one may have helped thousands."

Livingston fumed. "He couldn't help me!"

"But he tried. They all tried!" said Dent.

Livingston tried to hold back his tears. "Well, they should have tried harder!"

At that, Dent couldn't argue. He just nodded. "You're right."

Livingston broke down. After years of suffering through sickness and pain, plotting his doctors' demises, and implementing a hard-fought mission of vengeance, everything was coming to a head. He lost years off his life, his career, and the woman he loved.

"It . . . was so hard," the big man mumbled. "Being sick . . . so long. No one knows . . . can imagine. Waking up every day. Riddled with pain." Tears welled in his bloodshot eyes. "My body eaten alive, burning up inside . . . dizzy, hungry, alone, scared." His voice lost its edge. Dent knew the doctors on Livingston's list suffered those symptoms one at a time. Livingston felt them all at once. Constantly. For thirteen years. With no doctor able to cure him. And many making him worse. The idea was almost too much to fathom. Livingston's shoulders slumped; he loosened his grip on the shotgun and wiped the tears from his cheek. There was no doubt Dent sympathized with him, but he also knew this was his one and, perhaps, only chance to save himself. *WHISH!* From out of the water, he swung a heavy branch, knocking the gun from Livingston's grasp, sending it plunging beneath the murky surface. Livingston bent for it, but before reaching it, Dent tackled him, splashing into the swamp. And thrust the big man's head into the ambulance carcass. The two wrestled back and forth, exchanging blows. Pounding flesh with bare knuckles. Pressing faces beneath the water. Ripping and roaring at each other's throats, clawing with every bit of strength they had to try and gain the upper hand. Until *WHAM!* Livingston flipped Dent's soaking body onto the burning wreckage of the fan boat. Protruding from a cracked storage bin was a steel grappling hook. Livingston lunged for it and swung. Dent ducked in time and the hook stabbed into the fiberglass. With what energy he had left, Dent took hold of the chain hanging from the hook's end and wrapped it quickly about Livingston's throat. The big man managed to get a couple of meaty fingers between skin and chain, but it was little use. Dent just assumed cut his fingers off to strangle him.

"Where is she?" asked Dent. But Livingston only gasped. So, Dent pulled harder.

"Where is she?!"

"You won't . . . find her . . . without me," uttered Livingston.

Dent had no patience for reindeer games. He assumed Riley was already dead. And wanted only to hear a location. So, he pulled harder. The big man spat water, air, blood.

"Where is she?!" Dent belted again.

Now there was nothing Livingston could say if he wanted to. His face turned purple, his eyes bulged from their sockets, and his tongue was about to explode. Dent had him right where he wanted him, his grip tight on the soiled chain. And then, it happened. The moonlight crept through the fog, allowing Dent to catch his reflection in the shattered windshield of the broken boat. In that moment, he realized the monster he had become. Eyes wild, snarl carved, nostrils enflamed. And it scared him half to death. In one fell swoop, he relented, letting go of the chain. Livingston crashed into the water, and Dent fell back against the boat.

Livingston coughed back to life, peered up with tired tortured eyes. "Why?"

Exhausted and exasperated, Dent simply responded . . . "You've suffered enough."

With that, Livingston simply broke down and cried. Finally, someone understood him.

And that was that. A moment of peace.

Until the flashing lights of the nearing SWAT teams washed over them. Dent and Livingston knew. . . no matter the détente agreed between them, no authorities would subscribe.

"I can't go to jail," said Livingston.

"I know," said Dent.

"Not after what I've been through."

"I know."

Livingston slowly stood and calmly limped over to where the fallen shotgun lay. He picked it up, placed it under his chin, and promptly blew his head off. Blood splattered, and Dent recoiled. He had seen heads explode before but never from this close. He heaved a breath and took it all in. Until from out of the water came the glowing eyes of Big Bertha. Dent scurried backward from the bloodbath onto the refuge of the smoldering boat and watched as the enormous gator pulled Martin Livingston's remains down into the darkness.

SWAT trucks pulled to a stop on the distant road behind Dent, their blue lights swirling over him through the thick fog. He released a heavy sigh of victory, or defeat, depending on perspective. Livingston was dead. But so was Charlie. And Riley was nowhere to be found.

CHAPTER 70

BUTTERBALL

BAM! Federal agents kicked in the front door of Livingston's condo. A bomb squad already swept the exterior to make sure the doors were not wired. Two-by-two, a team of six young agents wearing black flak jackets over blue FBI parkas flooded the high-end beachside condo and covered all three bedrooms in a well-rehearsed routine.

"Clear! Clear! Clear!" was all Dent heard as he entered calmly behind them. Frankly, he wasn't sure what he wanted to hear. "Got her!" would be preferred. But that could mean: One, they found Riley safe and sound, sitting in an easy chair, sipping a tall glass of lemonade; or two, they found her little body cut up in pieces and scattered across all four corners of the master bedroom. He had seen both, and neither would surprise him.

"Agent McCreary."

Dent's heart sank. He steadied himself and followed the agent's voice to the top of the stairwell that led to the garage. Slowly, his weary legs descended the steps toward the light below where three armed agents stood waiting. One woman nodded solemnly to the closet which had been jimmied open by agents with a jar bar. Dent angled nervously toward it, his pulse pounding, brow sweating. He peered past the brooms and boxes to the crate in the corner. Slumped inside sat . . . Frodo, Livingston's faithful Labrador . . . hungry, scared, and alone.

The screen door of Donna Livingston's ranch house burst open across town. Barreling out of the door and down the driveway, high-tops churning a mile a minute, came Riley. Arms outstretched and tears in her eyes, she flung herself into Dent's open arms as he knelt to catch her in his strong chest. Armed agents stood at the perimeter of the black SUV behind him.

"It's okay, Butter. I'm here, I'm here."

It was hard to say in whose eyes there were more tears—Riley's, Dent's, or the agents', but suffice it to say, they were all tears of joy.

"You came," was all she said. And all he ever needed.

Donna Livingston emerged from the door behind Riley, wiping her hands on a checkered apron, finishing up baking a ham. Livingston knew he and Shayna would never deliver on his mother's dream of having a grandchild but hoped Riley would somehow serve as consolation, at least for a while. Soon, Donna would learn the horrible truth about her son and be left with but the taps and yaps of her Daisy Dog to keep her company. But for now, she just smiled, relishing the sight of the little girl, who briefly occupied her home, swinging round and round, silhouette in the sun, in the arms of the man who must have been her father.

CHAPTER 71

KANSAS

Sundown on McConnell Air Force Base came with vibrant hues of golds, reds, and oranges painting the military aircraft in a rainbow of color. In the center of the tarmac sat a Boeing C-17 Globemaster III, the pride and joy of the military's shipping fleet with a seventy-six-ton capacity. Today's mission was but a hundred and twenty pounds. It was charged with bringing the body of federal law enforcement officer Charlie Norris home for burial in Kansas. In attendance were her mother and father, her older brother and younger sister, their spouses, children, and two hundred fifty-four troops from the base. One for every day Charlie served in the homicide division of the FBI. Dressed in decorated blue uniforms and immaculate white gloves, two dozen of the soldiers lined the jetway from the plane's loading ramp to an awaiting hearse. Stepping down the ramp in formation, carrying the shiny black coffin, was Colby Lewis and the rest of his basketball-playing platoon from Camp Pendleton. Colby had the option of sitting out the procession but opted not to. He had to do something to keep his mind from turning inside out. He did his best to hold back his tears in tough-guy fashion but failed miserably.

Behind the family and friends stood Dent, sporting a tie nearly pulled to the top. He looked half-respectable, though his clothes were old and his face tired. He had buried too many friends over the years, and it never got easier. In fact, for him, it got harder. Like carrying a burlap sack of pain on your back, with each funeral, it got heavier.

Charlie devoted her life to her country, swore to uphold the Constitution, and sacrificed herself to protect the oath she took the day she left the academy. But all that was horseshit on days like today. She was a daughter, a sister, a fiancé, and a mother-to-one-day-be. She had become more than a partner to Dent in their short time together. She was a friend, a confidant, a conscience. Someone who believed in him when few did and trusted him with her life.

In the coming days, there would be the customary pomp and circumstance for Dent, patting him with medals, compliments, and back-slaps for his courage and commitment in bringing down the FBI's number one most-wanted criminal. Some of which were validating. Some of which churned his stomach. He felt—*no, he knew*—he was responsible for Charlie and let her down. Her name would be immortalized forever on the wall at Quantico, and the Myakka River tactic would be taught to incoming candidates for years to come. But that was never enough.

"Ain't your fault, ya know," said a familiar voice.

Dent craned to find Pac-man stepping up beside him. He looked good too. Black suit, black tie, black glasses. "Christ. They let anyone in here?" asked Dent.

"Nigga, please. Who gonna turn away this?" he said tugging his coat sleeves, showing off his custom fit.

Dent just shook his head.

"Suppose you're gonna spin a yarn on this?"

"Nah, man. Some things are sacred."

Dent waxed curious. "Then why are you here?"

Pac-man didn't say a word. Just looked ahead as though he didn't hear the question. But Dent knew. He was there for *him*. And it meant everything. Together they stood. Side by side. Brothers from other mothers. And watched as Charlie Norris's body was pushed into the back of the hearse for her last ride.

CHAPTER 72

AFTERMATH

The next day, *The New York Times* reported doctors across the country had finished living in fear. The witch was dead. But now, their real worries began. From that day on, they would be under a microscope to ensure they would *do no harm* to anyone. Anywhere. Anytime. After all, they never knew when another Livingston would come along. A copycat killer. Following in the madman's footsteps. Doing whatever it took to make wrongs right. The great irony was that was what Livingston wanted all along.

Waves crashed onto the sandy shore of Newport Beach. Families frolicked in the surf. Coeds baked in the sun. Lifeguards twirled whistles on stands. At a beachside playground, one little blonde girl spun on a merry-go-round with light in her eyes—Riley. Spinning the ride with encouraging cheers was Melody, happier than she had been in years. Maybe thinking she might lose Riley made her finally appreciate her. Or maybe it was the idea of never having to deal with Tiny Tim again. But for the first time since he met her, Dent saw Melody with joy in her heart. He watched mother and daughter from afar, sipping a Slurpee quietly from the boardwalk above. Melody looked up, spying him, and mouthed words he never heard from her before. *Thank you.*

Dent wondered for a moment if it were in the cards for him to have a child of his own one day. At forty-four, the prospects were slim, the suitors few and far between. But he found peace knowing he would always have Riley. Or at least the memory of what they had together. As the ride slowed, Riley caught a glimpse of him watching from afar. Without missing a beat, she brought her little fingers to her eyes, then pointed them at Dent as she spun round.

I'm watching you.

Without missing a beat, he did it back.

I'm watching you too.

And somehow, she knew he always would be. When the merry-go-round turned for the last time . . . he was gone.

As the sun began to set, a dented Gold Star taxi rumbled into the parking lot of the seedy motel in Culver City that Dent called home. Trash blew across chipped pavement. A maid cart sat idle with dirty laundry. A few homeless lingered by a rusted ice machine. It wasn't much, but at least it was a place he could lay his head, close his eyes, and get some rest. The rear door swung open on the cab and out bounded Frodo, the faithful Labrador—tail wagging, tongue flapping, and apparently happy to be with Dent on the west coast.

"Hang on there, Froyo," Dent said. He paid the cabbie, grabbed his bag, and lumbered toward his room with the dog by his side. To his dismay, he found a note posted on the door: EVICTION. He had been evicted from his motel room, which, of course, he only took after being evicted from his apartment. *Great to be back,* he thought. He dumped a breath, looked around at what his life had become, and took a seat on his worn suitcase. He patted his coat for a cigarette. Then remembered he let those go in Atlanta. All he found in his pocket were the matches for "The Wild Goose" he picked up when he checked into the motel.

Frodo looked at him. *What are we doing here?*

"I don't know, pal. I don't know," Dent said.

On the ground a few feet away, Dent spied the remains of a cigarette butt. It seemed to call to him. He thought twice about reaching for it. Until a car wheel rolled smack dab over it. Dent squinted up into the sunny haze, lifting his hand over his eyes to see. The car was a white Mustang. The top convertible. The driver, Evgeniia. Her long blonde hair dancing in the wind, her teeth shining like a thousand suns.

"Want ride?" she said in her broken Russian accent.

Dent just smiled. *Hell yeah*, he did. He rose to his feet, pried open the passenger door, and as if on cue, Frodo leapt in the back as if that's where he belonged—ironically, landing in the same spot a child's car seat would go. Dent climbed in and gave Evgeniia a heartfelt kiss. She smiled, hit the gas, and the car roared off down the road blasting "Slow Ride" by Foghat. As they disappeared into the setting sun—for the first time in a long time—Dent felt like everything was going to be all right.

ABOUT THE AUTHOR

Michael Lucker lives with his dogs, Rocky and Rambo, in the mountains of North Georgia. He writes books and movies and teaches others to write books and movies. His first book, *Crash! Boom! Bang! How to Write Action Movies*, is available wherever books are sold.

www.michaellucker.com

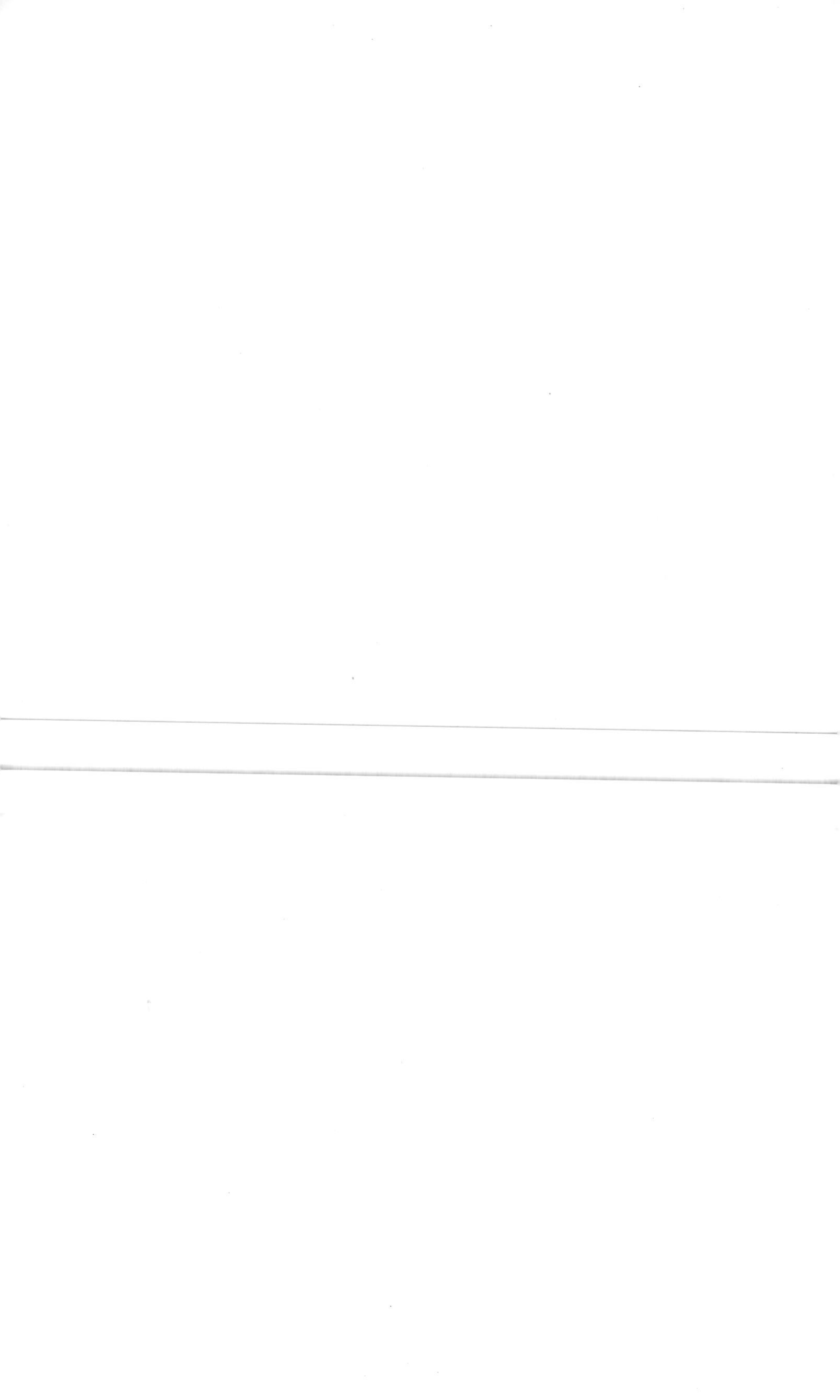